Crypto da Vinci

a Peter White mystery

SIMON BUCK

D0126590

An Alnpete Book

Crypto da Vinci
First published in Great Britain by Alnpete Press, 2009
An imprint of Alnpete Limited

Copyright © Simon Buck, 2009
Illustrations © Alison Buck, 2009
All rights reserved

Alnpete Press, PO Box 757
Dartford, Kent
DA2 7TQ

www.alnpetepress.co.uk

A CIP catalogue record for this book
is available from the British Library

ISBN 978-0-9552206-2-3

Printed by CPI Antony Rowe, Chippenham, Wiltshire

Foreword

Much as I abhor pretension in fiction, it became clear as this book took shape that certain devices would be necessary to assist you, gentle reader, without distracting from the narrative. Therefore I have felt it justified to leave footnotes from the translator in Leonardo's text – I would not presume to edit Leonardo's own words! Furthermore, to obviate the need for such annotations in Peter White's text without resorting to affected didactic speeches between characters, I have added (very brief) notes on some of the historical players overleaf – for those readers with little schooling in European history (such as our friends over the water); read them as if they were notes from a talk given by Peter's friend Al on a cold winter's evening in your local village hall. Al has also supplied a very limited bibliography for anyone interested in pursuing some of the themes touched upon. Finally, I have not resisted the temptation to continue, in the same vein as in the previous novel, to use the literary deceit of presenting fiction as if it were a transcript of real events communicated by the chief protagonist (but then claiming it as fiction in order to protect the identities of the other parties involved). *Caveat lector* †.

Simon Buck, Kent
Spring 2009

---

† Which is, of course, another pretension adopted by certain authors – using foreign quotes or phrases in the original language without a translation (not even in a footnote) for those of us without such an all-encompassing education. *Caveat lector*, as you will be aware, means... oh look it up yourself.

The events documented within this story occurred during the summer of 2003. In general, I have used participants' real names, except where they have requested otherwise. One or two locations have been altered slightly to protect identities, and some timescales have been shortened to improve the narrative – I justify this as dramatic licence (which I got from a Post Office for ten bob in 1968!)

You may feel that Al seems to spend a lot of time lecturing me, as I had a limited historical education. You probably think that this is merely a device to ensure that the reader knows what's going on, but, in fact, she actually spent even more time explaining things to me than is recorded here!

If you've been affected by any of the issues in this book, then Al has suggested some relevant titles for further information (which you may even be able to get from Mint Books).

Peter White
Spring 2009

Dramatis Personæ†

The Good Guys

Peter White — Security consultant, proprietor of PW Consulting. Quiet, shy and unassuming, but brilliant and very brave. Al's hero.

Al Mint — Antiquarian book dealer (that is, dealer in antiquarian books; not antiquarian dealer in books). Peter says she's the smartest person he knows (she thinks he must have a very limited set of acquaintances). Heroine.

Lucia Cicchinelli — Professor of medieval literature at Florence University. Peter's cousin (one of many).

Lynn Dentry — Al's Godmother, although they hadn't seen each other for years. Apparently very senior in SIS.

Barry Barnes — Private investigator, physical security consultant. Ex-colleague of Peter's.

The Bad Guys

Manley Trubshawe — Professor. Academic historian in Oxford, acquaintance of Al.

Eleanor Trubshawe — American wife of Manley. Leading light in Oxford chapter of Daughters of the American Revolution (DAR).

Bob 'Seldom' Lord — CIA London bureau chief, embassy 'cultural attaché'. Renowned for arranging extraordinary renditions throughout Europe, avoids prosecution by asserting diplomatic immunity and skipping the country (hence soubriquet as he's seldom around for long).

Cenobite Skrump — Cromwell junkie, anti-papist. Bit thick.

Mothers — Militant wing of the DAR, dubbed Mothers (short for a well known expletive) of the Revolution by the intelligence community. Well-connected in Washington and the Pentagon.

HoHO — *House of Hanover Organisation*, an unofficial political lobby group protecting the interests of the House of Hanover. Rather old-fashioned in approach.

RPG — *Rhineland Palatinate Group*, an unofficial political lobby group protecting the interests of the Electors Palatinate of the Rhineland. Technically quite savvy.

WARTS — *Westminster Association for the Republicanisation of The State*, pro-Cromwell organisation and political lobby group promoting republicanism.

---

† Compiled by Al – she hopes it will help.

The Historical Guys

Leonardo	Artist, engineer, mathematician, cryptographer (apparently), cyberneticist and robot designer, genius. Archetypal Renaissance man!
Francesco Melzi	Leonardo's assistant / secretary at the time of his death, to whom he bequeathed his notebooks etc.
King François I	King of France (1515-1547). Brought Leonardo to his court at Amboise.
Luigi of Aragon	Cardinal, Pope wannabe, gave (!) Leonardo the Mechanicart commission.
King James I	King of England, Scotland and Ireland (1603-1625) (James VI of Scotland 1567-1625).
Anne of Denmark	Queen Consort of James I. Mother to (among others) Elizabeth. Friendly (!) with Frederick IV.
Elizabeth	Princess, daughter of Anne and James (?). Married Frederick V. Mother of Duchess Sophia.
Frederick IV	'*the righteous*'. Elector Palatinate of the Rhineland (1583-1610), father of Frederick V. Knew (!) Anne.
Frederick V	Son of Frederick IV. Elector Palatinate of the Rhineland (1610-1623). Married Elizabeth.
Duchess Sophia	Daughter of Elizabeth and Frederick. Named in the Act of Settlement 1701 as heiress presumptive to the British throne. Mother of George I.
King Charles I	Son of James I. Succeeded James as King of England, Scotland and Ireland (1625-1649). Beheaded after losing the civil war.
Oliver Cromwell	Regicidal dictator, led the army in the civil war to defeat Charles I. Lord Protector of England, acting as effective monarch (1653-1658). Posthumously hanged, drawn and quartered after Restoration of monarchy.
King Charles II	Son of Charles I. King of England, Scotland and Ireland (1660-1685). Exiled after father's execution. Invited to restore monarchy after death of Cromwell. Died without heirs.
King James II	Son of Charles I. King of England, Scotland and Ireland (1685-1688). Succeeded Charles II. Deposed by William and Mary (his own daughter).
Queen Mary	Daughter of James II. Married William of Orange. Invited to depose her father. Ruled jointly with William (1689-1694). Died of the pox without heirs. William reigned on his own until his death in 1702.
Queen Anne	Daughter of James II. Succeeded William. Queen of England, Scotland and Ireland (1702-1707). Queen of Great Britain and Ireland (1707-1714). No surviving heirs, resulting in Act of Settlement 1701 naming the Duchess Sophia as heiress presumptive and bypassing Catholic descendants of James I.

King George I	Son of Duchess Sophia. Succeeded Queen Anne as her closest Protestant relative. King of Great Britain and Ireland (1714-1727).
James Stuart	*The Old Pretender.* Son of James II. Led unsuccessful Jacobite uprising in 1715.
Charles Stuart	*The Young Pretender. Bonnie Prince Charlie.* Grandson of James II. Led unsuccessful Jacobite uprising in 1745.
Saint Germain	Comte de Saint Germain. Adventurer and charlatan, described by Walpole as "mad and not very sensible" and by Casanova as "an astonishing man".
John Dryden	Poet, critic, playwright and translator. Made first Poet Laureate by Charles II, sacked by William and Mary. Translated various classical authors, culminating in the *Works of Virgil* (1697).
John Witherspoon	Presbyterian Minister. Went to America as president of the college that would became Princeton. One of the signatories of the US *Declaration of Independence*.

Others

SIS *aka* MI6	British Secret Intelligence Service.
SS *aka* MI5	British Security Service.
Simonetta	Museum guide at Leonardo museum in Vinci.
Carter Philus	Sold the Dryden volumes to the Brigadier.
Brigadier	Book collector. Bought the Dryden volumes from Carter Philus. Recently deceased.
Iris	Brigadier's widow. Sold the Dryden volumes to Ernest.
Ernest	Bookseller. Sold the Dryden volumes to Hugh.
Hugh	Peter's oldest friend. Bought the Dryden volumes as a birthday present for Peter.
Cecil	Curator of the Leonardo collection at Windsor. Has known Al for years.
Sarah	Al's oldest friend, looks after her shop when Al is away.
Ethel	College-friend of Al, now researcher in Oxford.
Larry Doors	US multi-millionaire entrepreneur. Cyberneticist.
Henri Menier-Tudor	Curator of the library in the castle at Amboise.

Further reading

A. E. MacRobert	*The 1745 Rebellion and the Southern Scottish Lowlands,* 2006, Melrose Books
Charles Nicholl	*Leonardo da Vinci: The Flights of the Mind,* 2004, Allen Lane
Mark Elling Rosheim	*Leonardo's Lost Robots,* 2006, Springer
Bruce Schneier	*Applied Cryptography: Protocols, Algorithms and Source Code in C,* 2nd edition, 1995, John Wiley and Sons

For Iris

'Tis enough for me, if the Government will let me pass unquestion'd.
John Dryden, 1697

Prologue

I don't usually bother with birthdays. I go out of my way to try and make sure people aren't aware of mine. But family and close friends know. Despite my wishes they still insist on cards and presents and cake. Okay, I like cake. These days there are too many candles to fit on top so at least I'm spared that embarrassment. But I don't like getting presents. People usually buy me things they assume I'd like rather than things I actually want. It's rare that I get something worthwhile. But I feel I have to be grateful and cheerful and feign excitement over the jumper or the book by some unknown author – "...I knew you'd love it, it's like the one I got you last year...". Don't get me wrong, I love giving presents, although I always find out in advance what the recipient really wants.

My last birthday, though, was different. That's when I got a present that turned out to be a lot more exciting than anyone could have imagined. It was a book. Now, I enjoy books, they're my only real vice (if you exclude food, but I see that as a necessity rather than a vice). The thing is, I prefer to choose books myself – I'm very picky about the authors and genres that I read and I tend to be very critical of literary style. So I'm usually wary of books that I'm given. This was an old book, a good book admittedly and what's more it was a book I already had. But there was something special about this particular book that I felt almost immediately, although it took me a while to realise exactly what it was. Just a book. Then again, not just a book but, quite literally, the key to uncovering a mystery that had remained hidden since the 1500s and which involved some of the most charismatic and intriguing characters from the Renaissance; a secret, intended to have been revealed as a result of political intrigue in the 18th century, that could have fundamentally changed the course of English and European history; a disclosure that, even today, could have serious repercussions for many powerful people, so much so that by deciphering it my best friend was in danger. The story starts with my birthday – although I guess it really started 500 years earlier in France, but let's not get ahead of ourselves…

Gift

"Happy Birthday!" said Hugh, "I found this in a little second-hand bookshop down in East Malling. I knew you'd love it because you've read Virgil before haven't you? I'm sure you told me that. Damn I've told you what it is now!"

Hugh handed me a small beautifully wrapped package. Silver paper with holographic stars twinkled up at me, trapped in place by a white ribbon with miles of tight curlicues.

"I'd have found out in a few seconds, anyway."

I grinned, carefully unpicking the ribbon and sliding it off the package, liberating the holograms. The silver paper sprang open as if alive and revealed the contents of the bundle. A set of three volumes. I could already see from the spines that it was John Dryden's translation of the works of Publius Virgilius Maro.

"Dryden. How appropriate."

"Why?"

"It's his birthday today too."

"Oh, I didn't know that. It wasn't a deliberate choice on my part. I don't really know anything about John Dryden."

"Just an added bonus then." I grinned.

I carefully opened volume 1 and looked at the title page:

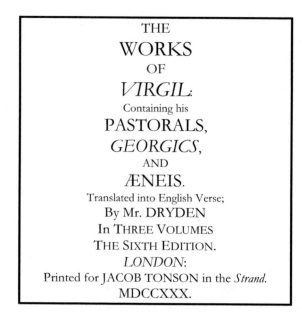

THE
WORKS
OF
VIRGIL.
Containing his
PASTORALS,
GEORGICS,
AND
ÆNEIS.
Translated into English Verse;
By Mr. DRYDEN
In THREE VOLUMES
THE SIXTH EDITION.
LONDON:
Printed for JACOB TONSON in the *Strand.*
MDCCXXX.

"1730. The sixth edition. Thanks Hugh." I said.

"You don't already have it do you? Should I take it back and get you something else?" Hugh was starting to look worried, so I thought I'd better not upset him.

"No I don't have this already. It's wonderful, thank you." It wasn't really a lie, I don't already have a copy of the sixth edition, my copy is the rarer fifth edition. Still there was something about these volumes that was attractive.

"The old chap in the shop said that he thought they'd been rebound at some time, because he was sure that they weren't the original end papers. Too clean, he said. But it looks like an old binding to me."

Hugh looked at the books with a frown.

"What do you think?"

"He's right. The binding doesn't seem to be the

original, but it's still almost as old as the pages inside. I wonder why it was rebound when it was still almost new? Maybe the covers got spoilt." I turned the volumes over in my hands and examined the edges of the pages. "Although there's no sign of any damage to the paper. Oh well I guess we'll never know. Thanks again, they're really nice."

"You're welcome." Hugh smiled.

I flicked through the first pages of volume 1 until I came to the dedication to Lord Clifford.

"Did you know John Dryden was the first Poet Laureate?" I asked Hugh.

"No."

"Apparently he impressed the King who decided he wanted to keep him around versifying. Then the King died and there was another one, or two. I can't remember the details. Dryden had decided to become a Catholic and the latest king was very anti-Catholic, as a result Dryden refused to swear allegiance and was promptly sacked. I think he's the only Poet Laureate ever to be fired. So then he started to translate the Classics, but needed to find patrons to pay for them. When he found one he was almost pathetically grateful. For example, there are twenty pages of grovelling thanks to Lord Clifford at the beginning of Volume 1."

I handed the book to Hugh and continued.

"He says that it was easier to do the translation than to find a patron who would support him. Clifford paid for the Pastorals. Then there is a dedication to the Earl of Chesterfield for the Georgics. He says that he was very nervous and put off approaching the Earl to ask for his patronage for seven years."

I picked up volume 2.

"Finally here at the beginning of volume 2 there's another one, where is it?" I searched for the dedication.

"Ah, here it is. A dedication to the Earl of Mulgrave that goes on for ..." I flicked through the book "...over a hundred pages, in much smaller type. But really it's an essay on Virgil and the nature of poetry. Followed, of course, by the Aeneid itself. Then at the end there's a postscript where he mentions a few others who've said nice things about his book despite the nasty comments some people have been making about him. Hang on..." I put the book back on the table and picked up the third volume, turning to the Postcript to the Reader on page 1001.

"Here we go. *What Virgil wrote in the Vigour of his Age, in Plenty and at Ease, I have undertaken to Translate in my Declining Years: struggling with Wants, oppressed with Sickness, curbed in my Genius, liable to be misconstrued in all I write; and my Judges, if they are not very equitable, already prejudiced against me, by the Lying Character which has been given them of my Morals.*"

I closed the book and grinned at Hugh.

"Poor old Dryden, desperate to find some patronage among what was left of the educated nobility so he could spend his time doing what he wanted, while being vilified for his choice of religion."

"I'm jealous. I'd like to find a patron who would pay me to do what I want all the time," said Hugh.

"I thought you enjoyed your job? You always seem to be happy."

"I do, yeah. But. Well. You know what I mean. Anyway, how come you know so much about this book?"

"It's a collection of all Dryden's translations of Virgil rolled into one edition. It's very well known." I hoped I sounded convincing enough. I didn't want Hugh to think I was ungrateful.

"I've never read anything by Dryden," said Hugh, "or Virgil for that matter. I had a flick through before I wrapped them up. It needs translating from the translation if you ask me. Couldn't really understand it. F instead of S and strange spellings. Music spelt with a K on the end. Might just as well be in the original Greek."

"Latin." I said, involuntarily.

"What?" asked Hugh.

"Virgil was Roman not Greek."

"I though the Aeneid is about the Trojan War."

"Not really, it's about the aftermath. Aeneas, the hero, escapes from Troy when the Greeks win the war and sails around a bit having adventures."

"Like Odysseus?"

"Sort of."

"But who was Aeneas? Why write the story about him?" asked Hugh.

"He was a nephew of the King of Troy, although his mother was the Goddess Aphrodite. He has a walk-on part in Homer's Iliad, when he fights Achilles and others, but survives. Then he is prophesied as the eventual ruler of the Trojans by the God Poseidon."

"Weren't the Trojans all killed when the Greeks sacked Troy? Wooden horse and all that?"

"Not quite, Aeneas and some others escaped out of the city by the back door." I laughed.

"Really?"

"Oh yes! Aeneas has adventures, Cyclops, harpies and so on. Hangs around in Sicily for a while where some of his followers settle. Then he goes on to Carthage and Queen Dido falls in love with him. But he leaves because he's told in a dream that his destiny is in Italy. He lands in what is now Tuscany, allies with the Etruscans and has a series of battles against the Latins, which he eventually wins. His son founds a city there and it's his descendants who eventually found Rome. So the Romans look back to him as their most illustrious ancestor."

"But I thought Rome was founded by Romulus and

Remus … and a wolf. Or something?" Hugh was looking puzzled now.

"Right. But they were descendants of Aeneas – the brothers, not the wolves – so he provides a heritage that goes back long before the founding of Rome. To the time of the Etruscans, demonstrating domination over the Latins, and even further back to those Trojans who survived the sack of Troy, demonstrating superiority over the Greeks. Which is why Virgil wrote the story as an epic poem like Homer's Odyssey and Iliad. For both cultural and political kudos."

"Why political?" Hugh was looking puzzled again. We'd been at school together where we had been taught no ancient history, I'd picked it up from reading the classics but Hugh had had other interests.

"The first emperor, Augustus, had just won a decisive battle. He was now sole ruler and Rome was the master of the western civilised world. So Virgil used the story of Aeneas to establish a divine origin for the State and the inevitability of its great destiny. He was a very good poet so he pulled it off too, not turning out patriotic drivel but such an epic that in his own lifetime it was the cause of great national pride and a sense of true destiny, even for ordinary Romans."

"No-one would ever guess that you're half Roman would they!" Hugh laughed. "The way you talk about Rome and the Romans it's obvious that you identify with them."

"We're all slaves to our own destiny." I said, grinning.

Putting the books down on the table I led Hugh into the kitchen to get a drink. I didn't think about Dryden, Virgil or Aeneas again until later that evening when I was clearing up.

~

As I scrunched up the silver paper, consigning the stars to the eternal darkness of landfill, I looked again at the covers of the Virgil. There was something about them that was nagging at me but I still didn't know what it was. I picked them up to take to the spare room that was lined with bookcases and that I grandiloquently called my Library. Making some room on the shelf next to the other edition of Dryden's masterpiece I carefully slotted the three new volumes in place. As I stood looking at them, alongside the previous edition, it was clear what had been nagging at me. The spine was decorated not with fleur-de-lis, as would have been common when it was printed, but with a key. The sort used in icons of St. Peter, the key to the gates of heaven. A very odd sort of motif to use on a book spine in post-Reformation England. Presumably it had been put there when the book was rebound, replacing the original decoration. But I was tired and decided to leave any further speculation for another day.

~

Over the next few days I thought very little about Hugh's gift. I had various pressing engagements and diverting activities to fill my time. The next weekend, however, I was at a loose end and wandered into my Library in search of a little entertainment. While trying to choose between the surreal humour of Robert Rankin and the quiet wit of Lindsay Davies' Falco, I remembered the Virgil. Rather than humour, I decided that the day's entertainment should be to investigate those books and deduce why the binding had been replaced with the new strangely decorated covers.

I retrieved all three volumes from the shelf and dropped into my soft reading chair. I love this chair. As you sink into it you are enveloped by warmth and cosiness. It's so cosy that you can easily imagine you're relaxing on a warm evening under the Mediterranean sun. But it's fatal to close your eyes or a whole day goes by before you know it. My eyelids fluttered, flirting with a snooze. I nearly succumbed, but managed to recover. Snuggling down further into the chair, I kicked my slippers off and scandalously rested my feet on the coffee table. What would my mother have said if she could see me? I grew up in a house where manners were important and sensible etiquette observed – no feet on the coffee table, no elbows on the dining table. As a result I was programmed to be just as fastidious about the same things as my parents had been. Except that we never had a library – plenty of books dotted around the house, but no specific place to read them. So, in my Library, I make the rules; and the first rule is to be as comfortable as possible while reading – if that means feet on the coffee table then so be it!

I re-read Dryden's grovelling to Clifford, cringing and smirking as I did so. Then I turned back to the cover and the end papers. Hugh had been correct, they were very clean; too clean. There was nothing written on them at all. No indication of previous owners. Over the years it would have been common practice for a well-to-do owner to paste an *ex libris* plate inside the cover of every book they owned proclaiming their ownership and, they hoped, their erudition, to the world. Lesser mortals would have made do with carefully writing their own name inside the cover, in their best handwriting. But these volumes had no such disfigurements. No-one had laid claim to them. Nor were there even the faintly pencilled marks of a second-hand bookseller pricing up his stock. Nothing. No stains. No marks. Just clean paper. But it was yellowing. It was yellowing the same amount as the pages inside. So I guessed that it was roughly the same age. My previous feeling that it was rebound while still new seemed to be justified. I held the book up to the sunlight streaming through the window making dust motes dance about in the quiet and otherwise still room. The end papers were obviously made in the same way as the rest of the book, although slightly heavier. The watermark was identical, in the same orientation as the pages. Then, quite by chance, I noticed that there was a different watermark, but not on the end papers. On the page with the illustration of Mr John Dryden that faced the title page. The watermark was oriented horizontally across the page whereas the other pages had a watermark oriented vertically. Curious. I flicked through to the next illustration and it too had a watermark in an orientation orthogonal to that on the other pages. I knew the printers would have taken more care to be sure that all the pages had similar paper with the same properties, including being laid in the same direction, so that the pages would lie flat together.

Reluctant to move, I nevertheless dragged myself out of the chair and extracted the first volume of my copy of the previous edition of the Dryden. Resettling myself comfortably I examined the watermarks on the pages of that volume. As I expected, the pages, illustrations included, were all made from identical paper with congruent watermarks. I returned to the sixth edition. Each of the illustrations was on a page of paper with disoriented watermarks. I worked my way through all three volumes checking every illustration, thirty-three in the first volume, thirty-eight in the second and thirty-one in the third. It was almost as if the illustrations had all been replaced with newly printed versions. But why would anyone replace the illustrations and rebind the books, unless they had wanted to change the images? I checked a couple of them against their equivalent in the fifth edition. They looked the same. It didn't make sense. I put the books down, shut my eyes and fell fast asleep in my soft, comfortable reading chair. By the time I awoke it was dark outside. I was conscious just long enough to get out of the chair, undress and tumble into bed. That night I dreamt of books being ripped apart and having their pages turned this way and that. Pictures were removed and replaced. Keys were inscribed on spines and the faces of both Dryden and Virgil swam before my eyes. I don't usually remember my dreams once I wake up, but that night's dream was still in my mind when the dawn chorus determinedly suggested I get up.

~

I'm not a morning person. I know people who wake up and bounce out of bed full of energy and ready to take on whatever the day brings. That's not me. When I wake up – or more usually when I'm woken up – I try to pretend I'm still asleep. If I have to get up at a particular time I set my alarm clock to allow for at least two thumps on the snooze button. Those extra eighteen minutes make all the difference. Finally I summon up the courage to emerge from under the duvet, sit up (usually blinking into slowly expanding awareness), find my slippers with my feet and stagger upright. If I'm lucky I avoid hitting my head on the low beam that's just above the edge of my bed (one of the few disadvantages of living in an old house). By the time I've made it downstairs, via the bathroom, to the kitchen, I'm *compos mentis* enough to make the coffee. I've always liked espresso and used to kick-start my day with a *doppio* made from freshly ground Arabica beans. That zing you get behind the eyes when you skol an espresso would be enough to awaken a zombie. But just at the moment my system seems to be rebelling against such strong coffee. Medical opinion is that I should stick to decaf. I ask you! How can you get a cup of decaf to wake you up in the morning? But the consequences of having an espresso first thing currently make the rest of the day a misery (don't ask, it's not pleasant). So decaf it is. I think it's the mental torture of having to drink decaf instead of espresso that actually wakes me up rather than the coffee itself. The sugar hit from the compulsory caramel biscuit helps too!

So, as usual, I dragged myself out of bed and down to the beckoning jar of instant decaf. I know you can get decaf espresso but that's just sacrilege. At least instant coffee isn't pretending to be the same thing as espresso.

I sat down at the table, drank my coffee, and chomped on the biscuit. The sunlight was pouring in through the window, unimpeded by the blind that I had forgotten to lower yesterday evening in my short stumble from Library to bed. As full consciousness wormed its way into my mind I started to think about my dream and the disoriented watermarks from last night. Why would the illustrations have been replaced by apparently identical pages? There must be some difference between them, even though they looked the same to a cursory examination. The only solution would be to take a more detailed look for which I would need to use some modern technology. I drained the last third of the mug in one huge gulp, licked the biscuit crumbs from my fingers and stood up refreshed and with a sense of purpose. Now, where had I put my trousers?

Illustration

As well as having a spare room lined with books and grandly called a Library (the capital L is very important, of course) I have a reception room that has a desk, more bookcases and a couple of racks of computer equipment. It's known as the Office (again, the capital O is significant), mostly because so much of my work is done there. I think of it as a mixture of study, laboratory, den and office. It has a thick wooden door that disguises the heavy steel bolts that are embedded in both door and frame. Very few people are allowed in here, and no-one has ever seen me unlock the door – concealed handprint sensor in the door frame (yes, it's a very wide door frame, but then it's a very old house) and keypad to enter a PIN. It's even programmed with a duress code – if I were being forced to open the door under duress, perhaps by an intruder, I use a different PIN which appears to open the door as usual but also triggers three other things: a silent alarm at the nearest police station, the automatic shutdown of the Office's main file server which is hidden in a secret compartment in the floor and the startup of a honeypot server to replace it, complete with fake files and misinformation. Maybe I'm paranoid, but that is the world I inhabit.

Apart from the security features, the Office contains some very fast, cool Macs along with a high-resolution scanner and state of the art image manipulation software. I've got video editing software, music authoring programs and lots of software development tools. But they're all for fun. What I spend most of the time doing for clients is writing reports with a simple word processor. That may sound dull, but if the report tells a large multinational bank why they should tighten their security, it can be great fun.   Especially when I point out to them that their current security is no better than that used by a toy shop or porn site.   Sprinkle in a few statistics about service outages, recovery times and computer viruses and they start to get worried.   Then calculate the bottom line impact and the numbers are so big that they sit up and take notice.   On occasions I've even woken up dozing Board level Directors with a jolt during a presentation when I got to the numbers that started with a £ sign. Unfortunately, I don't mean my fee!

Having got dressed, I brought the first volume of both editions of the Dryden to the Office and sat down in my chair.   Before doing anything else, as usual, I started up iTunes to play my favourite music.   Background music helps me both relax and work more efficiently.   It acts like aural lubricant, smoothing over the distracting noises that always surround us.   Today's playlist started with some Pachelbel, followed by Evanescence, Cockney Rebel, Muse and Queen.   I adjusted the volume and closed my eyes for a few seconds to let the Canon wash over me. I've liked baroque music ever since I was a child and used to listen to it as I did my school homework.   In recent years researchers have found that baroque music is effective in increasing learning ability and creativity.   Well I could have told them that a long time ago.   The vibrant strings resonated in my mind and in my soul.   Ready, now, to start work, I sighed and opened my eyes, swinging my chair round to the desk where I had deposited the books. I opened them both at the first illustration, John Dryden looking over his left shoulder.   He seems a bit superior in that portrait, not quite looking down his nose, which is just as well as it's got such a pronounced upwards bend at the end that he wouldn't have seen anything beyond it, but definitely as if he felt that the reader owed him a great debt for devoting his life to the cause of poetry. With his modern hairstyle, he wouldn't look out of place in a trendy club in the heart of Mayfair today.

Laying the volumes side by side, face down on the glass plate of the scanner, I clicked the 'Scan now' button and waited for the whirring of the moving scan head to stop, the noise grating against the music. As soon as unadulterated Pachelbel was restored, an image of the two pages sprang into life on the large screen in front of me. I cut both pages out of the scan, creating a separate layer with each. Overlaying one on top of the other with transparency enabled, I could see the original through the later version. They seemed to be the same. Any differences must be quite subtle, I thought. I zoomed into the centre of the two images but could still see no obvious difference. I tried moving the top image around slightly to highlight any differences but to no avail. I would need to use some more sophisticated techniques. Selecting the top layer I changed it to display a difference setting, so that only differences between the two images would be visible. After a second the image was almost entirely solid grey. I used the arrow keys to move the top layer sideways one pixel at a time until the images were once again perfectly registered. With the last depression of the arrow key the screen went white. I zoomed out to see if there were any differences showing elsewhere on the image. Near one corner there was a small mark, no more than a tiny squiggle. I zoomed back in to look at it more closely.

ᴧ

It was a little curve. Almost nothing. A squiggle. It didn't look like anything important. As I scrolled to the right, another mark appeared. This was less of a squiggle, more like a definite mark of some kind.

$\lceil$

It looked like a square bracket or possibly part of a rectangle. I should have realised at the time, but didn't, that it also looked like a letter I. As I continued to scroll around the image it became apparent that there was a mark near each corner.

⌐ $\lceil$ ⋃ ρ

The last one looked like a 'p'. With that insight I decided that they all looked like hand-written letters, maybe 'r' 'I' 'u' 'p'. But what could they mean? Even so, there was something strange about these letters which I couldn't immediately put my finger on. I turned to the second illustration in each volume. This was an engraving of a bust of Virgil with wide, almost staring, eyes and a very pointed nose. The laurel wreath and toga served to identify him as a Roman. But his hair, like Dryden's, was very modern in style, long and curly like a Rock star (which, in a way, is exactly what he was in his own time). I placed them back on the scanner's glass surface and pressed 'Scan now'. Once again I cut each page into a separate layer and applied the same difference filter. Carefully moving the top layer until the image registration was precise, I found four more squiggles, again near the corners.

ξ ϶ ο ⊣

Although they too looked hand-written, they were not immediately recognisable as letters. Maybe the first was a 'z' and the third an 'o' but what the second one was I had no idea. The last one looked like a 't' but in reverse, as if it had been written backwards. Just at that point the words of the Evanescence song *Taking over me* that was now playing seemed to break through my consciousness as if sent deliberately by the Gods to tell me to look in the mirror. It made me reflect on reversed letters. If the last squiggle really was a 't' backwards what would the second one be? It was hard to visualise it backwards as a letter although rotated 180 degrees it could possibly be a 'G'. If they were all reversed the 'z' would become an 's' and the 'o' stay an 'o'. But why would there be reversed letters hidden in these illustrations? Who writes backwards. No-one. Who has ever written backwards? Certainly not John Dryden. In fact, no-one except, of course, Leonardo da Vinci and his famous mirror-writing. He was left handed and being largely self-educated he wrote in the most natural way for a left-handed person, from right to left and in reversed letters. Right to left. I looked at my notes of the two pages of squiggles, reading them from right to left.

$$\mathcal{u p \wedge \Gamma}$$

$$\mathcal{o}\mathcal{\exists}\mathcal{?}\mathcal{-9}$$

It still didn't make sense. I turned back to my screen and copied the squiggles from each of the two pages onto a new blank image on the smaller screen. Then I reversed it.

$$\mathcal{I \wedge q u}$$

$$\mathcal{e \cdot s \mathcal{f}_o}$$

Now it made more sense. Not a rotated 'G' but a reversed 'e'. This was looking hopeful. Insert the missing punctuation and this would read *"In questo"* Italian for "In this". A good start for a sentence, maybe. I sighed, realising that I would need to repeat the process of scanning and comparing every illustration with its previous edition to retrieve the rest of the text. A quick mental calculation, one hundred pages at about five minutes each would take me over eight hours. So that was the rest of the day gone. Hoping it would be worth it, I flicked to the next illustration and set both volumes back on the scanner, then took them off again and examined the illustrations by eye. Now that I knew where to look I could immediately see the differences between the two pages. It stood to reason that if these characters were hidden in the book two hundred and fifty years ago for someone to find, they would have to have been recoverable without recourse to modern technology! Over the next few hours, as I examined each pair of illustrations, extracted the squiggles and added them to my list, I wondered why anyone would write a text in what looked like Leonardo's handwriting and then go to all the trouble of hiding it in a copy of Dryden's Virgil.

I took a break for lunch and sat in my kitchen. The refrigerator had disgorged some cheese and black olives. The bread basket offered the remnants of yesterday's focaccia. The chiller provided apple juice with elderflower to wash it all down. Any other weekend, with such pleasant weather as this, I might have had a glass of Frascati or Soave followed by the inevitable nap in the sunniest spot in the garden, but I wanted to stay clear-headed for my new-found project. Even while eating, my mind was running around in circles trying to guess any possible connection between Leonardo, Dryden, Virgil and whoever had rebound these books. However, abstaining from the wine had not helped me come up with any reasonable ideas. I would need more information before I could hope to understand what was going on. I went back into the Office. My list of letters was growing. Not just letters now, there had been some numbers too. Hopefully it would make sense when I had finished; and translated it, of course. Would my long-unpractised Italian be up to the job? I'd have to wait and see. Refreshed, I returned to the task at hand with renewed enthusiasm. But half an hour later I was brought to an abrupt halt. One of the illustrations was missing. In volume 2 opposite page 571 there should have been a picture but wasn't. Even on closer examination I couldn't see any evidence that it had been there originally, so it must have been cut out very close to the binding with a razor sharp blade. I made a note of the missing page and left four blanks in the text that I had been slowly typing on my computer. I kept going without a further break, hoping to finish before my stomach insisted that I make supper. By nine o'clock in the evening I had built up a string of 404 characters and 4 blanks. I reversed the text and could make out a few obvious words embedded within the long string. After inserting some of the more self-evident punctuation I was still left with various long unintelligible sequences of characters. Supper and sleep were called for. A fresh start tomorrow would undoubtedly help; as would an Italian dictionary.

You might think that nine o'clock is a bit late to start making supper. Especially when you're eating alone. A few years ago I would have agreed with you and just made myself a sandwich or a quick plate of pasta tossed in some olive oil and garlic. But these days I enjoy the process of making the food almost as much as eating it. Obviously it's most fun when you're cooking for someone else too. I like entertaining and love to have a dinner party with six or seven guests. I tend to be a bit extravagant though. A starter might be thinly sliced avocado halves in a raspberry coulis or something as simple as tomato slices with a huge dollop of pesto on top. For dessert I would normally put together a fruit salad, along with a less healthy option like rhubarb crumble, sometimes with home-made ice cream melting over it. But most of all I love to try out interesting dishes. I have a few standard favourites that I can make in my sleep and can always fall back on for ad hoc meals or unexpected guests. Pizza, pasta and risotto fall into that category of course. But my personal favourite, the meal I make when I'm in need of cheering up, calming down, or inspiration, is *Melanzane alla Parmigiana*. Aubergine slices layered with mozzarella and veggie 'parmesan' cheeses and a tomato sauce, baked in the oven and ideally served with fresh focaccia bread and a peppery rocket salad. At lunch time, when I had finished yesterday's focaccia I had thought far enough ahead to put the ingredients into the bread maker for some focaccia dough. I know it's cheating but life's too short to do all that kneading by hand. I just want fresh focaccia to eat every day, not the arm muscles of a body builder. So while I was preparing my aubergines and tomato sauce the focaccia was rising, ready to be baked. I finished the dough and the aubergine bake and put them into the oven. I took rocket, apple, orange and green peppers from the fridge and made a salad. By the time that was ready the oven's timer had beeped and I sat down to my favourite meal. It cheered me up but failed to inspire me. I still had no idea why this text (if that was what it actually proved to be) should have been hidden in these images. I put the plates and cutlery into the dishwasher, turned out the lights, locked the Office and went to bed.

Text

Another morning. Another dawn chorus. Beckoning decaf. But today I was determined to solve this puzzle. For once I got out of bed almost as soon as I awoke. Dressing, coffee and biscuit were just temporary hurdles on the way to being ready to tackle the challenge of the day. Amazing. I hadn't felt this enthusiastic so early in the day for years. Not since… Oh, never mind. I opened the Office, switched off the SETI screensavers and started up the music. Today would be a day that called for inspiration. I needed any help the baroque music could give me. I set up a playlist of Albinoni, Bach, Purcell, Scarlatti and Vivaldi, with some Barber and Einaudi thrown in for good measure.

After a quick canter up the stairs to the Library, I returned to the Office with my Italian dictionary. I had momentarily considered using a translation website, but from previous experience I knew that they were not much use for unusual vocabulary. I sat down at my screens and opened the text file from yesterday. Luckily the word processor had an Italian spell-checking option, which helped to identify some candidate words in the unpunctuated strings. From the spelling of certain words, though, the dictionary entries suggested that this was not written in modern Italian but in renaissance Florentine. The language of Leonardo! Just as well I hadn't bothered with online translators. As it was it took all morning to turn the string of characters into an intelligible piece of text. The meaning was already beginning to emerge as even my rusty Italian could make sense of some of it. The old style of writing and use of renaissance language started to convince me that maybe this text had been written by Leonardo after all. I continued without lunch, impatient to read whatever he'd written. As I flicked through the dictionary, checking on various words and making sure I was interpreting the endings correctly the text was coming together piecemeal; but I had still not read it all through in one go. By mid-afternoon I had more or less achieved what I had set out to do. The text was largely translated; for a couple of words, alternative interpretations were possible; and there was that gap enforced by the missing page. I sat back in my chair, rubbed my eyes and printed out the translation. Despite all the high technology in the Office and the fact that I spend a good deal of time writing at a screen, I still only really feel happy reading things on paper. I need the physicality of holding the printed page in my hands. That's why I don't read e-books, you can't print them out. I don't think I'm that unusual, so I'm sure real books will continue for a long time despite all the advances in desktop publishing, PDAs and electronic paper.

I picked up the sheet of crisp white paper from the output tray of the laser printer and turned it over. All this hard work to produce just eleven lines of text. It hardly seemed worth it. But it's quality that counts, not quantity. Standing at the printer, I read the text. Then I sat back down in my chair and read it again.

In this way I can hide knowledge in plain sight. Drawings are unwise as a philosophical painter will appreciate even 1 particular line out of place although the crowd looks upon art incapable of comprehending its clear meaning, never mind any truth hidden within. Using ???? with the numerical methods identified above it is quite conceivable to conceal the meaning of any writing without the disadvantages suffered by the ancients. But reverse method and signs. Use prime numbers larger than 4973. Only they can easily be combined into a product that is not susceptible to examination.

In the name of the King over the Water keep this hidden from
sinister forces.

I didn't know whether to be elated or disappointed. On
the one hand it made some sense, rather than turning out
to be the load of gibberish I had feared. On the other
hand, it was clearly the end of a longer text which detailed
what appeared to be a mechanism for cryptography or,
more likely, steganography. This was intriguing, especially
as cryptographic techniques are the lifeblood of the
industry that pays my bills. But I couldn't remember
reading about any cryptographic techniques invented or
even described by Leonardo.

I reached over and pulled a book from my reference
shelf. *Applied Cryptography* by Bruce Schneier is the
cryptographer's bible. If you want to know about a
particular algorithm, how to write a program to
implement it or how it can be broken, you look in this
book. I haven't read it cover to cover of course, no-one
does. But I have delved into it often enough to be sure
that I had never seen any reference to an algorithm
attributed to Leonardo. I checked the index and there
were no references to him at all, nor did the brief
steganography section at the front include any specific
examples from the Renaissance. Of course it wouldn't be
that easy! What would be the point of going to all the
trouble of hiding something in the Dryden if it was
already in the public domain. Mind you, the public
domain was a lot less public in the 1700s.

I had an appointment with a client in London later that
day, but there was still time to try and do a little research
on the internet. I fired up Safari and spent an hour
fruitlessly looking for relevant pages which referenced
both Leonardo and cryptography. I started to look at
reproductions of his famous notebooks, some in private

hands but most in public libraries or museums. But I was running out of time, I would have to continue this quest later.

~

Luckily, my meeting was in the Bloomsbury area of London, near the British Museum. But, more importantly, near Coptic Street, home to my favourite antiquarian book dealer. So in the dusty warmth of the late afternoon I turned the brass knob on the polished oak door and ducked as I walked into the shop. The small brass bell suspended above the doorframe tinkled and I heard a rustling noise from behind some shelves, followed seconds later by the appearance, around the end of those same shelves, of Al Mint, proprietor of this delightful literary hideaway. Al is the smartest person I know. She has numerous qualifications in a variety of subjects covering science, art, literature and the humanities. If she had put her mind to it she could have been very effective in any number of professions with money, power and all the other trappings that go with success. Instead she had been ensconced in this quiet bookshop for years, happily reading, occasionally buying and selling old books, manuscripts and other literary ephemera. As well as being intelligent she is good looking, but not in a calculated or ostentatious way. She has poise, style and grace. When she's wearing her reading glasses she is rather sexy too! I have been an admirer of Al's ever since we first met, introduced by a mutual acquaintance who suspected that our common interests and philosophies would lead to romance; we are both vegetarian, catholic and somewhat distrustful of authority, but also independent and inclined to become engrossed in what we are doing to the exclusion of all else. We have been close friends ever since and neither of us has felt the need to change the nature of our relationship.

Al smiled broadly at me as she removed her reading glasses.

"Peter. Lovely to see you. How are you?"

"Very well thanks. You?"

"Can't complain. Well, I could but I won't. As it's you!" she grinned and her eyes twinkled.

"Hang on." she continued, reaching past me to flick the snib on the door lock and flip the sign to read 'Closed'. She looked at me and planted a kiss firmly on my cheek. "Right, come on, let's have a drink out the back and you can tell me why you've honoured me with your presence."

"Do you think I only come to see you if I want something?"

"I didn't say that at all. Sounds to me like guilt talking!"

"Not at all. I had a meeting in Great Russell Street so I thought I'd come and see you as I was so close."

"When's your meeting?"

"Finished ten minutes ago. I'm yours for the rest of the day."

"Ooh. And what am I supposed to do with you?"

"Whatever you like."

"Promises, promises."

While swapping our usual mildly risqué banter, we were walking through the piles of books, past the table which must once have had a beautifully varnished top but now seemed to consist of an abstract pattern of intersecting white rings where countless hot mugs had been carelessly deposited in times long past, and through to the small back room where an electric kettle, china teapot and, incongruously, a state-of-the-art coffee maker were precariously balanced on a worktop that was much too narrow.

"Do you still have a habit, or are you being good now?"

She looked at me quizzically. "I've developed my own blend, pure Colombian but then cut with a little something extra. It's great in the nose."

"Well…" I wavered, "I had given up." Should I indulge? No-one else would know. Our little secret, Al obviously wouldn't tell anyone. I eyed the small bags that she had just retrieved from their hiding place. "I don't know."

"The Colombian has a subtle caramel overtone and a hint of chocolate, while these gorgeous beans from El Salvador hint at fruit. It's really delicious, a subtle aftertaste and a perfect crema."

"I'm supposed to stick to decaf. Doctor's orders."

"I can make decaf if you want. Don't let me force you."

"As I've often said before, I can withstand anything except pain or temptation. After your sales pitch just now, how can I possibly refuse your personal blend?"

"Okay, while I'm faffing about making the coffee, you can tell me why you're really here."

"Al. I told you."

"Yes and I don't believe you."

"Well. As I'm here anyway, I will tell you about an interesting discovery I made, and you can help me understand it better."

"Sounds intriguing already. Tell me more."

She separately measured out beans from each bag into her grinder and put the bags back into the freezer compartment of the mini-fridge. As she ground the coffee beans, carefully mixing the powders in precise proportions using a set of stainless steel measuring spoons, and packed it into the filter, I told her about the Dryden that Hugh had given me, the new binding, the orthogonal watermarks, the mirrored letters hidden in each illustration and the text I'd recovered and translated. The machine was disgorging two perfect espressos just as

I reached my conclusion. I had brought a copy of the text with me and laid it on the table in front of her.

"So it's obviously the end of a treatise on cryptography or steganography." I concluded.

"Or both. It refers to hiding knowledge in plain sight and also using numbers, especially prime numbers. Isn't that rather advanced for the sixteenth century?"

"Maybe. Mersenne was born at the end of the sixteenth and Fermat at the beginning of the seventeenth. From anyone other than Leonardo it would seem a bit suspicious, but he was a genius and very interested in maths. In terms of applying prime numbers to cryptography, then that is very advanced, assuming he's using them in the same way as public key cryptography. Which is why I need to find the rest of the text. One possibility is that it might be hidden elsewhere, perhaps in another book. Maybe it was split into chunks and hidden in a whole library and I just got lucky and found the final paragraph."

Al sat down after placing the two stainless steel espresso cups on saucers, which she had already put on the table. She pulled the sheet of paper towards her and read through the text for herself.

"Are you sure that this was written by Leonardo?" she asked.

"Well it seems to be, it's using his mirror writing and is in Renaissance Italian."

"But this last line, the reference to the King over the Water must be later."

"Why? Do you know what it means?"

"Yes of course. It's how the Jacobites referred to James Stuart."

"The actor?"

Al raised an eyebrow.

"Not Jimmy Stewart, James Stuart! The King. Or

rather the Pretender."

"When was that?"

"Early 1700s."

"So contemporary with this edition of the Dryden, if not Leonardo."

"But, of course, it may just be the last sentence that's later." Al mused. "If the rest really is by Leonardo, the approach would be typical. One of the things that he frequently did was deliberately sabotage his work."

"What do you mean?" I asked as I lifted the cup to my lips. The smell of the coffee was even better in the cup right under my nose than it had been when Al was grinding it. She was right, it spoke of caramel, chocolate and fruit. I savoured the aroma with my eyes shut, breathing it in deeply, and had almost forgotten my question when she answered.

"He was very worried about espionage. It's most obvious in the war engines he designed for the Duke of Milan. Almost all of them are flawed. If you build them as they're drawn they don't work. For example the design for the armoured vehicle."

"The tank shaped like a UFO?"

"That's the one. If you built it as he drew it, it would never move because the crank handles turn the front and back wheels in opposite directions at the same time. But we know he wasn't stupid. He designed very complex geared devices, he wouldn't make a simple mistake like that. The same thing is true of lots of his designs. So it's obvious that he was deliberately drawing blueprints with errors so that if his design was stolen or built by someone other than him it wouldn't work. If he built it himself he would know where the errors were and what he should actually build instead. He was probably paranoid, but on the other hand his whole livelihood was based on what today we'd call intellectual property."

"So you think that's what's going on here?"

"Of course. Look at what it says '…But reverse method and signs. Use prime numbers…' I think he's telling the reader of this paragraph that he's deliberately flawed the rest of the text by using non-prime numbers and reversing the method and signs in it. If we find the text and apply those changes then we'll have the real method."

"You're suggesting the rest of the text isn't hidden somewhere, just won't work without applying these changes?"

"What does he say? 'I can hide knowledge in plain sight'. I think the text is in an existing manuscript or notebook, and this postscript was intended only to be seen by Leonardo's genuine disciples. So we have to find a mathematical treatise by Leonardo that doesn't work and then try applying this reversal to see what happens."

"Well I came up with nothing when I searched the 'net for works by Leonardo on cryptography, effective or otherwise."

"Leave it with me, I'll see what I can dig up. I have access to bibliographic systems that may be more helpful." So saying Al lifted her cup and drank the espresso in one go. "Now, what would you say to a nice Italian meal?"

"I'd say 'Hello nice Italian meal' !"

"Very funny. Come on there's a new place just opened around the corner that I've been dying to try and I'm prepared to allow you the privilege of taking me there. They have loads of veggie dishes."

"Sounds great." I said as I finished my coffee. I left the paper on the table for Al, but picked up the two cups and saucers and moved towards the sink.

"Leave them, I'll wash up tomorrow. Come on let's go."

She stood up, turned, plucking her floppy felt hat from

the hook on the wall behind her and strode off into the shop. I followed in her wake.

Leonardo

For the next couple of weeks I was busy with various projects for clients. I never forgot about the Leonardo text, but I had more pressing things to occupy my thoughts and didn't have a spare moment to myself.

On Friday lunchtime I came out of a meeting to find a message from Al on my phone.

"Come to the shop this afternoon if you can, I've got some interesting news about Leonardo."

I finished up what I had to do, cried off from the inevitable drinks party and hopped in a black cab.

"Coptic Street please."

"Which end guv? There're terrible jams over that way. Russell Square's a nightmare."

"New Oxford Street. But anywhere nearby will do."

"I reckon we can get to the end of High Holborn. Will that do you?"

"Fine."

"There's trouble or something at the Museum. Havoc it is, havoc."

"Never mind, do your best."

I took out my mobile phone in what I hoped would be a subtle attempt to shut the driver up.

"Traffic gets worse all the time."

"Yeah." I answered as absently as possible while dialling Al's number.

"Hi, Al? It's Peter. Listen, I'm on the way in a cab but apparently the traffic's quite bad so I don't know how soon I'll be there."

"Where are you?"

"We're just going past St. Paul's. So, will you tell me

49

what you've found or are you going to keep me in suspense?"

"It'll wait until you get here." Although she sounded calm, I could hear the smile in her voice.

Apparently she was keen to tantalise me; she wouldn't even offer a clue. But within five minutes of hanging up, the taxi stopped at the end of Coptic Street.

"So much for the terrible traffic," I said as I paid the driver.

"Yeah. Dunno what happened to it. Must've just been lucky or something."

Two minutes later I was at the shop and ducking my head through the doorway once more.

"Good, you're here. Flip the sign over and lock the door. Then come and look at this."

"Is it wise to close the shop during the day. Don't you need customers?"

"There's no passing trade today. There was some sort of incident at the museum, so it's been closed, as has Great Russell Street. The police are diverting everyone away."

"What happened?"

"No idea. There's been no-one coming this way for the best part of an hour, so I haven't been able to find out. I'd already decided to close early anyway, when you rang to say you were on the way over."

So, without further argument, I did as I was told and joined Al at the pockmarked table hidden behind the bookshelves. At the far end was her iMac with the display almost completely filled with the image of two folios of a manuscript with the now-familiar reversed handwriting of the Florentine genius. Al turned the display so I could see it more easily.

"Leonardo I presume?" I ventured.

"Of course."

"What does it say?"

"That's what's so interesting. It appears to be a mathematical treatise on the cryptographic manipulation of text. I found a reference to it in an obscure paper in an otherwise unremarkable volume of conference proceedings from the early '80s. Once I knew what to look for I found an image of it on the 'net. It's quite beautiful. I think you'll appreciate the subtlety."

"In what way?"

"It's written to appear completely consistent and effective, but the paper from the conference documented experiments by the author, someone called Russ Anderton, that showed that there were serious flaws in the method and that it could never work effectively as written. Rather than pursue it, Anderton wrote it off as a pathetic attempt by Leonardo – 'dabbling in concepts that he obviously didn't understand' was what he wrote. The only enduring thing that his paper did was to give the treatise a name, the Leonardo Algorithm or Leo1."

"Not very imaginative."

"But better than the 12 digit folio number from the museum collection's catalogue!"

"So what's the subtlety?"

"Even with my limited understanding of the underlying maths, I can see that applying the principles of the text you found in the Virgil…"

"Using primes?"

"…and reversing the signs and method, yes. Applying all that, the scheme he describes appears to work and, hey presto, the flaws that are supposedly the result of pathetic dabbling are solved. Leo1 might not be much use to cryptographers, but I think Leo2 would be."

"Leo2 …?"

"Well you come up with a better name" she grinned. I shook my head and she continued.

"But you're the cryptography expert, you had better look at it and see what you think."

"It sounds like you've done all the hard work already. Do you have a translation of Leo1?"

"Here," she pushed a few sheets of paper towards me, "and here it is with the amendments applied. I hope I got it right." She picked up a few more sheets of paper and held them out to me.

"Okay I'd better get reading. Have you got any scrap paper I can scribble on?"

"Help yourself, it's in the recycling bin at the end of the desk."

I sat down in Al's visitor's chair. A straight-backed, wooden chair much like the ones I had to suffer at school. But somehow this one was much more comfortable and I soon became engrossed in Leonardo's treatise, completely forgetting my surroundings.

Al had also printed out a copy of the Anderton critique from the Cambridge conference. I had been making notes of my own and these largely agreed with Anderton's comments. However, unlike him, I knew that Leonardo was no pathetic dabbler and nor am I so arrogant to think that I am smarter than the greatest star in the Renaissance firmament. With the benefit of hindsight it was now obvious to me that Leonardo had deliberately flawed this method, just as Al had predicted. Working through the amended version, it was clear that all the flaws in the original had been very carefully constructed to appear genuine, but hide the truth of Leonardo's real method. I ticked off each of my notes as they were remedied until, when I came to the end, there was nothing left to tick. It all seemed to be right. But did it actually work? I couldn't tell. I would need to try it out on a real piece of text and see what happened. There was, however, a slight problem that would hinder any further progress. Those four missing characters.

"This looks good, but we can't really be sure until we find the lacuna."

"Does it have to be a specific value? What if you use a different one?"

"It's not entirely clear, in fact it's rather ambiguous. But even if it is just a random value, it's crucial to know what it is if we're going to be able to decipher anything that Leonardo's hidden himself. Assuming he ever used it. Do you know when this was originally written?"

"Not for sure. Apparently it was among notes that can be definitely dated around 1500, but that doesn't necessarily mean anything. A lot of his notebooks were haphazardly combined by his secretary Melzi and others after his death so it's not certain. However the date would seem to fit, there was a quote I found. Hang on I have it here somewhere…"

Al picked up her mouse, clicked on an icon and a series of widgets zoomed into view. In the middle was a yellow pad of virtual sticky notes, with some annotated quotes. She un-shuffled them quickly until she found the one she was looking for.

"Yes. Here we are. Between 1500 and 1501, Fra Pietro da Novellara wrote that Leonardo's *'mathematical experiments have so distracted him from painting that he cannot even bear the brush'*. So if he was engrossed in devising a cryptographic algorithm it would make sense that it should have been around that time."

"And there were another 20 years before he died. So there may be something, somewhere, that he encrypted and that's still waiting to be deciphered." I suggested.

"Actually I've got another pertinent quote here too, this time from the great man himself, *'Let no man who is not a Mathematician read the elements of my work'*."

"Interesting that it says 'read' – so he's presumably

talking about his notes, diaries, essays and other writings. So much for the idea that he hid secret messages in his paintings!"

"I don't think anyone intelligent really believes that, do they?" Al asked.

"There are conspiracy theorists who are desperate to hang their own weak ideas on any famous name."

I shook my head in despair.

"Actually I read another text where Leonardo talks about just that. I don't have the quotes to hand but to paraphrase, he said something along the lines of 'the whole purpose of art is to make the hidden visible', he said most commissions are religious in nature and intended for display in churches or public buildings, with the express purpose of helping the illiterate understand the stories, allegories and parables in scripture. 'What then,' he asked, 'would be the point of including hidden meanings in such art? The illiterate and uneducated would be unable to determine its presence; the initiated would already know whatever had been hidden; and if the art of concealment were such that only one versed in the performance of that art could discern it, then the meaning would be revealed only to rivals and competitors, the very last people that any adept would wish to enlighten'. He said that people had asked him about hidden meanings in his work, inferring all sorts of outlandish connotations from the gesture of a hand, the hang of a gown or the expression on a face. His reply was always the same."

"What?"

"That anything he produced was precisely and solely to provide the clearest representation of the subject matter in hand. If he had wanted to hide a message he would have written it on the back of the canvas."

"Hmm! I wonder why so many commentators on his art have chosen to ignore that then? Straight from the horse's mouth, as it were."

"Perfect fodder for conspiracies. As Mandy Rice-Davies said, 'he would say that wouldn't he?'"

"Catch 22. Damned if you do, damned if you don't." I paused, "Conspiracy theorists can't lose can they? Maybe I should start inventing some of my own and publish them to see what happens. How about a lost manuscript, a secret organisation. Oh and throw in the Vatican for good measure!" I laughed.

Al looked at me and raised her eyebrows.

"Anyway, what do we do now?" she asked, after a short pause.

"I guess we have to try and find some of his texts that were encrypted, to prove not only that it works but also that he designed it and actually used it himself." I replied.

"We still need to find those four characters, too."

"I'll do that. I imagine the page must have been removed fairly recently. You've told me that literary vandalism has become big business in the last few years. There's a good chance it'll be in a shop somewhere here in London. I'll phone a few dealers and see if I can track it down."

"Do you want me to do that?" Al suggested, "I know some of the more likely suspects."

"I don't think so. If you talk to them, they'll suspect some professional interest and may be more cagey. If I approach them they may anticipate a sale and be more open. Anyway you're the Leonardo expert," Al raised her eyebrows at that, "so you're more likely to unearth an encrypted text somewhere."

"Okay. I'll get started right away."

"Well I'm sure there's time to eat first. I'm starving, I missed lunch, so why don't we try something else on the menu of that place round the corner. I saw a rave review in the paper only yesterday, so we'd better make the most of it before it becomes too popular for us to get in without a reservation."

~

We left Al's shop and sauntered down the street to her newly discovered lunch venue. It seemed eerie for there to be so few people around here in the middle of the day, but at least it meant we had no problem getting a table. In fact, as we walked in the manager looked relieved that he had some customers at last. He came over to greet us.

"Dottore!" he said to Al, inclining his head slightly.

"Sir," he added in my direction. Then, indicating a table near the window, he led us to our seats. When he had called out to his waitress to bring the menu, he turned back to us.

"A bottle of Frascati, Dottore? On the 'ouse." He smiled.

"Thank you," said Al, "that would be lovely, if it's okay with you Peter?" she looked back to me and I nodded.

"Right away."

He beetled away to fetch the wine while we looked at the menus. There was such a wide selection of antipasti suitable for vegetarians that we were spoiled for choice. Then the Frascati arrived.

"Well, Dottore, he obviously remembered you, but not me," I said as we toasted each other with the wine.

"I have to admit that I've been here a couple of times since then. A little extravagant, but I came for lunch and I was eating alone so the manager got chatting to me. Then when I paid with my credit card he noticed the title and now insists on calling me Dottore."

The wine was a surprisingly fine example, most unexpected given that it was free. At that moment the manager arrived with two plates.

"Ah!" I said with eager anticipation, "Our antipasti."

"No sir," he corrected me, "this is just what the Dottore ordered. But yours will only be a moment." He put both plates down in front of Al. One had a selection of grilled vegetable slices artfully arranged, including courgette, aubergine, red pepper, shallot, tomato and wild mushroom. The other was empty. Another waiter arrived with a basket of breads and two cruets. From the first he poured olive oil onto the empty plate to make a shallow golden pool. Then, over the oil, he carefully tipped the second cruet, gently drizzling balsamic vinegar which swirled around making patterns like a Rorschach ink blot test. The interactions of the two very different liquids was almost mesmerising, the shimmering slick golden green of the thick oil contrasting with the deep dark infinite blackness of the thinner vinegar. He finished pouring with a well-practiced flourish. As he left the table, the waitress brought my plate – just the one. Slices of firm but ripe, deep red tomatoes with basil pesto on top. The oil from the pesto was already suffusing through the tomatoes and making a green pool on the plate. It all looked delicious.

"Is the wine satisfactory?" asked the manager.

"Very nice thank you." Al replied.

He smiled again and said "Enjoy your meal", turned and walked away.

The food was as good as it looked. We had both ordered a primo piatto that was new to us: I had *carcioffi al forno*, baked artichokes, which were superb; Al had *linguine al limone*, its more subtle taste complementing the strong flavours of her starter, although there was rather more cream in it than she had anticipated. We both decided to give desserts a miss and finished with just an espresso.

It was very pleasant to spend such an easy time with Al. I realised that it had been too long since I had been able to enjoy her company and I now regretted that wasted time. We have much in common, similar tastes, the same sense of humour (although she may deny that), a very similar outlook on most major issues. In fact the more I thought about it, the more it was clear that she and I were ideally suited. But perhaps it was too late. We had settled into our deep friendship and maybe there was no chance to turn back the clock to reorient the direction of our relationship. In many ways I was too timid even to try. Would she be offended if I suggested we become more than just friends? Would she perhaps be repelled by the idea? Maybe I would just succeed in losing my best friend rather than gaining a partner. With these thoughts and confusions swirling around in my mind – the Frascati must have been stronger than I thought, because we only had one bottle between us – we left the restaurant. As we were about to cross the road outside, Al recognised one of the security guards from the British Museum crossing towards us. We waited for him to reach us and asked if he knew what had been happening at the museum.

"Some guy went berserk and started trying to wreck the place." he said.

"Why?" asked Al, wide-eyed.

"He had a fight with a toilet!"

"What?" Al looked askance at him as if he was the one who had just drunk half a bottle of wine.

"Who won?" I asked grinning.

"Actually, the toilet did. He doesn't speak much English, so we had to try and piece together what we could from the security videos. But as far as we can make out, he went to the gents, one of the newly refurbished loos near the great court. What happened next isn't entirely clear, but from what we could gather, he was sitting there doing what comes naturally when the loo flushed itself."

"No!" said Al, barely suppressing a smirk.

"That happened to me a few weeks ago." I had blurted it out before I could stop myself.

They stared at me, both grinning.

"Go on," said Al, "you can't just say that and then stop there."

I looked at them both, Al was now exhibiting a passable impression of concern on her face, but her security guard friend was still grinning. Oh well, I thought.

"They've put in fancy new loos that work by some sort of proximity sensor. You don't have to press a button or turn a handle, just move your hand very close to a little pad. But stupidly, if you ask me, the sensor is on the front of the cistern and not on top, so if you are wider than average or, as in my case, wearing a large jumper, and lean back …"

"What, in relief?" asked Al's unsympathetic friend, with an even bigger grin.

"…or just settling down…"

"…making yourself comfortable for the duration…" suggested Al with the grin returning to her face.

"As I was saying, you lean back and the sensor decides you want to flush. It was a bit of a surprise, I can tell you. I nearly jumped out of my…"

"trousers?"

"skin. Luckily I was only splashed with water, but even so I felt rather…"

"flushed?"

"Thank you." I fixed them both with my best glare, though not entirely convincingly thanks to the wine that had, by now, found its way into my bloodstream.

"Now that you've had a good laugh at my expense, finish telling us about your berserker."

"Oh yeah. Well I don't think he was quite as lucky as you."

"Lucky?"

"Well, without wishing to be too indelicate," he glanced at Al and then back to me, "I think he was flushed with more than just water and he didn't take it too well."

"I'm not surprised."

"It seems he thought that someone had been playing a trick on him flushing it from next door or something, so he leapt out of his cubicle and into the next one, which was empty.   He was infuriated, and probably very embarrassed, so he took out his frustration on the porcelain."

"That's a euphemism if ever I heard one."

"No I mean he smashed it.   Then he stormed out of the loo and just went crazy.   He ran around the court and tried to push over one of the sculptures."

"Which one?"

"The Roman guy on the horse."

"Did he do any damage?"

"No, we managed to stop him, but he got away from us and ran out into the piazza.   By then the police were arriving and they chased him, cornering him in Russell Square.   He knocked over a few elderly people on the way though."

"And now?"

"The Met took him away.   We've cleaned up the mess. Things will be back to normal tomorrow.   Anyway, I'm late for my Pilates class, so I'd better go.   See you around." He strode off towards Cambridge Circus.

Al decided she might as well go straight home, the shop was already closed up so I walked with her to the bus stop where we waited for 10 minutes.   She smiled and waved out of the window of the bus as it drove away, and I turned and walked back to Charing Cross to catch the train back home.

Lacuna

During the next few days I called various shops and galleries, visiting those that had what sounded like the illustration missing from my Dryden. But none of them were even the right image, let alone the doctored version I was seeking. It appeared that it was quite common for these 'liberated' plates to have been quite viciously cropped removing the artist's name and any other information that might identify the source volume. I spent more time searching on the internet, contacting various online galleries to confirm what images they had for sale but all to no avail; I was beginning to despair of ever finding this plate. What I found hard to understand, though, was why anyone should have removed this particular illustration and yet left all the rest. It was hardly one of the most inspired in the book. Dido and her priests making a sacrifice to the Gods and consulting the entrails of a sheep. Ironically of course, it was an appropriate allegory for our own quest, seeking what was hidden within to reveal a message from, well, not a God but certainly a great man.

After more than a week of abject failure I sat down in my Library with the Dryden before me, picked up the middle volume and flicked to page 571. Why would anyone cut out the plate from here? As I stared at the page I still could see no evidence of where the page had been cut out. Maybe it was never there in the first place? I carefully opened the pages as wide as I could without damaging the spine. There was definitely no stub left from a missing page. But that should mean that another page would also be missing, the other half of that sheet.

The book was stitched in 32 page signatures, glued together and bound. Each signature consisted of eight sheets sewn together in the middle, four pages to a sheet. The plates were positioned so that one sheet would carry two plates on one side, being left blank on the other. They could thus be inserted into the sheets of a signature without affecting the page sequence. If a plate was removed by cutting so close to the stitching that it wouldn't leave a visible stub, the other half of that sheet would inevitably become loose and fall out. But I knew there was no other plate missing, just the one opposite page 571. Flicking back and forth, looking at the pages around the missing plate, I discovered there was, in fact, a stub a few pages further on; maybe a page had been cut out after all. But there was no gap in the sequence of page numbers and no other missing plate, so I was still confused. It was quite some time before I finally realised what must have happened.

The plate had not been cut out of the bound book, it had never been bound back into it at all. When the books were rebound with the new illustrations, this whole signature was obviously reprinted so that the other illustrations could remain in the right place leaving no evidence of the missing plate. But reprinting the whole signature to ensure there wasn't even a stub where the plate should have been, was a lot of effort. Just to excise one illustration from the book. It must have been very significant. But then we already knew that the four characters missing from our text, the characters that would have been hidden on that missing plate, were crucial to using this algorithm.

The next day I went to see Al to tell her of my latest discovery and see what she could suggest.

"So you think that someone went to all that trouble to make it clear that the plate was not missing but deliberately excluded?" Al looked a little puzzled.

"It seems like the only rational conclusion. But I can't even guess why."

"Presumably, as this plate should have had four crucial characters, the deliberate exclusion was to indicate to the intended recipient not just that the plate hadn't been removed but more significantly that they should therefore look elsewhere for those characters."

"Of course. Diverse channels."

"Diverse channels?" Al looked puzzled again.

"Yeah. Standard weapon in the cryptographer's armoury. If you have to send the means of decryption to the recipient you don't send it with the message to be decrypted. You don't even use the same channel." Al still looked puzzled.

"Channel?"

"Route or mechanism. You use a diverse route to send a key or password. So, for example, if I was sending you something password protected attached to an email it would be stupid to tell you the password in the same email, or even in another email – if I'm so worried about someone intercepting your email that I think it's worth protecting the document then I should find a different way to send you the password, like telling you over the phone."

"Someone would have to be both intercepting my email and bugging my phone to be able to read the document."

"Exactly."

"So in this case, someone needs the Dryden to recover the text but also something else to complete it. Either on their own is not enough."

"Which means we're stuck unless we can figure out where the missing characters are really hidden."

Al looked thoughtful for a moment. "What if," she said, "they're hidden in the binding? It would be awful to have to cut it open."

"It would be a shame, and I think I'll keep that as a last resort. But, frankly, I think it's unlikely. If the wrong person had got hold of the books, they would obviously try dismantling it. No, I'm sure it would have to be somewhere else. Maybe in something that's well known, but that on its own is meaningless."

"Like a Leonardo painting."

"Something like that. Does it ring a bell? Anything by Leonardo with random characters in it?"

"Not that I can think of, but I can have a look through my research notes to see if anything turns up. It might take a day or two though."

"That's fine. Call me as soon as you find anything, or when you give up!"

~

"Hi Peter, it's Al."

"Hello. I didn't expect you to call so soon."

"Sorry."

"I wasn't complaining, just surprised."

"I've found something that might be what we're looking for. But I can't read the characters."

"Why not? No, tell me what it is first."

"I looked through all the existing Leonardo paintings and cartoons but couldn't find anything with unexplained characters. But at the back of my mind I had a nagging feeling I'd seen something before. So I went back through all my research notes, all the folios I'd looked at and finally some other material related to Leonardo – books, articles, that sort of thing. Eventually I found what I'd half remembered seeing. An engraving, from the seventeenth century, showing Leonardo's tomb at *Amboise*. I've scanned it and just emailed it to you."

"Yes, I can see it arriving now. Hang on a second while I open it. Okay I'm looking at the picture."

"What do you see?"

"A tomb in a chapel. Actually it looks remarkably similar to the missing engraving from the Dryden. Saints instead of gods and the tombstone instead of the altar with a disembowelled ewe."

"Oh, I hadn't realised that. Mind you, a lot of mediaeval chapels look like classical temples on the inside. It may just be coincidence. But what I meant was for you to look at the tombstone, what do you notice about it?"

"It's a tombstone. Wait a minute, there's a squiggle in each corner."

"Exactly. Which may be why the rest of the text was hidden in the corners of the illustrations."

"I can't make out what characters they're supposed to be."

"Nor can I."

"So if we look on the web for a photo of the tombstone we should be able to read it."

"Tried that, but it's not so simple. Originally Leonardo was buried in the church of Saint Florentin which was part of the castle. That's what the engraving shows. But by the time of Napoleon, it was in terrible disrepair, so it was demolished. Years later the church ruins were excavated and a skeleton was found below the fragments of an inscription identifying Leonardo's tomb. The remains were moved to the chapel of Saint Hubert, where they are now accompanied by a new inscribed tombstone. The tomb was recently renovated. But the current tombstone is not the one that was shown in the engraving, and it has nothing in the corners."

"You think they didn't bother to reproduce the characters in the corners?"

"I don't know. The corners may have been missing

after the tombstone was fragmented."

"Maybe there never were any characters actually on it. They could have been added to the engraving by whoever amended the Dryden illustrations. Is this full size?"

"I don't think so. But the original is in the library at *Amboise*."

"Sounds like I need to pop over there to inspect it and have a word with them about the tomb's renovation. Fancy a day trip to France?"

"Why not!"

"Okay I'll sort out some Eurostar tickets. Any days you can't make?"

"No. Whenever. I'll just shut the shop for the day."

"Great. I'll let you know."

~

A few days later Al and I met in Waterloo station at 6:30 in the morning. We were both in need of coffee to wake us up. Once tickets, passports and other formalities had been dealt with, we settled into our mouse-coloured seats in the luxurious air-conditioned premier class carriage.

"Sorry about the early start," I said, "but if it's any consolation I declined the online booking system's recommendation of the 5:34 train."

"Just as well; I had enough trouble getting here for this one!" Al grinned. "But at least it should be comfortable, even if these orange headrests are a bit of a strain on the eyes this early in the morning. I'm surprised how empty it is, even for midweek."

"Don't complain. If we're lucky we'll remain outnumbered by the staff. One of the advantages of first class."

We were provided with much-needed coffee and by ten past seven the train was pulling out of the station. As we sped through the South London suburbs we barely glimpsed flashes of the crowds of commuters waiting on platforms to travel in the opposite direction. The sun was still not very high but already harshly bright in the cloudless sky, the shallow beams of sunlight highlighting the trees with bright haloes and emphasising the open fields of the Kent countryside with their elongated shadows. Before long we were burrowing into the channel tunnel like a manic ferret going to ground. But behind the tinted glass of our carriage we were almost oblivious to the speed or depth of our travel. When we could next see anything outside the windows it was the countryside of the *Pas de Calais* – not very different from that of Kent, although the sparse buildings were very obviously French.

Arriving in Paris we decided to brave the *métro* rather than risk a mid-morning taxi ride across the heart of the city. Even so we had time to kill at *Montparnasse* before our connection. Anyone who's ever been to this station will know that it is an uninspiring monument to the utilitarian architecture of the latter half of the twentieth century. None of the grandeur of older Parisian stations like *Austerlitz* yet, conversely, too old to have any of the modern chic for which the French pride themselves. But we could at least sit in a bar, have a drink, and watch the tribulations of tourists struggling with excessive luggage in the midday heat.

Finally we were allowed to board the TGV, find our reserved seats and soon be on our way again, with an hour's headlong rush through the *Centre* ahead of us. However this too seemed to pass quickly. Al is a lot more familiar with France than I am, so much of the time was spent with her recounting anecdotes about places as we flew past; names such as ... *Versailles* and *Villiers-sur-Loir* ... which are the only two I can actually remember!

Until we arrived at *St. Pierre des Corps* our travel plans had been running as smoothly as clockwork, so it was inevitable that there should be some glitch on the final, shortest, leg of our journey. A wildcat strike meant that the local train to take us the final thirty kilometres had been cancelled. Our expected wait, already too long for comfort at ninety minutes, was now destined to be more like three hours. Luckily, outside the station we found a solitary taxi who agreed to take us along the Loire valley to the Chateau in *Amboise*. Half an hour later, having spent much of the ride admiring the architecture, vineyards and woods, we were standing at the entrance to the grounds of the castle. We were now an hour earlier than planned, so decided to look around before our scheduled meeting with the curator of the library. Finding the chapel of St. Hubert we gazed at the stone tablet, fixed to the wall with rusting iron brackets, commemorating Leonardo's latest resting place. We took a walk around the gardens and, at the appointed time, headed for the main building to seek M. Menier.

Part of my motivation for bringing Al along, apart from the pleasure of her company, had been her better command of French. But as it turned out our host spoke perfect English. The son of a French father and English mother, Henri Menier-Tudor was exactly the sort of faux aristocrat you would expect to find among the dusty shelves of a castle library. We explained our interest in Leonardo's tomb and he told us that the original tombstone, although in fragments when it was found by the excavators, had been sufficiently complete for him to be able to assure us that there were no inscribed characters in the corners. However the original of the engraving that had led us here was in the library and he agreed to show it to us. He told us that it had been a gift to Napoleon from a mysterious Comte who had brought it over from London. Napoleon had decided that *Amboise* was the most appropriate place for it and had sent it to the library for safekeeping. It had been reproduced some years ago in a scholarly work about the library by Henri's predecessor, but otherwise largely ignored. More than twice the size of the version we had previously seen, it did, indeed, show four characters, one in each corner of the tombstone. Henri was surprised, he had never paid much attention to it before so he had not noticed the discrepancy.

It was immediately apparent that the four characters spelt out the word *tono*, Italian for 'tone'. Expecting a number, I was confused. What could this mean? We thanked Henri for his time and hospitality and went back into the gardens. There was nothing further for us here at the castle so we sauntered out of the grounds and through the streets of *Amboise*, heading over the bridge and across the island in the middle of the river – which reminded me of *Tiberina* in Rome – towards the station. By now, we hoped, there would be some trains running again to take us back to *St. Pierre*.

As we walked, only half paying attention to the scenes around us, I was trying to understand the relevance of our latest discovery.

"Perhaps it is a reference to the general tone of the text," Al was saying, "or maybe he was using 'tone' like we would use 'key' for a piece of music today. Did you know that Leonardo was a virtuoso musician?"

"Really?"

"Oh yes. When he was introduced to the Court of the Duke of Milan it wasn't as an artist or engineer, but as a musician. Music and maths are inextricably linked, and Leonardo knew that. In his day, music was regarded as the highest form of science, capable of greater formality yet greater abstraction than maths and able to affect human emotions so powerfully. So maybe he is saying that the number you're looking for is in music."

"Okay. But there are two problems with that. First, how do you get a number from a piece of music? Would he have known the frequency of each note?"

"Maybe, I don't know. But that's not what I'm suggesting. Although maths and music are scientifically related, they are also linked together by gematria."

"What?"

"Numerology."

"Number magic?"

"If you want to call it that. But numbers turn up in music all over the place. Beethoven, Mozart, Bach especially. Leonardo also composed music, we could look at that."

"I'm intrigued by this notion of magic numbers hidden in music. Like Bach was writing Sudoku for the piano. But, getting back to Leonardo, the second problem with your theory is that it would only work for a text that had some musical component or was obviously linked in some way to a piece of music."

"Maybe that's it. Perhaps any text that was hidden using this algorithm had to have some music included with it to hide the key."

"That would be a bit of a give-away, wouldn't it? Unless every text had music associated with it anyway."

"Maybe there is a more literal interpretation." I suggested after some more thought. "Maybe he really does means tone. If a text is hidden in another text that is unrelated, maybe the 'tone' of that text is the clue to the key. So we should look at the apparently irrelevant text to determine that key."

"How?" asked Al.

"Don't know! I guess we'll need to try to extract a text that has been hidden, working it out by trial and error. At least we know the process to use, so we would just need to guess at the key."

"But first we have to find a hidden text." Al frowned as she looked at me.

"That's the first hurdle. But, I think that it's likely that a text containing another hidden one, would be a little disjointed. Not gibberish, but certainly not great prose."

"I'll look through some of the Leonardo folios that are regarded as inferior. There are even some that seem to be incoherent ramblings – they've been put down to a feeble-mind brought on by old age – maybe that's the place to start looking."

Crypto Da Vinci

Ramblings

Back in London, Al continued her research into Leonardo's writings and music over the next few days. She suggested we visit the Leonardo museum in *Vinci*. So we were soon travelling again, this time flying to Florence.

Vinci is a pretty little town a few kilometres outside Florence. Standing by a sculpture inspired by Leonardo's Vitruvian man, looking out over the steep-sided valley, the inspiration for much of the scenery in Leonardo's paintings was immediately apparent. After admiring the view we turned and crossed the small piazza back to the museum as it was about to open. Working our way through rooms with reconstructions of various of the great man's inventions it became clear how practical and down to earth he was. We all tend to remember the exotic and exciting: the parachute, flying machine, underwater breathing equipment, armoured tank; even the dubious, such as the violin and the bicycle; but here were endless examples of farming and industrial equipment such as improved drill gears. The museum was quiet, we may even have been the only visitors. In one room, surrounded by facsimile folios from various of his notebooks, we were quietly discussing the likelihood of finding suitable candidates for hidden texts. An elderly lady, one of the museum guides, had been sitting in the corner so unassumingly that we had hardly noticed her. She stood up and walked over to us, far more sprightly than would be expected. I was waiting to be scolded for talking too loudly in this shrine to genius, but, instead, she politely asked us, in faultless English, what we were looking for. I explained that we thought that Leonardo may have written some of his notes in a code to hide their real contents and that we were hoping to find some clues to which notes they might be and where they had ended up. I waited for the likely disdainful look and dismissal, but it didn't come.

"Quite so," she said. "I have spent much of my life reading and trying to understand everything about *Il Maestro*. I was born here in *Vinci* and, since the earliest times I can remember, he has been a part of my life. He was a distant relative, but *Vinci* is a small town, many people here are related." She gave a slight shrug and smiled.

"It's beautiful countryside here. A lovely place to live," said Al.

"Yes, but have you been to *Anchiano*? That is truly beautiful."

"No, where is it?"

"Three kilometres away. It is where *Maestro* Leonardo was born and grew up. The house is now a national monument." She beamed with obvious pride.

"We'll be sure to go." I smiled and nodded.

"But you won't find what you're looking for in *Anchiano*, or here in the museum. There are pages that have been translated from his notebooks but that make no sense. They are from his last days in France. The academics believe that they are the ramblings of an old man; inconsequential rubbish. Pah! He was coherent right up to his death. He may have become physically weakened, you know he had a stroke that affected his arm? But his mind was still as strong as ever. Even when he was on his deathbed he dictated his will perfectly clearly. So tell me why he would have written rubbish?"

"He wouldn't."

"Exactly. But would they be the sort of notes you're looking for?"

74

"It sounds precisely like what we're looking for," I agreed. 'Where are they?"

"In two or three of the Codices. But I have facsimiles of some of the pages at home. I can fetch them at lunchtime and make photocopies for you if you wish. Can you come back this afternoon?"

"Of course. That would be very helpful, thank you." I was trying to restrain my excitement at such a promising lead.

"We can go to *Anchiano* in the meantime," said Al. "What time should we be back?"

"If you can come back at four o'clock I will have had time to make the copies. Ask for me at the ticket booth."

"We don't know your name, Signora," Al politely reminded her.

"Oh, of course. I am Simonetta. Just ask for Simonetta."

"Thank you very much, Simonetta. My name is Al and this is Peter. We will see you again at four o'clock this afternoon."

We looked around the rest of the museum with interest, but were now completely distracted by the anticipation of what Simonetta would bring us later. When we left the museum we found a taxi to take us to *Anchiano*. There was not much to look at in the house. A couple of bare rooms, an outside bread oven, a stunning view across the valley. The crest over the doorway was quite out of keeping with the scale of the rest of the house. As in the museum, we were the only people there, apart from an elderly curator dozing in a shady corner.

Sitting on a wall in the garden we chatted as we soaked up the sun for a few minutes, enjoying the tranquillity of the location. Gazing down at the gravel that covered the ground in front of the house I noticed a small, light, flat pebble that seemed to have a letter engraved on it. I bent down and picked it up, turning it around in my fingers to show to Al.

"It looks like a reversed g. Just as Leonardo himself would have written."

"Maybe it's one of Leonardo's scrabble tiles. Perhaps he invented the game." I grinned. Al laughed.

We wasted a few minutes half-heartedly looking for more of Leonardo's scrabble tiles, but no others were to be found. Although the prospect of more idle banter in the sun was very attractive, we couldn't forget that our taxi driver was sitting in what passed for a car park with his meter ticking away. So we bade farewell to Leonardo's first home and were soon back in *Vinci* looking for some lunch.

In the end we bought ourselves some bread, cheese, tomatoes and figs just before the shops shut. Sitting on a bench overlooking the valley we had an impromptu picnic, washed down with a light and cheerful little wine that had been perfectly chilled in the shop. We moved along to another bench in the shade of a large tree and enjoyed a dozy siesta.

At four o'clock we climbed back up to the museum to meet Simonetta again. She handed us a sheaf of about twenty photocopies of folios from three separate codices. I offered to pay her for her trouble, or at least for the photocopier paper, but she refused.

"If you can decipher them," she said, "send me a copy of what they say. That will be enough."

We thanked her and headed back to Florence to our hotel.

~

Sitting at the small desk in my hotel room I was looking at three of the pages that Simonetta had given us. Although

I was convinced that they were exactly what we had been looking for, we still couldn't decipher them until we had found the right key. But there was nothing obvious to go on. Al had the rest of the pages spread out on the bed and was systematically examining each one for clues.

I was on the verge of giving up and suggesting we go out for a meal when Al took a sharp intake of breath, not loud but noticeable enough, in the quiet of the room, to make me turn and look at her. She was peering at one of the sheets of paper.

"What have you found?" I asked.

"Hang on…" she said, still staring intently at the page while beckoning me over with her free hand. All of a sudden she looked up at me, a huge grin illuminating her face. "I think I've found it."

"What? … Where? … How?" I was almost speechless. I found myself incapable of formulating a complete sentence!

"This folio has a small musical phrase tucked away in the corner. At first I didn't realise what it was. Musical notation has developed quite a bit since Leonardo's day. But look…" she held the paper up for me to see now that I had moved close enough, "… here" she pointed to a corner of the page, " a stave with five notes."

"What are they?"

"Re. Mi. Fa. Sol. La."

"Isn't that just part of a scale?"

"Yes. But it's more than that. In fact I've seen it before. It's part of a joke, or musical riddle on a Leonardo folio in the Windsor collection. In context it says 'Love makes me sob'."

"So how does that translate into the numeric key that I need?"

"Well. It could be straightforward. Re is 2. Mi is 3. Fa is 4. Sol is 5. La is 6."

"That seems a bit too obvious, and an easy sequence to guess without the key. Anyway, it's supposed to be a prime number, which 23456 obviously isn't!"

"Okay, maybe it's the same numbers in a different sequence. Would any of those be prime?"

"To be a prime it can't be even so the last digit mustn't be 2 or 6. Nor can it end in a 5. So it must end with the 3. That reduces the permutations to 24. Hang on, I can run a sieve to see if any of them are prime."

After a quick search on the net for a list of the first 10,000 primes I quickly narrowed the list of candidates down to 6.

"These are the only primes with those digits. But which one is it?" I was asking myself as much as Al.

"Do any of them make sense as words?"

"How do you mean?"

"Well, 23456 is Re Mi Fa Sol La which was part of the phrase *L'amore mi fa sollazar.*"

"Love makes me sob."

"Right. So do any of these six make sense?"

We tried each of them but the only one which came close to a meaning was 65423.

"*La sol fare mi.* The sun makes me?"

"No, sun is *Il sole.* Masculine. But it could be *La solfa remi.* Which seems to mean something like 'The same old story that you re-tell'. Not very convincing, but let's give it a try."

I used the number in Leonardo's algorithm and soon the text on the page was spilling out as comprehensible sentences, albeit in old Italian. When we had finished the first sheet we tried to translate it into English, but my vocabulary wasn't up to the job and I only had a small pocket Italian dictionary with me.

"I'll call a cousin of mine to see if she can help. She's a professor here in Florence. She'll be able to translate this for us."

I called Professoressa Cicchinelli. She was having the evening meal with her family, but when I briefly explained what we had found and why I had interrupted her supper she was keen to come round. Twenty minutes later she knocked at the door.

"Lucia. *Come stai?*"

"*Sto bene*, Peter. *Et tu?*"

"I'm very well too. Come in, come in."

She came into the room with hugs and kisses.

"Lucia, this is my friend Al. Al, this is my cousin, and good friend, Lucia."

"Nice to meet you, Al. From what Peter said on the phone it sounds like you've made a fantastic discovery. I can't wait to read it."

"We're pretty excited too!" Al grinned, picking up the sheet of paper with the results of our decipherment. "Here."

Lucia took the paper and slowly sank onto the end of the bed as she started to read it. She stood up and moved to the desk where she sat down, picked up the pen that was lying there and started scribbling on my notepad.

While Lucia worked, Al and I felt obliged to keep quiet. But the tension increased and our growing anticipation was tangible. Finally, Lucia looked at us both, blinked and smiled.

"This seems to be part of a series of notes that Leonardo made about a project he was undertaking when he was living in France in his old age. He seems to be rather ambivalent about the outcome, though. Have you deciphered any more?"

In fact, while Lucia had been working, Al and I had deciphered two more pages. We passed these over to her and waited a few more minutes.

"Well, this is not what I was expecting at all. On this

page he is struggling with the ethics of the project, and debating whether to complete it or destroy everything. While this page is an earlier note and tells us the name and nature of the project. I think you'll need to decipher all the pages and then I can translate them properly and we can get them into the right order. But for now I'll read you a bit of this page I've just been looking at..."

With that, she picked up the notebook and started reading aloud.

"The more I try to catalogue, analyse and categorise the work, activity and sequences of actions, the more I realise the immensity of the undertaking…"

"I will be creating a new breed of creature, which I have christened a Mechanicant."

As she read more, even these fragmentary notes from Leonardo's journal hinted at an incredible project, undertaken for a powerful Cardinal. A project that, ultimately, Leonardo could not, or would not complete.

Meccanicante

The text decoded by Al from the folios that Simonetta had given us, was roughly translated for us by Lucia that evening in Florence. Over the following few weeks Lucia made a careful and complete translation which she subsequently sent me. That full translation is included in the following pages for the benefit of the reader.

Crypto Da Vinci

I am Leonardo, son of Messer Piero from Vinci. I have had some success in my life as an artist, engineer, musician and mathematician. I have worked for Dukes and Popes. I have created images of the Divine and the mundane, although I see little distinction between them. I am sixty-seven years old and I do not believe that God's Grace will be with me much longer, if indeed it ever was. I am today to make my last will and testament, but first I must settle the matter of my final work. I have entrusted my quill to my good and faithful friend and secretary Messer Francesco Melzi, as I find that I am now unable to hold it steady. In these few sheets is a collection of annotated entries from my journal describing the gestation and stillbirth of what I once thought to be a Great Undertaking. If anyone should read these in days to come, I urge you to think and learn from my own wretched condition in order that it deters you from trying to reproduce what I have done.

23 April 1519

First, like a bard, I must set the scene...

In the year of Our Lord 1517 I was living in Anbosa[1] by the Era[2] at the invitation of King François, an intelligent young man who is much more interested in culture and the arts than his noble but warlike predecessors (although I have to admit that he invited me in person after he had re-captured Milan –

---

[1] Amboise. Leonardo often spelt foreign words phonetically, based presumably on his own accented pronunciation.

[2] Loire. Leonardo's rather individualistic spelling.

Francesco has suggested that his Majesty only took the city so he could meet me again, but I am not vain enough to entertain that idea). He has made a small 'castle' called Clu[3] available to me, near his own magnificent Chateau and we have spent many long evenings discussing art, music, philosophy and spiritual matters. He is cultured, literate and wise beyond his years – traits that seldom result from the privileged education of his high birth – as is his delightful sister Marguerite, who had originally suggested he invite me here to 'dream, think and work'.

I have been very happy here. The landscape is attractive and in many ways reminds me of my childhood days in Anchiano, Vinci and Florence. The Era is wide here and blue, but not as powerful as our own blonde Arno. Nonetheless I am happy to sit here pondering life's mysteries, listening to the sparrow hawk and the owl[4]. Francesco has a ready wit and is never afraid to rise to the challenge of a philosophical discussion. King François steals whatever opportunities he can to escape the attentions of his court and sneak through the tunnel that connects his royal chateau to Clu. Our discourses often range over a wide variety of subjects, invariably starting and ending with some theological impossibility such as whether animals have a soul, or why angels should want to dance on the point of a needle! Although robust in his ability to make and defend an argument, he does not have the arrogance that usually accompanies nobility – indeed he treats me with more respect than I deserve, even to the point of calling me 'Father', although I still have to determine if this is merely a witty reference to my age. I might digress here to make mention of the fact that I am

---

[3] Cloux.

[4] This may be a metaphorical reference to the two people with whom he spent most of his time at Cloux, King François and Francesco Melzi, even perhaps an 'in-joke' – which is the sparrow-hawk and which the owl? However Leonardo was very fond of birds so it may just be a reference to the local ornithological population!

perceived as impossibly old, even 'magickally' old, by many of the local peasants – one priest has told me that some folk have asked if he thinks I am a sorcerer. Apparently there is a story abroad that I am none other than Merlin of the recently popular legends, which is apparently proven by my long white hair and beard which they say 'cannot possibly be natural'.

To be honest, I was expecting to end my days here in quiet peaceful contemplation. But into my simple and happy life there came a challenge. A temptation sent, no doubt, by the evil one, just as he tempted Our Lord. To disguise his purpose he delivered this enticement in the form of a holy commission from an eminent Cardinal. Luigi d'Aragona in fact, cousin to the beautiful but tragic Duchess Isabella whom I came to know so well when we were both enjoying the hospitality of the Moor in Milan[5]. The Cardinal came to see me at Clu with his secretary Antonio[6] – a young man who was very taken with my library and spent much of his time here examining various of my Greek and Arabic texts while I spoke with his master.

"I have a vision to enhance God's glory a hundredfold," announced His Eminence. I told him I was no longer accepting artistic commissions. I had already offered to show him those works I had in my studio but he had waved the suggestion away with an irritated hand.

"I don't want graven images," he said, "pictures may help the weak or feeble-minded to believe the Gospels, remember the commandments, or understand man's covenant with God, but they are useless for the intelligent or educated. In fact they serve a base

---

[5] This is presumably intended as a sarcastic comment; Isabella was far from enjoying her time in Milan after Ludovico (the Moor) poisoned her husband the Duke to take the title. Some art historians believe that Isabella was the model for the Mona Lisa.

[6] Antonio de Beatis – the Cardinal's secretary maintained a journal in which a subsequent visit to Cloux is described in detail, but this first meeting is not recorded.

purpose, to aggrandise the artist or immortalise the patron. No! I do not value your skill at daubing."

I was somewhat taken aback. Much as I think of myself as humble, and fear the hubris that can come from creating what others hail as a masterpiece, I had never encountered quite such a vehement attack on my erstwhile profession. The Cardinal paused for breath and calmed himself before continuing.

"What we need is to be able to spend more of our time praising the Almighty, hymning, praying, and making rightful obeisance. It is regrettable, therefore, that man has too little opportunity to spend his days in such significant activities, for the land must be worked, food made, clothes washed, and someone must tend the young, the old and the sick. No I do not want pictures. I want time. Time for God's people to praise Him. I want the time that is taken up with their work."

"But doesn't Augustine himself tell us that every man's life is itself a sacrifice to God? That all work which is done is a true sacrifice?"

"Ah. You have read the City of God?"

"Many years ago." I nodded.

"But you remember it incompletely. Augustine says a true sacrifice is every work which is done that we may be united to God. He goes on to say, indeed, that man himself vowed to God is a sacrifice, but only in that he dies to the world that he may live to God. If the body rightly used is a sacrifice, a sacred action no less, how much more so is the soul?"

"So then a man's work is a sacrifice to God just as a hermit's prayers or a monk's chant." I answered.

"But I want to give every one of God's servants that opportunity, not just monks in their cloister, hermits in their cave or even the Holy Father in Rome. Everyone who has to work could be praying. I want their work. To be precise, I want workers to do it. I have heard much about your clockwork Lion, it is the talk of all the Courts throughout Europe. I have seen for myself the mechanical knight you created for the Duke of Milan.

It was wondrous at the time but I did not then appreciate its full potential. I do not want children's playthings. Instead of a knight to amuse and impress a Duke and his visitors, or a Lion with flowers in its chest to flatter a young King, I want you to create automata that can perform all the menial tasks that presently enslave God's children, so they can be free to spend their days worshipping Him as they should."

I was flattered by his request and not a little intrigued by his goal, but I told him it was impossible, many such tasks would require mobility and a complexity of action far beyond what my immobile knight could perform.

"Have you not been considering how to improve your knight, these 20 years? How to make it move around and perform more sophisticated tasks? As your lion did?"

I was forced to admit that I had, indeed, made various notes over the years, and more than a few experiments too, often in the process of designing some other mechanical device – a gear or drill or clock. But the more I tried to fend off this Cardinal's folly, the more attractive it became, Satan's glamour was obviously working on me. Eventually I agreed to think upon it and in exchange the Cardinal gave me a purse of coins in advance 'for my expenses'. I was not used to being paid in advance – although admittedly King François was himself paying both me and Francesco a salary to stay at his court. I failed to count the coins at the time but Francesco tells me there were 30 silver scudi. What irony![7]

His Eminence the Cardinal asked me to keep the commission secret so that "people's expectations would not be raised unnecessarily", especially as I was clearly

---

[7] Leonardo is undoubtedly referring to Judas Iscariot's fee of 30 pieces of silver for betraying Christ, but this may also be intended to indicate the paltry size of the Cardinal's advance – for comparison the King was paying Leonardo an annual pension of 1000 scudi, even Melzi was being paid 300 scudi a year.

not confident of the undertaking's eventual success. When I had achieved his goal, he would make a great announcement and demonstration in Rome. I must admit Francesco suspected the Cardinal was more concerned about raising his own stature in time for the next Papal election, than managing others' expectations. We knew of the stories about this Cardinal – that he had failed in his bid to become Pope after Julius; that he had ordered the murder of his own sister and her children and husband; that he was implicated in a conspiracy against the current Pope, Leo. Away from Rome he wears a sword beneath his cloak and appears to know how to use it – he has the air of a soldier rather than a priest. I had met him once, almost exactly two years before, when we had both accompanied His Holiness Pope Leo to meet King François at Bologna, but then we had only briefly conversed and about nothing of any consequence.

Despite my reservations, I have nevertheless agreed to his conditions. I was not swayed by his offers of money, I am living comfortably here in the French court at the King's expense and there is little I could think to spend the money on – although Francesco can always be relied upon to concoct a desperate need for expenses when encouraged. No, I am going to do this for the challenge itself. Oh, ... and for the Glory of God of course!

Having accepted the Cardinal's purse and commission, I sat down to review all my notes from previous automata. I have designed various mechanisms to enable a range of movements and actions; I had indeed, as His Eminence had noted, already achieved mobility with the mechanical lion that I demonstrated a few months ago here in Anbosa – it had been well received, even causing somewhat of a sensation at the time as it had seemed to onlookers to be capable of choosing where to go of its own volition, starting and stopping with no obvious external influence. Of course, this just encouraged the local story that I am a sorcerer with an enchanted lion that does my bidding – which may be a good thing after all, as it will surely discourage unwelcome visitors. But those who actually witnessed my little performance knew it to be merely a wooden likeness. It had no real characteristics of a lion and could just as easily have had a wooden carcass shaped like a duck, dog, horse or even a man. In fact I had made a wooden man before, to ring the bell on a water clock, but the knight that had so impressed his Eminence had only looked like a man because of the suit of armour in which it was encased. None of these automata had ever had to perform a genuine task in real environs. The wooden man had wielded a hammer, but it only ever struck the side of a bell that was always in the same place, and only did that once an hour – I knew that an automatic blacksmith would need much more force and would be working in very hot surroundings – not well suited to water power, or even clockwork! The knight had been situated in a grotto and I had made sure that the crucial joints, especially the neck, were protected against the damp – but it had no need to leave its place and the controlling mechanisms were well out of harm's way below the floor. My lion, while moving around according to a pre-determined path that I had encoded in its clockwork mechanism, would have been unable to deal with an unexpected obstacle or a slick surface causing its wheels to slip. While I had already solved some of the likely problems I would now face, it was in each case at the expense of some other capability. It would certainly be a great challenge to solve them all at once.

~

But what problems will I actually need to solve?

Francesco and I have started to make a list of the work that the Cardinal had in mind for this creation to perform. He talks about all God's people, men, women and children. I must admit to being somewhat surprised, most clergy I had ever met seem to undervalue women's work. However I noted also that they had always seemed to manage to come to my studio on some pretext when there was some undressed female model posing. But this Cardinal apparently values women's prayers along with men's and children's (everybody knows that children's prayers are the fastest to reach the ears of the Almighty); so we have begun our list with the domestic chores that are usually done by female servants – cooking, cleaning, washing, sweeping – all chores, in fact, that I myself had been required to perform on many occasions as an apprentice in Maestro Andrea's workshop. We have added seamstress, blacksmith and armourer, baker and butcher, wine and cheese makers, farmer, milkmaid, husbandman and many others. We are pondering whether the Cardinal had intended for us to include soldiers, sailors or watchmen – I have previously designed war machines for my patrons, but they all required operation by living men.

~

Now that we have listed the types of work we will be required to perform I have started to analyse the individual activities that will be necessary. Some, like farming, require much mobility, while others, like sewing, require little or none. All require hands with flexible fingers able to grip and manipulate objects. Some require legs. But, most difficult of all, almost all require sight, first among all the senses, in order to adapt to their surroundings and react to changes or the results of actions undertaken. I believe this will be the biggest challenge and will need to be overcome in a variety of ways to achieve each required effect in a simulacrum of vision.

Then there is the problem of how to power the machinery. I have previously used clockwork, water, weights; each of which suited certain situations. But I will need to find other sources of power for this undertaking.

The more I try to catalogue, analyse and categorise the work, activity and sequences of actions, the more I realise the immensity of the undertaking.

It was at this point that we started to talk of it as the Great Undertaking, in reference more to its size and complexity than any judgment as to its worth or significance. [8]

I have concluded that no one machine could do everything, just as no one person can. This insight has given me the confidence to continue as it allows me to adopt my usual approach of breaking a problem down into a set of smaller inter-related problems, which then often prove easier to solve individually. I will be creating a new breed of creature, which I have christened a Mechanicant.[9]

---

[8] Passages shown here italicised are parenthetical comments, annotations in the manuscript, that appear to have been added by Leonardo (or Melzi) to expand on the original journal entries.

[9] *Meccanicante*, a word presumably coined by Leonardo. There being no direct translation in English, a transliteration seems most appropriate.

Now I have completed my analysis I feel that I understand the variety of actions that will be required, although for some of them I am still unsure what this might entail. For example, neither Francesco nor I have ever milked a goat, so although we are sure we understand the basic principles, I have decided that we will need to do some practical research for various of these tasks.

In the past I spent much time understanding the workings of the mechanical aspects of the human body. I found golden ratios throughout God's design for man. I examined, understood and documented the way that muscles, tendons and sinews work together to control arms and legs, to keep a head erect or to enable a hand to wield a sword or hold a cup. I dissected cadavers to reveal the inner workings. I observed men, birds, horses, cats, dogs and other creatures walking, running, sitting, standing, flying, swooping, and sleeping to see the ways in which various muscles interact. But I have never taken the time to observe what muscles a blacksmith uses when forging a sword, a woman scrubbing and wringing out a shirt, or a baker kneading dough.

~

Francesco arranged for us to visit local artisans to observe them at work. I needed to see the way all their muscles work together as they perform each action, so I asked Francesco to ensure they did not mind working unencumbered. The blacksmiths and bakers were unabashed. The older washerwomen were a little more wary at first, but in the end I think they enjoyed the attention. But the most trouble has been caused by a fair young girl called Marie-Louise who came to Clu to let me observe her sewing. She was quite unashamed, almost keen, to sit unclothed in my room and sew – perhaps the dubious reputation which I now enjoyed among the local peasantry was in her case an added thrill; but don't misunderstand, she was still a maiden and quite naïve – pretty too. However, shortly after she had divested herself of her simple garments and started to make delicate patterns in the cloth, whilst I made sketches and notes of the intricate movements that she made with her needle, the required gyrations of her wrist and the subtle interplay of the tendons and muscles in her forearm, chest and back, her father came battering at the door demanding to know what evil magic I had worked on his daughter to lure her into my "den of iniquity". I don't know exactly what this hysterical man believed was taking place within my house, a pagan orgy maybe or some other devilish ritual involving the sacrifice of his virgin child, but he was very agitated, calling foul curses upon me and invoking all the angels and saints of heaven to save his beloved daughter. Luckily he was smaller than Francesco who managed to restrain him; nor had he thought to bring reinforcements with him, no angry mob of frightened townsfolk looking to burn a heretic as appeasement (or entertainment?). I bade the girl dress quickly and she ran to the castle to summon help, returning with no less a person than the King himself who vouched for my character and good intentions and presented the man with a gold coin to recompense him for his unwarranted concern. The man left with his daughter in train.

As I remarked to François, it is amusing that I should have such trouble now, when I am too old to be either desirous or capable of doing to the girl any of the things the poor man must have been imagining, whereas, when I was younger and would have been both able and willing to take advantage of a naïve girl in my studio, I had never had any problems at all with fathers (or brothers or husbands come to that). Apart from once while I was still in Maestro Andrea's workshop, I was imprisoned overnight after being falsely denounced for immoral activities with a boy who was modelling for me, but it was all a political game intended to cause trouble for our patrons the Medici. The King opined that it was more likely to be an indication of the difference between the 'sophisticates' of Florence and the 'unsophisticates' of Anbosa.

However the girl herself had seemed entirely oblivious to the worst fears of her raging parent, and I was sure it was not because she was a simpleton, merely sweet and innocent. Indeed she returned two days later while her father was away at market in a nearby town. She finished her sewing and I completed my observations. Strangely, François seemed to know when she returned and was on hand to offer helpful advice and draw attention to details of her form that he was worried might otherwise go unremarked. Francesco assures me that he hadn't told the King of the girl's return so he was either keeping a watch for her, or had directly intervened with her himself. She also seems to be spending more time around the castle now. As a result of the King's intervention I have been forced to confide the nature of my undertaking to him – he shares Francesco's misgivings over the Cardinal's motives but also my excitement at the magnitude of the challenge.

From this point on King François became a regular collaborator on the Great Undertaking, which ultimately helped to focus attention on the underlying moral concerns that would present themselves more and more forcefully.

After many days of observations of the actions of various actors I am now becoming more confident that I have catalogued the individual actions involved and how they are performed and controlled within a body. I know that I can design a set of mechanical parts to address each of these actions. By putting them together in different combinations and with the appropriate controlling mechanism I can build them up into assemblies capable of performing sequences. For example, to milk a goat I need a repeated sequence of a squeezing action and a pulling action for each hand, but synchronised half an arc apart; for the wielding of a hammer in a smithy I need a squeezing action to grasp the hammer firmly and a repeated sequence of a swinging action followed by a lifting action to beat the hot metal against the anvil; similarly for many other activities; so I need squeezing, pulling, lifting and the ability to repeat sequences. I have already designed a controlling mechanism like this to make my lion stop, start and change direction. Yes, I am starting to feel confident.

Too confident!

~

With my catalogue of required actions complete I can turn my attention back to what I had suspected to be one of the more intractable of all the undertaking's problems. Power.

I have rejected the usual means of harnessing water power for the obvious reasons.

It requires both a constant supply and good drainage so could only be a practical option for immobile mechanicants.

There has been little improvement in the techniques of employing water power since Hero[10] and despite the significant advances I have made with my own designs for clocks, fountains and various amusements, it would still not be a practical solution. Even though Hero created a fountain using water in such a way that it is returned to its starting container for re-use, I discovered, in my experiments, that this flow soon stops and I realised that this return mechanism ultimately requires more power than could actually be generated from the water itself.

Using steam produced by heating water was also shown by Hero to be a means of powering a machine and I too have previously experimented with steam power, but it has severe limitations. It does not rely on the weight of the water flowing downhill and can consist of a simple container, like a cauldron, requiring neither drainage nor constant supply; it merely needs to be filled with water at the start of an activity, making it much more suitable for mobile mechanicants. However, it also needs a constant source of heat to boil the water into steam and force it out of jets in order to turn the steam wheel. For many tasks this need for an intense source of heat will prove to be a significant disadvantage; it will damage cloth, spoil dough and other foods, curdle milk and discomfort the goats. For a few tasks such as those of a smithy it may be possible.

---

[10] Hero of Alexandria, a Greek inventor who lived in the first century AD and built steam powered devices and automata.

I have not entirely dismissed it, but only for such specialised purposes.

Gears, levers and springs, such as I have used frequently in my previous automata, are suitable for tasks that can be completed in a short time. The spring must then be retightened and gears reset to their starting position before the task can be repeated. In the calculations I have made based on the many such machines I have previously created, I believe that a mechanism sufficient to power any activity for a number of hours would have to be enormous, far bigger than a man, and would take a large gang of men to tighten. Springs are not, therefore, likely to be of much use in this project. Gears and levers, though, will be essential for controlling and directing the movement of the limbs of my mechanicants.

We were starting to despair of finding a suitable means of powering the Mechanicants, when François observed that it is so much easier for Man, God having provided food as the means of ensuring that we have the power we need to work. As a result we started experiments into using food as a power source.

During the last few weeks I have been trying to find a way to use food to create the power for my mechanicants. Francesco and I have been keeping a record of what we eat, and by varying our diet we have tried to understand the different effect of each food. We know that some food keeps us healthy, preventing disease. Country people will tell you that those who drink milk have stronger nails and seem to be less prone to broken bones, while it is well known that milkmaids are often immune to poxes. Our own experiments have confirmed that bread, cheese, beans and polenta all seem to give us the power we need to keep our bodies going – when we haven't eaten these we become weak and tire easily. We tried restricting our diet to raw materials and found that some were more effective than others. Honey we found to be particularly powerful.

Once I had discovered these potential fuels I still had to find a way of extracting and using the vital force contained within them. I read various alchemical treatises that were in the King's library, in the hope that they would provide me with some insight. Ignoring the cryptic language (of which I thoroughly approved) and the supposed goals of creating gold or the philosopher's stone (which I understand to be an allegorical reference to achieving gnosis), there are many well-described experiments for combining substances with interesting results. Some mixtures appear to create heat while others require heat to be applied. I decided to try some of these myself.

~

Today I once again had need of the protection of his Majesty, who never begrudges it. Francesco and I were trying to follow the recipe for an experiment involving vinegar and baking soda. The treatise that we were following suggested that the alembic would become warm. However, it reacted rather more quickly and catastrophically than we expected, with the result that there was an explosion with glass and foaming matter flying everywhere. We were carrying out this experiment in the kitchen, having sent Maturina[11] out for the day, so that little actual damage resulted. But the sound of the explosion caused much alarm to the King's servants and others in the vicinity. Within a few minutes, apparently, rumours were flying, once again, that the evil old sorcerer was conjuring up demons.

Soon we were besieged by a frightened and hostile crowd, groundsmen and farmhands armed with pitchforks and sticks, women with pots and pans, and even one of the King's armourers with a newly forged sword. A priest was propelled forwards through the crowd to act as spokesman and he challenged me to explain myself. Francesco was suggesting we make a strategic retreat to the royal chateau when the King himself arrived. He asked what we had done 'this time' and surveyed the mess in the kitchen. After listening to a brief explanation he strode to the door and invited the priest along with the armourer and one of the pan-wielding women to follow him to our kitchen. As they looked around, François bade me tell them what we had been 'cooking'. I recited the ingredients of our experiment and suddenly the woman burst out laughing. In between roars of laughter, the force of which caused ripples to move up and down the flesh of her thick arms – she was a woman of generous proportions who undoubtedly partook heartily of the fare she produced in the King's kitchen – she called us 'amateurs' and chastised us, saying that every French wife knows not to heat up such a mixture in a closed container and probably most French husbands too! She turned and left, still cackling to herself about 'ignorant Florentines', but at least she no longer thought me an evil sorcerer, merely a simpleton. The

---

[11] A cook and housekeeper, supplied by the King. A local woman, her name was Mathurine but Leonardo invariably calls her Maturina.

armourer watched her leave and then turned back to look at us. He seemed less easily convinced at first, but when the King raised an eyebrow and threw a disparaging look at me, he too seemed satisfied and removed himself. That just left the priest, who had actually appeared rather uncomfortable all along, smiling sheepishly at the King and then looking down at his feet, which he shuffled incessantly.

"Well Père?" asked François.

Shaking his head and mumbling semi-coherently about 'loud noises', 'frightened children' and 'superstitious women' he made his way out of the house. Grinning, François turned to me.

"I could hear the outcome of your... 'cooking', all the way inside my own chamber. No wonder they were frightened. But I assume you've found your power source now?"

"Maybe, if it can be controlled." I answered.

"Unlike you..." he smiled, and left us to clear up the mess, although he returned later to ask many more questions about our progress.

I have now overcome all the significant problems that stood in the way of effecting a basic mechanicant. Different types of mechanicant, for performing different tasks, still need to be designed, refined and built. But the essential nature of the creation is now certain.

I was determined to start with the most difficult tasks, in the belief that if we could create a mechanicant that would successfully perform them, then everything else would be achievable too.

When I was a child I had been fascinated by one of Antonio's friends, a small man called Mario who made and repaired water conduits. I had often watched him at work with his brother Luigi. I am convinced that if we can make a mechanicant capable of doing what Mario did with ease every working day of his life, we can do anything. So we have decided to build a mechanicant version of Mario; Francesco has dubbed it a SuperMario[12].

~

For the last two weeks we have been building the various components of SuperMario. The King has permitted his armourers to aid us by making some of the parts we require. The leader of the group that his Majesty has put at my disposal is none other than he who was wielding a sword in my kitchen after the explosion of the alembic. Unfortunately these supposed craftsmen are not as accurate in their craft as I need. Their construction techniques may be sufficient to make a deadly sword or a protecting breastplate, but they appear woefully inadequate for making my precision machinery. Whether this is through incompetence, carelessness, laziness, or a deliberate attempt to sabotage my design is unclear. But it has meant that Francesco and I have spent more time

---

[12] *Marioissimo.* 'SuperMario' seems a better rendition than 'Mario the Greatest'

correcting dimensions, filing down oversized gear teeth and generally reshaping every part, than we are supposedly saving by having the armourers' help.

But in the evenings François, Francesco and I have been considering the nature of my mechanicants. A mechanicant will be powered by food, just like a man. It will work at its assigned task all day, just like a man. I believe that it will need to rest at the end of the day too, like a man, otherwise the gears, levers and joints will become overheated and may warp. In so many ways a mechanicant will be like a man. Which, for me, raises serious questions. If a mechanicant is like a man in so many other ways, will it too have an eternal soul? We are told the 'Soul is the idea of the body' and a mechanicant will obviously have a body. Francesco has pointed out that animals eat, sleep and have a body, but we know that they do not have a soul – the Church Fathers tell us that.

The Cardinal's argument, supported by the works of those same great Doctors of the Church, especially Augustine, is that the work a man does is a sacrifice to God; but dedicating his soul to God allows an even greater sacrifice. By removing a man's need to work he can be enabled to achieve that dedication and make that greater sacrifice. But if the mechanicant is performing the work, is it not still a sacrifice to God but now offered by the mechanicant? If, in being like a man in those other ways, a mechanicant is making sacrifices to God, then surely he too has a soul.

François' response is that even animals work, such as oxen pulling a plough or horses pulling a cart. François believes that animals are mere automata. They have a brain, but no mind; a body, but no soul. He bade me remember my own experiments with the bodies of dead animals, that elicited movement and other responses; the kicking legs of a dead frog for example. Those animals no longer had any life left, yet were still capable of the actions needed to work. If an animal had a soul it would surely leave their body at death, yet that same dead body could still perform work. Therefore the ability to work is neither an indication of the presence of a soul, nor does it necessitate a soul.

I reminded him, in return, that I had demonstrated the same responses in human corpses. Did that mean that their owners too had had no soul?

For my part, I still do not understand why animals should have no soul. What will eternal life be like if there are no birds in the sky, soaring and swooping majestically? Will we have to content ourselves with watching the flight of angels?

François maintains that there will be animals with us in eternity, even though they have no souls. He still does not understand why I will not eat anything that has been killed, although he appears to respect my views; so he cannot appreciate the true gulf in our perceptions of the nature of animals or any other form of life. He asserts that although angels may have no soul, they nonetheless enjoy eternity in the presence of God, and have done since before man or animals were created. This just makes me even more concerned with the eternal life of my mechanicants. Both Francesco and François contend that the mechanicant does not have life now, so it cannot possibly have eternal life in the hereafter; without life, it cannot experience the death that is the precursor to eternity. But what is life? A mechanicant will eat, work, rest.

"What more is there to life?" I asked.

"Speech", suggested Francesco.

"The mute Henri sits in the market in Anbosa every week. He cannot speak. Is he not alive?"

"Understanding, then." Francesco tried. "Henri cannot speak but he understands what is said to him and can reply with signs and gestures."

"A village idiot cannot understand much that is said to him. But, again, I'm sure you would not deny that he is alive."

François laughed. "There are no village idiots in France. Perhaps they are a feature peculiar to

Florentine life."

Francesco nodded "Indeed, Sire. Milan has no idiots either, yet in Florence they often seem to be in charge."

François grinned and then, with a flourish, pointed his finger at me very determinedly, saying "Children. Your mechanicants cannot have intercourse and create a new mechanicant. You must build them all yourself. So the essence of life is to be able to create further life."

"Nuns and priests, bishops, cardinals, Popes, do not have children..." at this both of them laughed. Unperturbed, I continued "Many of them, then. But they are still very much alive."

"But they could create life if they chose."

"What about the Lady Claudette," I continued, "your sister's favoured attendant? She is barren. Is she therefore not alive because she herself cannot create life?"

"Of course she is, but the important factor here is potential not actual fecundity. What's more...", he added as a further thought obviously struck him, "this also answers your soul question, as we know that God himself creates the soul for each new person at the moment they are conceived when he breathes life into them. Your mechanicants are not conceived therefore they have neither life nor a soul."

~

These discussions have continued for some days now. The argument always returns to the same points over and over again. Like everything else about our understanding of God's realm, in the end it comes down to blind faith in what the Church Fathers tell us. I still find this difficult to accept, as I have spent most of my life making careful notes and observations in order to try and learn how everything in nature works. As I get older I realise that, however much I try to examine, understand, or explain, there is always far more waiting to be addressed. So, hard as it is, I must finally accept that I cannot understand everything; only God himself is omniscient.

For many years the Church's teaching of the restrictions on who, or what, may enter the Kingdom of Heaven has dissuaded me from a belief in the afterlife, or at least the orthodox view of the afterlife. I cannot examine, measure, or record any aspect of this life eternal, save only in my dreams, so I have chosen to ignore it as far as possible. But now, with the culmination of the mechanicant project almost in sight, I realise that it is an issue that I can no longer ignore; perhaps my increasing age and declining health have also made me more aware of my body's mortality and concerned for my own immortal soul. They say churches are filled with the young out of fear of the old, and the old out of fear of death. I still cannot reconcile the denial of immortality to animals or even those of other creeds (surely the great Greek and Arab thinkers are at least as worthy of an eternal life in God's presence, as a priest of the Church who pays lip service to his professed vocation while scheming and plotting and whoring and murdering?). Despite all these concerns, my work has led me to conclude that the Almighty must have a place for us after our death, else we are all even less than machines put here for no discernible purpose, mere automata as François believes of animals.

François had been concerned for some time lest I end my days without having reconciled myself with the Church – I feel that my conscience is now reconciled with God (which is what surely matters?), but for François' sake I have agreed to make overtures to his priests to return to full Communion.

The more progress I make towards building a working mechanicant Mario, the more concerned I become about the fate of these creations. It is clear that to be effective a mechanicant will need to be autonomous, and in that case surely the creation becomes a creature? But merely positing such an idea raises even more questions. The components of my first working prototype are lying on my bench awaiting final assembly. At what point does it metamorphose from a collection of parts into a creature? When I attach the last component? When I feed it fuel? Or when it starts to perform work? I have been sitting here in my studio looking at these things before me, considering how IT becomes HE[13].

Leo, my Papal namesake and most recent Medici patron, recently accused me of always thinking about the end of a project before I'd even started it and others have complained that I don't complete commissions (at all, never mind on time!) That may have been true upon occasion. But in this case I feel that I MUST NOT complete this work. Replacing God's children with mechanicants so that they can spend more time praising Him and saving their souls is very laudable, but I now fear that it will only result in the need to create something else to replace the mechanicants themselves in order to allow them, in their turn, to save their own souls. And so on, ad infinitum. Where would it end? Would every generation be compelled to create yet another creature to relieve the previous generation's from their work, freeing them to pray? With experience and increased knowledge maybe engineers could one day dispense with mechanical components and build a new race out of the components of life itself – after all it requires little effort on the part of a man to enable his wife to create a perfectly-formed child.

---

[13] In Leonardo's original Italian text he sometimes, as here, uses 'slave' (masculine) to mean 'creature' (feminine). As 'machine' is a feminine noun, this phrase is literally 'SHE becomes HE', but in modern English 'IT' seems to convey Leonardo's intent more effectively.

Perhaps in centuries to come men will in this way be attempting to play God, surely the ultimate blasphemy. I can foresee someone inquisitive and skilled, seduced by the glamour of discovery and invention as I have almost been, yet blind to the morality, attempting to combine the strength of the horse or the speed of the deer with the dexterity and intelligence of a man.

Maybe such was the genesis of the dog-men of which we have heard so many tales. I have always doubted the existence of such creatures; I have met many people who claim to know someone who knows someone who has seen them, but I have yet to meet anyone who has actually seen them himself.

~

I have written to the Cardinal, telling him that I cannot complete the project. He has replied by sending me another bag of coins (gold this time) and a firmly worded note reminding me it is God's work and that I have a duty to use my God-given talents in his service (although it wasn't clear whether the service to which he was referring was God's or the Cardinal's – perhaps he sees no distinction?)

Despite written and financial encouragement from His Eminence, I know I cannot complete this project. The more I consider the consequences the more I am convinced it must be against God's will. Francesco agrees with me, although I doubt he would ever seriously disagree with me about anything important.

Even the King has come round to my view. Our hitherto differing opinions on souls and the afterlife have been largely put aside. I suspect that he is now more concerned for my well-being than winning a theological debate. His concern may be justified. The worry has made me very tired – Francesco is fussing that I'm not eating properly and my health is suffering as a result, the irony of which, after our earlier experiments into the effects of food, is not wasted on me. I have also suffered an apoplexy – brought on, François' doctors now say, by a combination of age, overwork and anger. They originally blamed bad humours and poisoned blood, but I know that those are the standard responses of doctors to anything that they can not immediately diagnose. I am sure that it will eventually be doctors that kill me. I have been prescribed rest, theriac[14] – and leeches of course, but I have declined them (François was amused by my observation of the symmetry of employing bloodsuckers who themselves employ bloodsuckers – even though it is to him that these particular bloodsuckers are presenting their accounts for my treatment). At present I am paralysed in my right arm. Francesco has sent another note to Cardinal d'Aragona telling him of my incapacity.

~

I have been warned that the Cardinal is coming to see

---

[14] Theriac was the universal antidote from Roman times until the late 19th Century. It contains 64 ingredients including opium, frankincense and myrrh. The modern word 'treacle' is derived from it (but is not as therapeutic!).

me, on his way back to Rome from a visit to Spain. Francesco has hidden the prototype components and most of my notes, leaving out just a few early drawings from my research into limb actions and some sketches of Marie-Louise sewing, which will hopefully distract His Eminence.

~

The Cardinal and his secretary have visited us once again. It was a typical October afternoon here in Clu, neither hot nor cold, wet nor parched. Maturina served us refreshments and, while Francesco distracted Antonio with my copy of Fra Luca's Proportione[15], I took His Eminence upstairs to the studio. He cast only the merest glance over the paintings while I lamented that my recent paralysis had brought an end to my painting, drawing and engineering. By good fortune neither he nor Antonio had ever seen me work so they do not know that I am mancino[16]. I showed him my mechanicant research drawings and returned his bag of coins apologising that it was no longer possible for me to continue[17]. At that point the King arrived and the Cardinal, not suspecting that François knew of the project, became very circumspect in his language. He did, however, make it clear that he expected me to teach and supervise others to continue my work. The King expressed great concern at my current debility and assured the Cardinal that he would personally ensure that I was not overstretched or tired until my health improved. This, of course, was not what the Cardinal

---

[15] Fra Luca Pacioli, De Divina Proportione – Leonardo had produced the illustrations for this mathematical treatise by his friend Pacioli.

[16] Slang for left-handed.

[17] In his record of this meeting Antonio de Beatis, the Cardinal's secretary, laments that Leonardo can no longer paint or draw as his right arm is paralysed. Although some others had remarked on Leonardo's left-handedness, it was obviously not widely known at the time.

wanted to hear, but it was impossible for him to argue with His Majesty – not only would it have seemed overbearing, but with François in favour with Pope Leo and the Cardinal still somewhat suspect he could not afford to make an enemy of the King. Just then, Maturina appeared with a reminder from Antonio that His Eminence needed to leave for another appointment. I left François in the studio while I accompanied the Cardinal downstairs and outside to join Antonio and the waiting horses.

On my return François was studying the sketches of Marie-Louise and grinning smugly like a mischievous youth.

"I've never trusted that supposed man of God," he said shaking his head.

I thanked the King for his help and timely intervention.

"As payment you can give me these sketches".

Despite the closeness of our friendship he was a man even I could not refuse.

~

It is a few days since the Cardinal's visit and I have received another letter further exhorting me to train someone, he suggested Francesco, to continue with his mechanicant project. I eventually replied that I was hoping to recover enough to be able to pass on some of my experience of the various arts in which I have dabbled, but was not able to assure him that anyone, not even dear Francesco, would be capable of continuing with his project.

~

I have received a further letter from the cardinal. Unlike his previous correspondence, this is a formal missive – as well as a signature this one is sealed with his ring. The script is the same, I imagine it is Antonio's.

He exhorts me once again to train a successor; in fact, he says he has already identified a suitable candidate. A German engraver no less. While I have a great interest in the new mechanisms being developed for engraving with copper plates, ideal for reproducing designs and plans of machinery, they are not capable of as excellent a work as a painting. I would be insulted by the Cardinal's suggestion had this man and his work not already been known to me; he spent some time with my old friend Luca, learning the secrets of perspective, and then came to visit me briefly in Milan. Francesco tells me it is widely held that his engraving of Saint Jerome in his Study is modelled on me; I haven't seen it, therefore I do not know if that is so. I have examined a little of his work and hear many admiring comments from others who have seen more. They say he is the greatest German artist of all time, but Francesco points out there is little competition! Even François is impressed by his works and reputation, and it appears that the Emperor Maximillian has this artist salaried at his court in the same manner as I am here at Clu. François looked pleased when he told me and seemed to think he was the better off[18].

Francesco has replied on my behalf to say that the skills required are those of invention and engineering rather than of draughtsmanship, and to decline on my behalf.

---

[18] It appears that Leonardo is referring to Albrecht Dürer. It is not recorded elsewhere that they actually met, although many critics have remarked on the obvious influence of Leonardo's work on Dürer, especially after the latter's sojourn in Venice in 1505-7 and his visit to Fra Luca Pacioli in Bologna at the end of 1506.

For some months I have been incapable of truly finishing this project. Although I have decided that I must not complete the work or build even one mechanicant, I have found it impossible to destroy what I have done thus far. Whenever I thought I had the courage to burn the notes and plans, I faltered before I could even ask Francesco to bring the lighted candle. I am still torn deciding what to do. Should I obliterate everything? Francesco has tried to persuade me that once knowledge is found it cannot be lost. I am not convinced.

"Look", he says, "how in recent years we have rediscovered much that our ancestors knew and subsequent generations had forgotten".

Even in my own lifetime there has been a rebirth of art, the like of which has not been seen since the heyday of the mighty Roman Empire. This, Francesco remonstrates, proves that knowledge cannot be lost for ever. Even if I destroy my work and notes, who knows whether it too will be reborn in centuries to come.

~

I used to think of this as a Great Undertaking and yet now it seems rather to be a Great Conceit. In my life I have done wondrous things, I have built amazing artifices, I have stretched the sinews of man's mind (or at least this man's mind) and yet I fear that in this undertaking I have stumbled into the very heart of God's own realm. Not Paradise (or Hell), but Creation itself. There have been those who have decried my skills as vainglorious excess, I have always regarded such detractors as mere envies trying to distract from my work with their false accusations. But this time I have almost gone too far. Why? Because I could. Perhaps my envious critics were right after all.

~

The Cardinal died a few days ago, to the lasting grief of no-one. Finally I am free from his endless letters. Now, at last, I feel able to destroy everything I have made, although Francesco has recently persuaded me to keep some of my journal entries to record what could have been. I fear that they may represent my undoing at the hands of my enemies. So I shall obscure them using my cipher. If anyone has the skill to discover the truth, I pray they will have enough wisdom to understand what must, and what must not, be done.

La fine.

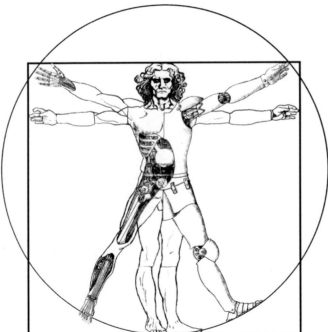

Crypto Da Vinci

Brigadier

As Lucia finished reading us her translation, a silence settled on the room, strangely emphasised by an uncharacteristic quietude outside the window. The street was suddenly empty and still. Even the rest of the hotel was silent. As if the whole of Florence was collectively holding its breath in awe of Leonardo's revelations. It seemed to last for an eternity, such was the incongruity of this absence of any of the sounds of the vibrancy and life for which this city is justly famous. But in reality it can only have lasted a second or two.

Al broke the spell.

"Wow. That was certainly unexpected."

"At least by me," she added.

"Are there no references anywhere else to this Mechanicant project?" I asked.

"Not that I've ever come across," said Al.

"Nor me," echoed Lucia, "and although I'm not an expert in Leonardo's writings I am what you might call an informed amateur. He's one of my heroes, if you will. I've read about his robotic knight and automated musical instruments, but I've never heard of such a sophisticated automaton as this before. He must have been serious about wanting no one to find out about it."

"I can understand his concern about letting the notes on the Mechanicant fall into the wrong hands." I said. "Wrong, that is, by virtue of being unable to comprehend the ethical dilemma that obviously haunted him and which may have led to his decision to abandon the project entirely. Wrong, even, in the sense of being less skilful as an engineer and misusing the notes to construct some inferior device that may endanger the very souls it was supposed to be freeing. Or merely wrong in the sense that they could inform the Cardinal that Leonardo had not, in fact, been unable to complete the project but had, rather, chosen to ensure its failure. In all of these ways, the wrong hands could have been dangerous personally, spiritually or morally. Given that he had already committed these notes to paper, albeit steganographed under his own algorithm, and had bequeathed them to Melzi for safekeeping, I could even understand that there would still be an intellectual or even egotistical imperative for him to ensure that the algorithm itself would remain accessible, as he said, to a suitable 'Man who is ... a Mathematician'. But that still doesn't explain how, or indeed why, the crucial key to that algorithm came to be hidden in a book printed over 200 years later."

"That's right," agreed Al, "by then Melzi had gone and his avaricious family had already sold the great man's notebooks. Leonardo had become more widely known among the crowned heads of Europe than ever before."

"So," I asked, "who would have been so keen to hide the text and why in this particular copy of Dryden's Virgil?"

Al looked thoughtful for a few seconds and then looking up she spoke.

"If the notebooks had been dispersed around various rich aristocrats, maybe one of them discovered Leonardo's cryptographic technique and was using it for his own purposes. In fact, come to think of it, that would explain the reference at the end to the King over the Water. Perhaps it was a Jacobite sympathiser after all who was using it, and he had it hidden in the Dryden to enable someone else to be able to decode his messages."

"So it's coincidence that we found it and have used it to decode the Mechanicant notes?"

"Serendipity rather than coincidence." Al smiled.

"I'm sure that Leonardo's Mechanicant notes are far more interesting than some Jacobite political intrigue. Leonardo's Mechanicant versus Jacobite machinations. I know which I'd rather read." I grinned.

It was clear that the only way I could possibly come close to trying to answer these questions would be by investigating the provenance of the book.

"When we get home, I'm going to go to the shop where Hugh bought the book and see if I can find out a bit more about its history."

"If you're still interested in having some help..." Al looked at me quizzically, to which I nodded and smiled, "I'll carry on looking for other Leonardo folios to decode. Maybe there's more about this Mechanicant project waiting to be found somewhere, or perhaps some other notes that he didn't want too public either."

"Meanwhile we need to decipher the remainder of these pages from Simonetta."

"*Amici*," Lucia stood to take her leave, "I must go home to my family, they'll be wondering where I've got to. Call me if you find anything else, I'll be happy to translate any pages that you decipher. In fact I'm very interested, so maybe I will do some research too, like Al, and see if I can dig up any more suitable folios."

"That would be great." I said.

"And if you're going to publish something eventually, let me know; I have contacts with some Italian publishers. I'm sure there'd be a good market here. Leonardo is still one of our national heroes."

"Okay, thanks."

Lucia left, amid the usual Italian ritual of cheek kissing and hugs, and Al and I were once again alone. I raided the mini bar to get us a night cap and we both drank in silence, each in our own reflective mood. Soon, Al had finished her drink; she stood, bade me goodnight and went back to her own room.

In the morning, for once, our travel plans worked like clockwork. Early wake-up call, breakfast, packing, check-out, taxi to the airport, check-in and boarding. Before we knew it we were airborne en route home to England. As we flew across Kent and banked to circle in to the airport I was, unusually, sitting by a window that gave me a good view of my own village – I could just about pick out my house – followed not much later by a view of Al's home in Dulwich. We landed and caught the tube back into London. Al was heading straight for her shop so we parted company at Oxford Circus. While I was sitting on the train out of town towards home, once again travelling in the opposite direction to the hordes of passengers who were, this time, inbound as the cheap fares kicked in, I phoned Hugh to confirm where he had bought the Dryden. Later that day I would drive out into the heart of Kent to meet the bookseller and see what more I could find out about this curious book.

~

When I got to East Malling I parked next to the triangle of grass, surprisingly neat and tidy, opposite the second-hand bookshop through the windows of which could be glimpsed an unsurprising jumble of volumes stacked on shelves, next to shelves, under shelves and leaning against shelves in gravity-defying piles as tall as a man (albeit a below-average height man in stockinged feet, with a pronounced stoop – which, amazingly, was a perfect description of the chap sitting deep in the bosom of this repository of print). I hadn't been here for at least ten years, but this fellow looked very familiar, as did many of the volumes with which he was surrounded.

"How's business?" I asked him as I strolled through the already open door.

"Mustn't grumble," he said, then added "but that won't stop me of course."

He looked up with a sardonic grin.

It was the same fellow who had been here all those years before, I realised. I remembered he'd made the same quip then too.

"Looking for anything in particular?" he asked.

"Well actually, a friend of mine bought a copy of Dryden's Works of Virgil from you recently."

"I remember, the 1730 edition. Three volumes. Surprisingly clean end papers."

"That's the one."

"I doubt if I can get another copy if that's what you're after," he said, shaking his head gently.

"No. He gave that one to me as a birthday present. But I wanted to trace its provenance, I'm intrigued because it had been rebound and I'm curious to know why, and when."

"That's what I thought. I told your friend too. Nice job though. Why're you so interested?"

"As I said I'm just curious. I'm a bit of a bibliophile. I already have a set of the 1721 edition and I compared them. The new binding seemed to have been done in order to change some of the illustrations and remove one altogether."

"Probably just cut out, there's a lot of vandalism these days."

"No. Definitely removed before it was rebound. So, my interest has been well and truly piqued. Do you remember where you got it from?"

"As a matter of fact I do. I very nearly kept those volumes for myself, you know – occupational hazard really. My wife Olive, God rest her soul, always said that

I'd never be a commercial success as a bookseller because I'd buy lots of books that interested me and then never want to actually sell them. She wasn't that far from the truth either. Perceptive woman. I miss her so much, you know. Don't get much company these days either."

"No grandchildren to fuss over?"

"We never had children. Couldn't. Biggest sadness of Olive's life, God rest her soul." He gazed into some distant horizon that only he could see and tears started to well up in his eyes. After a few seconds he suddenly came to, as if he had just remembered where he was. "What about you?"

"Me?"

"Kids?"

"No. I'm single. Never had the courage to settle down. Always too busy."

"But there was someone you should have settled down with."

"Why do you say that?"

"I can see it in your eyes. I'm right aren't I?"

"If you'd asked me a few days ago I would have said no."

"And now?"

"I've recently come to realise that there is a person I should probably have married a long time ago."

"And now it's too late?"

"Yes... Well, no... maybe. I don't know."

"Take my advice, don't leave it any longer. I had the happiest years of my life with Olive, God rest her soul, and I miss her dreadfully." He sniffed, wiped his eyes with a handkerchief he had removed from his breast pocket, and pulled himself together.

"Anyway, you were asking about the Dryden."

"What?" I had almost forgotten why I was here, I had been thinking about Al.

"Oh yes. Do you remember where you got it?"

"I do. One of my best customers. The Brigadier. Lived over in Larkfield. Jolly good chap he was. Knew what was what. Died a few months back and left his library to his widow. She doesn't particularly care for books and just wanted to clear them out. To be honest, I think she needed the money. They'd retired to quite a decent-sized house but I imagine it must take some upkeep. Anyway, she asked me to come over and take his complete collection and sell them on for her. He had some lovely volumes that I managed to place with London dealers. She raised a decent amount, and gave me a fair cut. I bought the Dryden for myself but then thought of what Olive would say, God rest her soul, so I put it out on the shelves here. Your friend came in the very same day, I hadn't even had time to price it up. It was a Thursday and he was the first customer I had had all week."

"Almost like it was meant to be!"

"You believe in that sort of thing?"

"Sometimes." I grinned. "So," I prompted him, "the Brigadier's widow. She still lives in Larkfield?"

"Yes."

"Do you think she'd mind if I went round to talk to her?"

"I doubt it. Tell you what, I'll give her a call and ask for you. What's your name?"

"Peter White."

"Okay. The phone's in the back. Could you keep an eye on the shop for me while I ring her?"

"Sure. And if a customer wants to buy something?"

"Very unlikely," he shook his head, "but on the off chance I'm sure they'll wait till I get back. If not you could take their money for me, if you wouldn't mind. Everything's priced." So saying he disappeared into the bowels of the shop.

A few minutes later I could hear him talking on the phone, but I couldn't make out what he was actually saying. Then he came back holding out a small piece of paper to me.

"This is her name and address. She's expecting you. Do you know Larkfield?"

"Vaguely."

"You can't miss the house, it's the biggest one on Lunsford Lane before you get to the new estate."

As far as I could recall, the 'new' estate had been built in the 1950s.

~

"Hello, my name is Peter White. You must be Iris." I smiled, as a neatly dressed, silver haired lady opened the door. She was fairly short and had a smooth, smiling face. In fact she reminded me of the recently departed Queen Mother.

"Ah yes. Ernest telephoned a few minutes ago about you. He said I could trust you. Do come in." She held the front door wide to let me in and guided me towards the first room on the left of a long hallway. I walked into what she undoubtedly still thought of as the drawing room. A tiled mantelpiece surrounded the fireplace which had been replaced at some point in the past with a gas fire. The décor was cheerful, but a little old fashioned for my taste.

"Do sit down young man. The kettle has just boiled, would you like a cup of tea? I was making myself an Earl Grey, I'm afraid that's all I have. It's a bit of an acquired taste, but my husband and I have preferred it for years."

"It's a taste I've never acquired, thank you. Do you have any coffee?"

"No, sorry. Not even instant. I've just run out. I had a

whist morning here today and the ladies drank me out of coffee – none of them appreciate Earl Grey either!" She smiled apologetically. "They ate all the shortbread biscuits too, I'm afraid. Not that I really mind of course. I'm grateful for the company; and now, more company. I'm really being spoiled today. Can I offer you a cold drink perhaps?" All this time she had remained standing, making me feel awkward in the comfortable and enveloping armchair into which she had ushered me.

"Some water would be very welcome, thank you."

"Do excuse me while I go to the kitchen, Mr White. I'll be back in a jiffy."

Moments later she was back with a glass of chilled water in one hand and a teacup and saucer in the other. She handed me the glass, carefully put her own drink on the coffee table and sat down opposite me in another armchair.

"I'm afraid I have no cake or even biscuits to offer you, they all went this morning…" she trailed off.

"At the whist drive? Please don't worry. I really shouldn't be eating cakes or biscuits anyway." I grinned and patted my stomach.

"Nor should most of us in the whist drive," she laughed, "but that never stops us. I'm sure we'll all go through diabetes or worse. At our age, though, you stop caring. Anyway, you didn't come here to talk about a bunch of silly old women. Ernest said you are researching for a book. How exciting. What is it about?"

"Actually, I'm not writing a book. I'm researching into the history of a particular book that I was given. One that a friend of mine bought from Ernest's shop. He told me that he had bought it from you."

"It was my husband's library. He died eight months ago."

"I'm sorry."

"Thank you. It was difficult to cope at first. But everyone around here has been very helpful. We have two grown up children, with their own families and they have been wonderful. In fact, I've seen more of them in the last few months than in the previous twenty years."

"They live far way?"

"No. Less than half an hour's drive. But they had different attitudes, shall we say, to my husband Tom. He was in the army."

"Ernest said he was a Brigadier."

"That's right. Well our children grew up in the sixties and were attracted to the lifestyle of the hippies. Quite different from that of a career soldier. Tom believed in traditional values, Queen and country. Duty. That sort of thing. They were pacifists, got involved in anti-Vietnam demonstrations and so on. He couldn't understand what they were up to, couldn't accept their views."

"And you?"

"Goodness. Free love and flower power? Burning bras? No, no. I accepted their decisions once they were adults, but as a lifestyle it wasn't for me. I'm far too old and boring. Even then." She smiled, almost wistfully, I thought.

"Anyway," she continued, "once they'd left home we hardly ever saw them. When Tom retired we bought this house and came to live here, halfway between where the children now live. But, still, we rarely saw them. Now I see one or other of them every week. And my grandchildren. That's a blessing. Even so, I'd still rather have Tom back." She looked down sadly and I was ready to retrieve a handkerchief from my pocket for the likely tears. But she looked up, forced a smile and continued. "But I mustn't be maudlin. A particular book you said? I asked Ernest to sell them all for me. There were some quite old ones apparently and he managed to sell them in

London for a lot of money. I wasn't really interested in them, you see. Never had been. These days my eyes aren't what they used to be – the diabetes does that – so I wouldn't be able to read them even if I wanted to."

"I was hoping you might know where your husband bought this book." I had brought all three volumes of the Dryden with me in a small briefcase, so I took them out to show her.

She glanced at them. "I'm sorry, but I really haven't any idea. I never took an interest, so Tom rarely even bothered to show me what he bought. He went on 'expedishions', he called them, you know like Winnie the Pooh, to London to look for bargains. Sometimes he would get back really excited about something special that he'd found, but he knew there was no point in trying to enthuse me."

"Oh well, never mind."

"But all is not lost, Mr White. On the contrary. One of the benefits of military training is discipline and a respect for order. My husband maintained all the paperwork for his bookish transactions in a file in his study. It's obviously rubbed off on me, because when Ernest sold the library for me I filed the invoices, or receipts, or whatever they were, in the same file. I still have it. If you'll excuse me again I'll go and get it and you can look through it for your book."

All the time she had been speaking, she had been holding her teacup in her right hand, hovering about two inches above the saucer in her left. Now that she had stopped talking, she raised the cup to her lips and demurely took a couple of sips before putting it back on the saucer and returning them to the coffee table. Then she stood up, smiled and once again left the room. I could hear her footsteps clacking on the wooden staircase and then in the room above. Soon she came back down the stairs and entered the room with a large expanding file which she held out to me.

"It will all be in chronological order, and I don't know when Tom bought that book, so I'm afraid you might have to wade through the lot. While you do that, I'll go and make some cakes."

"Please don't bother on my behalf."

"Young man. This is my house, and if I want to make cakes I'll make cakes. I would make them even if you weren't here. But as you are, you can choose. Cherry cakes or fairy cakes?"

"Well I must admit I'm partial to cherry cakes. But I'm a strict vegetarian, so I doubt if I'd be able to eat them anyway."

"What don't you eat that's in cakes?"

"Eggs, or animal fat. Or margarine, because it has fish in it."

"Margarine. Heaven forbid! Is butter all right?"

"Yes."

"Fine. During the war we couldn't get eggs and my mother made cakes with vinegar and bicarb. Worked just fine. I've got both. I can do that. Then you'll have to stay to tea out of a sense of duty." She grinned at me and winked conspiratorially.

"You win. Thank you, I would love to stay for tea." I smiled back.

She went out to the kitchen and I could hear the sounds of cake mixture being prepared and the oven being heated while I was working my way methodically through the receipts in the Brigadier's file. He had obviously bought a lot of books in the last twenty years and, as Iris had said, he had kept all the paperwork for each purchase. More than one receipt identified a book that I would have loved to have seen and I found myself paying more attention to the books I wasn't looking for than the one I was. In fact

I almost missed the relevant receipt because it was handwritten on a scrap of paper and just identified the purchase of 'Dryd. 6ed. 3Vol'. There was an address in Cheyne Walk in London and the name Carter Philus. It was dated in 1997. I made a note of the details and put the paper back into its rightful place in the file. By now I could smell the cakes baking, but Iris hadn't yet re-appeared from the kitchen. So I looked through the rest of the receipts to see what else this library had contained. I was surprised at the breadth of subject matter that had obviously appealed to the Brigadier, including some titles that I knew to be quite rare. Over twenty years he had made some very shrewd purchases and had, indeed, found some very special bargains. When I came to the last items, I saw that Ernest had done a decent job of selling the contents of the library on Iris's behalf and had charged her a very small commission. The Brigadier had not only bought titles that were of interest to him, but in the process had built up a sound investment to provide for Iris. As I was replacing the final receipt in the file, the chink of plates on a tray alerted me to Iris's imminent return. Soon the coffee table was covered with plates of cherry cakes, fairy cakes, cucumber sandwiches (with the crusts removed) and a pitcher of what turned out to be home-made lemonade. It was like being ten years old again. Iris passed me a plate.

"Tuck in. It's all vegetarian."

"I thought you said cherry cakes OR fairy cakes?"

"I was intrigued to see if I could make the cakes with this vinegar recipe like my mother did. So I decided to try to make both. I hope they've worked."

"They look delicious…"

"The butter cream is just butter and sugar and a drop of vanilla essence. That's okay too isn't it?"

"You shouldn't have gone to so much effort."

"It was no effort. Anyway, I need the practice because one of my granddaughters has just decided to become vegetarian so I need to be able to make suitable cakes when she comes to see me. Did you find what you were looking for?"

"Yes. Thank you. Your husband bought the books from someone in Chelsea in 1997."

"Well I never! Chelsea. His uncle was a Chelsea Pensioner. He used to go and see him now and again. I didn't go though, old soldiers reliving campaigns. You know the sort of the thing."

"I can imagine. But this was an address in Cheyne Walk."

"That's posh isn't it?"

"Rather."

"Then, it can't have been someone he knew. We didn't have any rich friends. Was there a name?"

"Carter Philus."

"No. Means nothing to me. Will you go and talk to them?"

"If the same person still lives there, hopefully I can have a chat with them."

"Well, you know, young man, you've rather intrigued me with your quest. But you haven't told me why you are so interested in the history of this book."

"I haven't pieced together the story myself yet, that's why I'm trying to track down the book's history, but what I know so far starts with Leonardo da Vinci."

Iris picked up a fairy cake and two cucumber sandwiches and popped them onto her plate, then settled back on her chair and said "Really, tell me more".

~

After I had told Iris all that Al and I had found out so far, she made me promise to let her know what else we uncovered. She said it sounded intriguing enough to become a book itself, maybe even one that she would read. I promised that if it did I would dedicate it to her. After that she had also insisted I tell her all about Al. Finally she wanted a description of Florence, a city she had dreamed of visiting as a young girl, a dream she had never managed to fulfil.

I eventually left for home just as it was starting to get dark, full to bursting with cherry cakes, cucumber sandwiches and lemonade.

Crypto Da Vinci

Spy

A week later I was in Kensington for a meeting which was finished by lunchtime, so I thought I would take the opportunity to check out that address in Cheyne Walk. Before long I had found the right house. It was not very wide but quite tall, with three storeys visible above the ground, and obvious signs of a basement too. Once upon a time it must have had a good view of the boats passing by on the river, although the smell would probably have been quite off-putting then. Now, of course, there is a Victorian embankment and its trees acting as a screen, even from the top storey windows.

A few seconds after I had rung the doorbell, a short, balding, elderly gentleman opened the door. He was wearing a dark suit and tie with a beige cardigan over a white shirt. While not exactly threadbare the clothes had obviously seen better times, probably quite a while ago. It was difficult to tell if he was the owner of the house or some sort of servant.

"Good afternoon, sir. My name is Peter White. I'm looking for Mr Carter Philus who I believe lived here in the late nineties."

"Still does, and it's Philus," he said, pronouncing the name to rhyme with 'feel us' rather than 'file us' as I had done. He looked at me suspiciously.

"What do you want?" Although abrupt, he was firm but not rude, obviously used to dealing with unwanted visitors.

"I'm trying to trace the provenance of a copy of a book that he sold in 1997."

"Why? Was it stolen?"

"No. Well, not as far as I know. It was given to me as a present and I noticed some anomalies."

"Anomalies?"

"All three volumes had been rebound and all the illustrations had been replaced."

"Except one, which was removed." He corrected me. "You're talking about Dryden's Virgil."

"That's right. You know something about it?"

"Maybe. Very well, you seem genuine enough. I am Carter Philus. Come inside where we can talk more comfortably than here on the doorstep." He beckoned me in. "Can't be too careful these days. Lots of strange people about."

He showed me into a small library with two rickety chairs either side of a large desk piled precariously high with books.

"When did you get the Dryden?" he asked as I tentatively lowered myself into one of the chairs. Surprisingly, it didn't collapse. It didn't even creak.

"A few weeks ago. A friend of mine bought it from a little bookshop in Kent as a birthday present for me."

"Kent? And the shopkeeper had bought it from the Brigadier?"

"No, from his widow. The Brigadier died eight months ago."

"That's a shame. He seemed like a nice chap. For a military man."

"I never knew him. She showed me his receipts and that's how I found out he had originally bought it from you."

"Indeed."

"I was hoping you could shed some light on its history. Do you remember where you got it?"

"I do. Very well. In fact I was quite taken with those volumes for a while." He was about to sit down when he stopped and seemed to suddenly brighten up.

"But where are my manners? What a poor host. My sister Martha would have a fit if she were here."

"Does she live with you?"

"Not any more. Both she and my younger sister Mary passed away a long time ago."

"I'm sorry."

"Don't be. I haven't mourned them in years. Now, let me fix us a drink. Do you care for white wine?"

"I do, thank you, but I don't usually partake in the afternoon."

"Nonsense. I have lived alone for a very long time young man, so a glass of wine at any time seems like an indulgence, not to say a vice; whereas a drink in company is a social necessity. So you see, my hospitality isn't entirely altruistic." He smiled. "Please join me in a glass of wine so I don't feel guilty."

"Put like that, how can I refuse?" I smiled back indulgently, aware that I was the one being manipulated to feel guilt.

He disappeared from the room but was back moments later carrying a small silver tray on which were perched two of the largest wine glasses I had ever seen, filled with an almost colourless liquid with just the slightest suspicion of green. The glasses were beaded with condensation from their obviously chilled contents. He carefully placed the tray on the desk in a space that seemed to be made for it. Sitting down he lifted a glass and offered it to me. I accepted it, waited for him to raise his own drink before I took a sip of the cool, dry, clean, wine. "Very nice." I said.

I'm not much of a wine aficionado so I can't tell you what variety of grape it was made with, which vineyard it came from, or even what country. I can tell you though that it was very refreshing. Fruity, almost nutty. Perhaps even as enjoyable as my favourite Frascati. I wanted to keep a clear head to remember whatever this affable gentleman had to tell me, so I took a small sip and replaced my glass on the tray. As I looked up, my host was savouring his own wine, with a faint smile playing on his lips and a decided twinkle in his eyes.

"You were saying?" I prompted.

"I was? Oh yes, I was, wasn't I. I had that Dryden for very many years. When they first came my way I read all three volumes from cover to cover. Let me tell you, it was a very pleasant experience, the mixture of obsequiousness and arrogance in Dryden's dedications contrasting with the elegance and beauty of his translation of Virgil's timeless poetry. His assessment of the characters of some of his critics was spot on. It was refreshing to read someone who wasn't afraid to speak his mind, I'm afraid that had been a dangerous luxury for many years, especially after what's now called the Reformation. For years afterwards, I enjoyed each opportunity to bathe in the richness of language spoken in those days. English now has become so much more utilitarian and homogenised. When I first came to this country, it was still regarded as a sophisticated tongue that every educated person in Europe wanted to be able to speak. Mind you, in those days I still had an accent and got into trouble for sounding too foreign. They even thought I was a spy! Me." He laughed.

"But I'm digressing again. Where was I? Oh yes. Dryden. His translation of Virgil was the best I'd seen. My Latin had never been that good, occupying forces and all that, we needed to communicate but weren't intending on immersing ourselves in their culture. It was years later that it became clear that understanding Latin was the only way to be educated. Then you could be whoever you wanted. Someone obviously educated couldn't possibly be lowly born. Assume a title of somewhere no-one's ever been and you've got an entrée into the highest echelons of society. Look at young Jack…"

"Jack?" I asked, puzzled.

"Giacomo. Casanova. It worked for him in France, nearly worked in England too. But eventually you have to move on." His voice trailed off as if he was reliving old times. His eyes seemed to take on a faraway look.

"Latin never was my strong point." I ventured.

"Doesn't really matter these days does it? But Dryden's translation was very evocative. Took me back to better days. So evocative. Don't you think? Ah, but you've only just got them, you probably haven't had the time to luxuriate in his language yet."

"Actually I already have an earlier edition, so I read it some time ago. And I agree with you, it is a very special book."

"Indeed. Anyway…" so saying, he stopped talking long enough to have a sizeable sip of his wine, making his smile more beatific. "…I studied the illustrations," he continued, "and reread the text many times, especially the Georgics. Then I was given a copy of the fifth edition."

"That's the edition I already had."

"Ah, so we have even more in common." He nodded sagely, and took the opportunity of the momentary pause to take yet another deep draught of his wine. I was sure his smile was becoming wider with each mouthful.

"I had only glanced through them at first, but sometime later, when I felt the need to revisit Virgil's Pastorals I thought I'd read them in my latest acquisition instead. That's when I realised that there was an illustration missing from my existing copy. I was furious, assuming that someone had hacked at it just to remove the plate. I couldn't imagine why, though, as it's hardly the best picture. So I looked a little more closely and realised that

135

all the illustrations had been replaced on paper with the wrong orientation."

"The watermarks gave it away, didn't they. That was what I noticed first. The original would never have been printed that way."

"Indeed. I already knew it had been rebound, that had always been obvious, but it was only then that I started to suspect that there was more to it than merely a repair of some sort." He had been looking into his glass while talking, but now he looked up at me and, for the first time, I noticed the piercing blue of his eyes, reminiscent, I thought, of Paul Newman.

"I suspect the rebinding was done not long after it was originally bound and published." I suggested.

"I'm sure you're right. That's why I had previously assumed that it had been done to effect some sort of repair. Maybe there was some damage to the original binding caused by careless mishandling or even an accident in a library."

"Reading by candlelight must have been a particular hazard."

"It was. And bad for the eyes too. All that flickering. I'm so much happier with electric light. But why rebind all three? It would have had to have been a serious accident to damage all three volumes, yet none of the pages seems in the least affected. No water, fire, or even wax damage. So I concluded that they were rebound deliberately, for a specific purpose, rather than through necessity." He paused, then asked "Did you notice the spine?"

"Yes, decorated with the keys of St. Peter. Somewhat surprising choice given the prevailing anti-Catholic sentiment."

"Exactly. But only if they had been rebound in England or one of the other northern European protestant countries. Quite understandable if they had been rebound in, say, France, Spain or Italy."

"You think they were rebound on the continent?"

"I'm sure of it."

"But then, back in England, they'd stand out from any other copies."

"Indeed. So you could be sure that you had the right copy."

"Right copy for what?"

"Haha! That's the question isn't it? I never could work it out. Perhaps it's literal – the key to something else."

"But if you had become interested enough to speculate about their history, why did you sell them?"

"I was upset about the missing plate."

"Really?"

"Well... Okay. That, and because I had suspected all along that there was something more, let's say, sinister, about those books."

"Sinister? What do you mean?"

"When I originally had them I was given the name of someone to pass them on to, when I reached London."

"I don't follow. You bought them on behalf of someone else?"

"I didn't buy them. I was given them in Paris, before my trip to London. I was supposed to deliver them. Like a courier."

"For whom?"

"Louis."

"Louis?"

"Never mind. Let's just say, the government in Paris. They wanted me to deliver the books to a writer here in London who had political leanings in common with them. They didn't tell me why. But when I arrived I was arrested as a Catholic spy..."

"The police thought you were spying for the IRA?"

"No, this was long before they appeared on the scene. They were arresting many people coming from the continent at that time, there was rampant paranoia. They eventually let me go for lack of evidence, even the prime minister who had decided that I was obviously mad, had to admit that I had done nothing wrong. But I was being closely watched so I had to be very careful. I couldn't safely deliver the books and I had to return to Europe. I was unable to come back here for many years, by which time he was dead."

"So, who was this writer you were supposed to deliver the books to?"

"If I told you, I'm sure you wouldn't believe me. He's dead now, so it's irrelevant anyway."

"And you have no idea what he was going to do with them?"

"No."

I was now baffled. I pondered for a moment, considering my wine glass, then looked up at him.

"I don't understand what a code by Leonardo could have to do with the French government."

He looked surprised.

"Leonardo? As in da Vinci?" he asked.

"Yes."

"What has that got to do with the Dryden?"

"I found a text hidden in the illustrations, apparently written by Leonardo, explaining how to use a steganographic technique on text."

"Steganographic? Covered writing?"

"Hidden writing. From the Greek."

"Yes, that's what confused me. I know a little Greek. There were a lot of Greeks around when I was a child. They were generally regarded as the intellectuals. But explain more. How is steganography different from cryptography, which I understood also to mean hidden writing?"

"Essentially the difference is that with cryptography you have a message, say, that has been encrypted with a code so that its meaning is hidden, whereas with steganography the message itself has been hidden. The earliest examples go back to the ancient Greeks."

"Hence the name."

"Exactly. If you wanted to send a secret message you would scratch it on a wooden tablet and cover the tablet with wax, then write something innocuous on the wax. Only your recipient would know to remove the wax to read the real message. "

"Well, even at my age I can learn something new. And how ironic that it is ancient knowledge, even older than me." He smiled, then added "But where does this 'da Vinci code' fit in?"

"It would be a Leonardo code," I grinned back, "and it's an algorithm rather than a code. But I can't really answer your question. I found the text in the Dryden, as I said. It was the key to a treatise that Leonardo wrote providing a very effective algorithm to hide one text inside another. A friend of mine has tracked down some of his folios that we have decoded to find notes about some bizarre experiments he did towards the end of his life. But I don't think that has anything to do with why the key to the algorithm was hidden in the Dryden. If you say that the French government wanted the books sent to someone here in London, then presumably they wanted whoever it was to be able to use Leonardo's algorithm to extract a hidden message from something else. But I don't know what."

"Hmm. I might be able to help after all. Of course it could be a coincidence, but when I came to London with the Dryden volumes I also brought something else, that I was supposed to deliver to the Royal Society. Two folios from one of Leonardo's notebooks. I didn't pay much attention to them at the time."

"What happened to them? Did you deliver them to the Royal Society?"

"Not directly. I had them with me when I was arrested. It was the Excise men as I recall who actually interdicted me. They took the documents. Said they looked foreign and probably in code, obvious proof I was a spy. Eventually someone a bit more literate recognised them for what they were. Once I admitted that they were destined for the Royal Society I never saw them again, so I had always assumed that they were delivered there. However, I noticed one of them in the recent Windsor exhibition, identified as having come from King Charles the First's collection. But it was definitely one of the sheets I brought over, the only thing I had noticed about either sheet was a funny little design on that one, almost like a doodle in the margin. At the time it had reminded me of the pattern on a scarf my mother had when I was a child. I recognised it at once. So presumably both folios were somehow added to the Royal collection."

"I don't suppose you made a note of the catalogue number?"

"No, sorry. But I can sketch out the design for you if you want to try and find it again." So saying, he opened a small drawer on his side of the desk. A drawer I hadn't even noticed. He extracted a fountain pen and a sheet of paper and quickly drew a sketch of the design. "I'm no artist I'm afraid, but it looked roughly like this." He picked up the paper and blew gently on the ink to dry it, before handing it to me.

"Thank you. It sounds like more than just a coincidence, so maybe it will help solve the mystery. I'm sure Al will welcome anything that can narrow down the search of Leonardo manuscripts."

I carefully folded the paper and put it into my pocket.

"Who's Al?" he asked.

"The friend I told you about, she tracked down the other Leonardo folios."

"Oh, a young lady. Alice? From the name Al I was expecting…"

"It's short for Alison."

"A lovely name, Alison. Do you know what it means?"

"No, or if I did I don't remember."

"It means noble."

"That's most appropriate in this case."

"I knew someone called Alison once. Wife of the Scottish ambassador in Venice."

"I didn't know Scotland had their own ambassadors."

"No, not any more. She was a very good dancer. Noble. Noble character as well as being of noble birth."

"What happened to her?"

"Oh, she's dead now. Virtually everybody I've ever known is dead now. Except me of course. 'Twas ever thus." He sighed a very dolorous and heavy sigh. "One day, hopefully."

"Don't say that," I said, somewhat taken aback, "there's plenty to live for. Solving this mystery for a start!" I laughed, hoping to lighten his suddenly morbid mood.

"You have no idea," he said, "you're young…"

"Hardly." I objected.

"Everything's relative, as my old friend Albert used to say. Compared to me you're young, because I'm so much older than you can imagine. But I hope you do solve this mystery. And when you do, please let me know."

"I've already promised the Brigadier's widow that I'll publish something. I'll send you a copy too."

"That would be most kind." As he spoke he suddenly seemed to wilt before my eyes. His steel-blue eyes were now half closed and looked very weary.

"I don't mean to rush you out, but I'm feeling very tired all of a sudden. Too much excitement for one day, maybe. I'm sure there's nothing else I can tell you that will help, but if you leave me your address I'll let you know if I remember anything. I'm sorry. I think maybe I need to just sit here quietly for a while. Do you think you could show yourself out?"

"Of course. Is there anything I can do? Do you want me to call someone?"

"No, no. I'm sure I'll be as right as rain if I just have a little nap. Please don't concern yourself about me."

"If you're sure?"

"Positive. Please. It was nice talking to you."

"And to you too, sir." I stood up, took a business card from my pocket and laid it on the desk in front of him, then turned and let myself out of the library and then the front door. I paused on the doorstep collecting my thoughts for a moment before setting off back to Victoria Station.

Jacobites

While I had been tracking down the recent history of the books, Al had been pursuing her theory of a Jacobite connection. I had scanned and emailed her the design that Carter had sketched for me in Chelsea, but I was surprised when she called only a couple of days later to say she had already made some progress. We arranged to meet for lunch at our favourite restaurant, Il Fornello in Southampton Row.

I arrived at 12:30 to the usual warm welcome from the staff. Al and I have both been coming here for over twenty-five years and there are still the same people behind the bar and waiting at table. All, like us, looking a little older but otherwise largely unchanged. It's very much as if a restaurant from Parma has been uprooted and transplanted from Italy into Central London. You always feel more like you've been invited to eat in a family home, despite the printed menus and plethora of tables – there's no fake cordiality as you find in so many restaurants, no unnecessary sophistication or expensive trappings. Good food, a pleasant environment, warm friendly people, and usually a familiar face or two at some of the other tables. Everyone is made to feel welcome: tourists from the nearby hotels in Russell Square; passers-by on their way to the British Museum or Holborn or Covent Garden or back to the great railway termini of Euston, St Pancras and Kings Cross; locals who appreciate value for money; and occasional patrons like us who only come to eat here when we can, but are still welcomed as if we were the mainstay of their business. Once, I had been working away from home for nearly three years and hadn't had the opportunity to visit London during that time, but when I next walked through their door it was as if I had never been away. I brought my mother here once, many years ago, on one of her rare trips to town. She was very touched by the fuss they made of her, treating her like a VIP and chatting with her in Italian. She was really pleased to discover the option of fresh figs for dessert, a luxury that she couldn't find in her local shops. After that, the staff always asked after her whenever I came in to eat – until she died, when we drank a toast together to her memory.

Al was already sitting at the table she had reserved for the two of us and was just tasting the wine that was being poured as I took my seat. We ordered our food straight away, both unimaginatively having the same, an *insalata tricolore* to start followed by *risotto ai funghi*. While we waited for our salads, I lifted my glass, clinked Al's and took a good swig.

"Second time this week. How decadent."

"Second time what?" asked Al with a puzzled look on her face.

"Drinking in the afternoon. I had a glass in Chelsea when I saw Mr. Philus."

"You must tell me more about him, he sounds fascinating."

"He's certainly a character. He used emotional blackmail to force me to join him in a drink."

"The bully!" she grinned. "So what's your excuse today?"

"Pleasant lunch with my favourite person."

"But you have to be drunk to face it?"

"No!" I protested, putting my glass back on the table. "One bottle is hardly going to make either of us drunk, anyway."

Still grinning, Al took a deep sip from her glass.

"Right. And thanks for voting me your favourite person."

"No voting required. It's obvious. Well, to me anyway. Isn't it to you?"

"I couldn't say." The grin was still spread across her face and her eyes were brighter than I had ever seen them.

For the first time in years I was suddenly nervous, even tongue-tied, and not entirely sure what to say next. In mild panic I blustered "So, tell me what you've found out."

Al's grin faded slightly and her eyebrows betrayed a hint of a frown.

"Found out?"

"About Leonardo, Philus' design and the Jacobites."

"Oh." Her grin faded completely and a faintly disappointed look fleetingly overtook her face, quickly followed by a deep intake of breath and a somewhat resigned expression. "Right then."

I had never been nervous around Al before. I was thinking about her a lot more lately – not just because we were working on this mystery together. I was still pondering why I should be feeling like this when I realised that she had already started to reply.

"… connection. As I suggested in …"

"What? Sorry I missed that."

"Are you alright? You don't seem yourself. You look a little, well, distracted."

"I'll be fine. Lots of things preying on my mind at the moment. I'm really sorry, what were you saying?"

"I said that I was looking for a Jacobite connection, as I suggested when we were discussing this in Florence with Lucia."

"And have you found one?"

"I hadn't until you sent me that little sketch. Then everything seemed to fall into place. But rather than answering questions it seems to have raised more."

"Typical. Tell me why."

"Will you listen this time?"

"I'm really sorry. Yes, I'm listening." I think she was just teasing me but I couldn't be entirely sure.

"Okay then. You remember the 'King over the Water' reference in the original text hidden in the illustrations?"

"Yes, of course. You said it wouldn't have been Leonardo's term, it was used by the Jacobites."

"Some two hundred years later, that's right. So this is the first clue that the Jacobites were somehow involved. For now, let's make some simple assumptions. One, that a nobleman, probably French, possibly even the King, came by Leonardo's algorithm and the enabling key."

"The what?"

"Enabling key?" she repeated tentatively. "I was trying to use your sort of terminology. I meant the text you found in the Dryden that enabled us to make Leonardo's algorithm work properly."

"Not really a key but who cares. 'Enabling key' it is."

"Now you're just being patronising. I was originally going to call it a corrigendum. My sort of terminology!"

"Okay then, the 'Corrigendum'. Actually I prefer that."

"Anyway!" She glared at me, but this time I could tell that she wasn't serious. "The next assumption is that this same person is a supporter of the Jacobite cause."

Just then our salads were delivered. They looked delicious, of course. Deep red slices of plum tomato alternating with creamy white slices of mozzarella, interspersed with large basil leaves. I knew the dressing on this salad would be absolutely superb. It always was.

Many years before I had been eating here with a German friend, Karl, who was always very proper in such situations and could never really comprehend the Italian passion for food. When I asked the waiter, Giuseppe, for some more bread, Karl looked at him, raised his eyebrows and said "He wants to soak up the dressing," expecting this to horrify any self-respecting waiter. Instead Giuseppe asked me "You like the dressing?" "Yes," I replied, "it's wonderful." He beamed a huge smile, said "*Sì*. Is my father's recipe," and then proceeded to explain to me the exact proportions of oil, vinegar and other ingredients. Karl had looked on in bemused bafflement, completely incapable of understanding any Italian's relationship with food.

Despite the beautiful presentation, neither Al nor I hesitated in tucking in to our food. Our conversation had made us even more hungry than we had realised and we decided to forgo further discussion while eating. Food is generally the only thing that shuts me up! Once we had both enjoyed our starter and I had replenished the wine in our glasses, I sat back in my chair.

"I'm still a bit hazy on the Jacobites." I said. "So, they were trying to put a different king on the English throne?"

"Not the English throne, the British throne. By then it was already a union of the kingdom of England and Wales with that of Scotland. Officially called the Kingdom of Great Britain. The Jacobites wanted to replace George with a Stuart king, a more direct descendant of James II. Hence the name Jacobites."

"You've lost me again."

"Your Latin is ..." she was searching for the polite description.

"... virtually non-existent!" I suggested.

"James in Latin is Jacobus."

"So George wasn't the legitimate king?"

"That depends on your point of view, of course. Didn't you do any British history at school?"

"Not really, it was all tedious stuff about laws and taxation. I was always much more interested in Classical history. So explain to me these different viewpoints."

"Okay. Briefly. James the Sixth was a Stuart King of Scotland in the latter half of the sixteenth century. When Elizabeth the First died she had no heir, so James was invited to take the English throne because his mother, Mary Queen of Scots, had been Elizabeth's cousin. Thus he became James the First of England and Ireland at the beginning of the seventeenth century."

"So that was when the kingdoms were united into Great Britain?"

"No. Although he was the King of England, and hence Wales, as well as Ireland they were separate kingdoms for another hundred years or so. But he did actually call himself King of Great Britain, even though there was officially no such kingdom."

"Semantics!"

"Politics!" she replied, raising her eyebrows.

"So James is King. Then what?"

"When he died his son Charles the First becomes king."

"He was the one who was beheaded during the Civil War."

"Yup. So then there was the short-lived republic of the Commonwealth, with the Puritan Cromwell's somewhat tyrannical rule as virtual monarch, and eventually the restoration of the monarchy with Charles's son Charles the Second."

"When was that?"

"1660. He died without heirs twenty five years later so his brother James gained the throne."

"That was James the Second?"

"He was James the Second of England and Ireland but James the Seventh of Scotland. Within three years he had upset lots of people who were already suspicious because he was a Catholic. So a group of aristocrats invited William of Orange to invade, depose James and take the throne."

"Why William?"

"Because he was married to Mary, James' eldest daughter. They reigned together."

"Ah! William and Mary. I've heard of them. Or am I thinking of Peter, Paul and Mary?"

"Honestly. Sometimes I'm not sure whether you're being deliberately obtuse, trying to be funny, or are just plain ignorant! You know that march by Purcell that you like so much?"

"Which one?"

"Music for the Funeral of Queen Mary."

"Oh yeah."

"Well the clue is in the title. When Mary died, William reigned alone for a few more years. But they had no children so, when he died, Mary's younger sister Anne became Queen."

"That's Queen Anne with the bandy legs?"

"What?"

"Didn't they model Queen Anne chair legs on hers?"

"Idiot!" said Al with a resigned sigh. Then she continued "But yes, it was that Queen Anne. She died with no surviving children either. But parliament had passed the Act of Settlement in 1701 which basically explicitly excluded any of James' Catholic descendants and ensured that the crown would pass to the closest protestant descendant. Which, as it turned out, was George the Elector of Hanover, a German who couldn't speak English – which led to plenty of ridicule when he took the throne."

"Who was he?"

"Charles the First had a sister Elizabeth who married Frederick, Elector of the Palatinate. Their youngest daughter was Sophia who married the first Elector of Hanover and George was her eldest son."

"And HE was the closest relative who could take the throne?"

"The closest who was allowed to inherit. The legitimate heir after James' death at the beginning of the eighteenth century should have been his own son, who would have become James the Third and Eighth. In fact the French, Spanish, and various others, recognised him as such anyway. He's buried in St. Peter's in Rome along with his wife and sons and the inscription entitles him as James the Third."

"Oh yes, I've seen the Stuart memorial and one for his wife, Maria Sobieska or something like that. I only remember because I always thought it was odd for English Kings to be buried in St. Peter's."

"That's right. In England he was known as the King over the Water by his Jacobite supporters and the Old Pretender by his opponents."

"Ah! I've heard of the Old Pretender. And the Young Pretender?"

"His son Charles. Known as Bonnie Prince Charlie in Scotland."

"One of the sons buried in St. Peter's?"

"Yes, with the title Charles the Third."

"Okay so I think I get it now. The Jacobites wanted the Stuarts back on the throne instead of some German who couldn't even speak English. But we still have Germans on the throne today so they obviously failed. Why didn't anyone help?"

"The French supported an attempt by James to take back the throne."

"Hang on, which James?"

"The Old Pretender."

"That's James the Second's son?"

"That's right. But the French ships were chased off by the Royal Navy so they gave up."

"When was that?"

"Can't remember exactly, some time around 1708 or 9. George came over from Hanover in 1714, the Whigs won the General Election in 1715 and arrested lots of Tories who they accused of supporting the Jacobite cause or of being traitors and supporting the French. There was an uprising in Scotland, with James coming over to set up court, but there wasn't enough solid support and they failed to win any battles against the government army, so James high-tailed it back to France leaving his men to fend for themselves. It was clear they needed more support from a European monarch so they persuaded the Spanish to help. But it was a half-hearted effort by the Spanish invasion force, most of whom failed even to get as far as England. It was twenty five years before there was another serious attempt. By then the English and French were in conflict again, although not officially at war. King Louis planned an invasion for 1744 and invited Charles to join them. He rushed from Rome, where he was living with his father James, to take part, but the plans were defeated by a storm. Louis suddenly lost interest in Charles and the Jacobite cause."

"Isn't it a bit petty to cancel invasion plans because of one storm and then lose interest completely?"

"There's obviously more to it than that, in fact that's probably where the Dryden comes in, but let me finish the history lesson first."

"Yes, Miss!"

Al looked at me with a schoolmistressy glare and then continued.

"The failed attempt had excited Charles, so he decided that he'd go it alone and set sail for Scotland in 1745 with two ships, only one of which arrived. He managed to raise an army and achieved some success. His army made good progress through England, getting as far south as

Derby. But he had become very difficult to deal with and was no longer on good terms with his general. He assured his supporters that a French invasion fleet was preparing to sail from Dunkerque to help, but they didn't believe him. The army returned to Scotland, to the relief of the government, and Charles spent his time sulking. Eventually they were defeated at the battle of Culloden and Charles fled to France disguised as a girl. The Jacobite forces were crushed and the cause was pretty much over."

"So that was the end of the Jacobites?"

"There are still Jacobites left today. Even some heirs, although none of them have claimed the throne for a few generations."

Just then, Maria cleared away our starter plates and cutlery so that Giuseppe could replace them with our risotto.

"*Buon appetito*," he smiled as he left us.

While the presentation of a *risotto* cannot be as photogenic as a *tricolore* salad, it was nevertheless an appetising sight. Arborio rice seems to make such perfect *risotto*, light yet filling, capable of accentuating the flavour of the mushrooms and olive oil. A twist of black pepper had added just the right piquancy. Again, our conversation petered out while we enjoyed the food.

When I had finished, I dabbed at my mouth with my napkin and downed the last of my wine. Al was not quite finished yet.

"I don't think I've got room for any dessert, I'll just have some coffee. What about you?"

Al nodded and, as she finished her mouthful, added "The same please."

I called Maria and asked for *due espressi*, and waited for Al to finish her last mouthful. As she was sitting back in her chair with a contented smile on her face, I leant forward.

"Okay, so now explain where you think the Dryden fits in."

"Right." She replied, pausing to take another sip of her wine. "There is a lot of academic conjecture that the reason the French had been prevaricating and then finally lost their nerve is because they had been expecting an uprising in London. While there was supposedly popular support for the Jacobite cause in Scotland and Northumbria, it was more muted and underground in London. What was needed was something to rally the diverse supporters to make a showing. There had been various attempts over the years but nothing had really worked. By now, most of the support was nothing to do with religion, but political ideology and dislike of the Hanoverians. In fact, as it turned out, Episcopalians outnumbered Catholics 7 to 1 in Bonnie Prince Charlie's army."

"The one that got as far as Derby?"

"That's right. And the Tories, many of whom supported the Jacobite cause, had been out of power for years. But there is a story, with little supporting evidence it must be said, that the French had come up with something that would instigate a significant uprising among the common people as well as politicians and nobility. Supposedly they had sent some damning evidence against George's legitimacy to rule, with massive propaganda value that should have had the desired effect. But it didn't."

"Why not?"

"Because it never arrived. No-one knows what happened. Anyone trying to bring seditious material into England would have been immediately arrested as a spy, so they would have had to conceal the text. What better way than to send it openly without disclosing the actual text to anyone, along with a means of ensuring that the right person would be able to recover that text? Now, back to our assumptions. We have a French sympathiser with knowledge of Leonardo's algorithm and the corrigendum. By then, the original of the Leonardo treatise was in the Royal Society in London, where it could be examined by members. So if there was a Fellow who was a sympathiser they would just need to be sent the corrigendum. Where else to hide it than in a book? What's more, an English book to reduce suspicion. Then... Oh my goodness..." she stopped talking and I could almost see a cartoon light-bulb come on above her head as I watched.

"What?"

"I've just realised why they specifically used the Dryden. Mind you it should have been a give-away..."

"What?" I asked again.

"Dido and Aeneas."

"What?" I repeated a third time, starting to get a little irritated.

"Oh, sorry. It was when we talked about Purcell a few minutes ago. That must have started a train of thought that just arrived as I was speaking. Purcell wrote an opera, called Dido and Aeneas, based on part of the story of the Aeneid. At the time it was suggested that Aeneas represented James II and Dido was the British people lamenting his departure across the water. I'm sure you'd recognise the aria, Dido's lament. They use it on Remembrance Sunday at the cenotaph. So it would be appropriate, even ironic, to use Dryden's translation as the medium."

"Especially as Dryden had only done the translations because he had been sacked by the king." I added.

"There you go. It was William who sacked him."

"So, back to your corrigendum?"

"Right. It's hidden in the Dryden and sent to a

sympathetic Fellow. As long as he's expecting it and knows how to extract the text he can reconstruct the algorithm and is then in a position to be able to recover the seditious message from its own concealment."

"But where was this seditious document concealed?"

"That's what I didn't know. When you sent that sketch I thought we might be on the right path. I tracked it down to a folio in the Royal collection, just as you had said. It was a fairly unremarkable page from one of Leonardo's notebooks. I tried to see if I could extract a hidden text from within it, but couldn't. I don't think there is anything concealed in it at all. So I'm stumped again."

"There's nothing special about that folio?"

"Not really. Unusual route into the collection but otherwise nothing."

"Unusual? In what way?"

"It's identified as being part of King Charles' collection that was found in a chest in Kensington Palace. But it doesn't really fit in with the rest. In Spain, Lord Arundel bought Charles a collection of folios containing drawings, mostly anatomical or natural history. Only a few have any significant amounts of text. This is one of them. I came across a story, probably apocryphal, that there were some folios that were actually added to the collection years later, after they were found in the Customs House – supposedly lost for years. It might be one of those, but frankly it seems fairly unlikely."

"Maybe not."

"What makes you say that?"

"The story Carter Philus told me seems to match in various details. I already told you about the sketch on the folio because it seemed likely you could track it down. But he said that there were two Leonardo folios confiscated by the Excise. They were supposed to be delivered to the Royal Society."

Al looked at me incredulously.

"Really?"

"And, what's more the Dryden was supposed to be delivered to a writer – he wouldn't tell me who – on behalf of the French. It fits your assumptions, the facts and the story. Except..."

"We don't know which was the other folio, who the intended recipient was, or who delivered them – or rather who failed to deliver them. However, I have quite a good idea. Have you heard of the Comte de Saint Germain?"

"I don't think so, but..."

"Hang on, let me try this theory out on you. Saint Germain was a larger than life character who appeared on the scene in the French court in the early eighteenth century. Although he never actually said so, he was widely believed to have discovered the secret of immortality or at least of incredible longevity." She laughed.

"Apparently, he talked of people from the past as if he had known them personally, including Jesus, Cleopatra, Henry the Eighth. He was very popular with King Louis and Madame de Pompadour and then later with Marie Antoinette. He popped up all over Europe for years, even long after his supposed death. Look on the net, there are people who, even today, believe he is still alive. Elements of his story have influenced popular culture like the Highlander films, even Doctor Who. Some think he was an occultist who mastered the secrets of the Qaballah, some think he was an alchemist, some say he was Merlin, others that he was a time-traveller or alien, some even think he was Lazarus."

"Why Lazarus?"

"There's a crackpot theory that after Lazarus was raised from the dead by Jesus he couldn't die again and so has been wandering the earth ever since destined to keep going until the end of time."

"But what has this got to do with our story?"

"In 1745 he came to London."

"Lazarus?"

"The Comte de Saint Germain." She glared at me again. "Probably on behalf of King Louis. He was promptly arrested as a Jacobite spy. In the end they found no evidence against him and had to let him go. Walpole described him as an odd man who was mad and not very sensible, but said that nothing had been made out against him so he was released. There is at least one account that he had some Leonardo folios with him, but they were taken when he was arrested. When they let him go he went back to France and over the next few years acted as an ambassador for Louis around Europe. So he may have been the courier. He could have brought the sedition hidden in a Leonardo folio, presumably fake, which was then confiscated. Along with the corrigendum in the Dryden that eventually found its way to your Mr Philus. He told you that there were two folios, so if we could identify the other one we could find out what the French were pinning their hopes on. That would be an interesting historical find."

By this time I must have been staring with a gaping mouth because Al looked at me quizzically and said, "What?"

"In the light of your theory, let me tell you the final detail of what 'my' Mr Philus told me. The courier who brought the folios and the Dryden from France, who was supposed to deliver the Dryden to the unnamed writer and the folios to the Royal Society, who was arrested as a spy – Catholic spy, he said – and who had to return to France unsuccessful was none other than the man himself."

Our coffees had been delivered and Al was cradling her

espresso cup in her hands.

"Who?" she asked, then promptly started to drink her coffee.

"Carter Philus." I replied.

She nearly choked on her coffee. Putting the cup back in the saucer, Al looked at me like I was either mad or stupid, or both.

"No!" She regained her composure and then spoke slowly as if explaining to a small child. "Maybe I wasn't clear. This happened two hundred and sixty years ago." She shook her head.

"You thought it was the Count of Saint Germain."

"Yes."

"Who was, is, immortal."

"Allegedly." She snorted.

"So he could still be alive and well, living in Chelsea under a different name."

"What? Are you serious?"

"Why not?"

"Other than the fact that immortality is impossible?"

"Run with it." I may have sounded a little more pleading than I intended.

"How can you even be considering it? You're a scientist."

"Engineer."

"Either way, you believe in the scientific method. Don't you? Which should lead you, with very little investigation, to conclude that immortality is impossible."

"I thought the scientific method was founded on an open-minded approach to the natural world?"

"There's open-minded and then there's totally uncritical! Why have you fallen for it?"

"I haven't fallen for anything, but I must admit I'd love it to be true. How cool would it be if it were true? Don't you think it would be amazing?"

"Incredible, not amazing. I mean that literally. Not credible. This is far-fetched, even for you!" She was staring at me now. "No I take that back, it's not just far-fetched it's completely doolally."

"No more so than any of the rest of your theory."

"I'm sorry! That is all backed up by evidence, albeit circumstantial in some cases, but physical evidence that we can see. Like the letters hidden in the illustrations in the Dryden, the text, the Leonardo algorithm. Even our successful extraction of the mechanicant notes. Facts. Evidence." Al was getting louder now. Luckily no-one else in the restaurant was paying any attention.

"Carter Philus IS a fact. I met him."

"But what he told you obviously isn't fact."

"Might be."

"And might just as easily be a load of ..." she restrained herself and slowly and quietly said "spheres."

"It fits with your theory and the rest of the facts."

"Did you consider that maybe he already knew those other facts and told you a tale that would be consistent. If I was reading this in a book," she looked me straight in the eyes and I could see that she was now less amused and more concerned, "it would be at this point I'd laugh and throw it away."

"But we're not reading it, we're writing it. We can't avoid the evidence so far."

"In which case, ignoring the ludicrous question of whether your Mr Philus is really hundreds of years old as opposed to the overwhelming likelihood that he is just a good storyteller who has taken you in, hook line and sinker, we should look for the other folio."

"Where?"

"If it was confiscated along with the one I already found, then presumably it's in the Royal collection too. I'll have to see what I can find."

"That sounds like a good plan." I agreed.

"But I still don't believe in immortal Counts," she muttered under her breath as she lifted the cup again to finish her interrupted coffee.

~

When I got home I was still feeling somewhat replete from our delicious lunch, if a little disappointed by Al's reaction. Despite her conviction, I had not been 'taken-in' by Carter Philus' story. In a childlike way I would have loved for it to be true, and the romantic part of my soul wished for that. But I had actually adopted the non-sceptical position in an attempt at playing devil's advocate. The rational, scientific, investigative part of my nature agreed with Al that Carter Philus could not possibly be the Comte de Saint Germain. I decided I should try to find out as much as I could about both of them, and any other reputed immortals. However, when I sat down in the Office to start my research I noticed an email waiting for me from Simonetta in Vinci. I had left her my business card and asked her to let me know if she came up with any more candidate folios for our quest. But I was completely unprepared for what she had to say. I called Al immediately.

"Hello Al, it's me."

"Hello again. Long time no see. Must be all of two hours!" she laughed but then stopped as she sensed the tension in my voice.

"I've had an email from Simonetta. You remember the lady in Vinci."

"Of course I remember her. How is she?"

"Worried. Apparently some American guy was at the museum yesterday asking questions about us."

"Us? What, by name?"

"No. At least I don't think so. She says it was her day off so she wasn't there when he turned up. But apparently he asked other museum staff about two Brits who had found some Leonardo folios with hidden texts. Of course, they had no idea what he was talking about, but he became quite angry and abusive when no-one would answer his questions, so in the end they had to get a security guard to escort him out. This morning when Simonetta got to the museum, one of her friends told her about the excitement she'd missed yesterday. She thought she'd better tell us. She's a bit nervous in case he comes back. It's obviously unsettled her."

"Does she have any idea who he was?"

"She says he didn't give a name. Her friend just described him as American wearing an expensive suit."

"Who might it have been?"

"I haven't got a clue. What about you?"

"Me neither. What should we do?"

"I don't think there's anything to do at the moment. I'll reply to Simonetta, tell her not to worry and ask her not to tell anyone about us unless she has to. Beyond that I guess we just see what happens."

Crypto Da Vinci

Folio

Over the next two weeks Al spent much of her time looking through the Leonardo folios in the Royal collection in Windsor. The curator Cecil, an old friend of hers, gave her more or less unrestricted access. Having identified a few possible candidates for our missing folio, Al applied the Leonardo algorithm assiduously to attempt to retrieve any hidden texts. None of the candidate folios had so far revealed any secrets and Al was beginning to lose heart. With only two left on her shortlist she had already resigned herself to having to widen her search or give up. But giving up was not Al's style.

Applying herself, in spite of her sense of likely failure, she considered the penultimate candidate on her list. Whereas with most of the others determining the key had been tricky, one might even say dubious, in this case a likely key stood out like a sore thumb. Encouraged, Al set to with the algorithm, which after so much practice she could now apply without needing to refer to her notes, and almost immediately a hidden text began to reveal itself. With growing elation she worked her way through the tight, handwritten, rambling text as it metamorphosed into a beautifully elegant piece of Latin prose. She was torn between completing the process of extracting the text and translating what she had revealed so far. Practicality won out over curiosity and she continued to apply the algorithm, recording the results in longhand on her notepad. Even so, as she went on, she couldn't help but notice various words and names such as Jacobus Rex, Anna, Frederick, Sophia. Her curiosity thus even more piqued, and the implication that this text really was in some way connected to the Jacobite cause and therefore nothing to do with Leonardo himself, she worked her way through the rest of the folio as fast as she could. At last she got to the end and had the complete Latin text extracted from the folio. She was amazed how long it was, Leonardo's small cramped writing style could fit a lot onto one page.

Al's Latin skills were reasonably good, so she could already see that most of this was couched in very formal Church Latin, while some was more conversational in style. There appeared to be a document with the title '*Confessio*' followed by a discussion or commentary. Barely able to contain her excitement she nevertheless went back to her shop to carry out the translation. As soon as she arrived, she grabbed her Latin dictionary and started to translate with enthusiasm.

Three hours later, after revising and finessing the result, she sat quite still and stared at the two texts in front of her in disbelief. She picked up her phone and called me.

"Hi, it's Al. Do you have a few minutes?"

"Of course, what's up?"

"I've found it. The missing folio."

"Where?"

"Exactly where we thought, in the Royal collection. I found it this morning."

"Well done. So now we have to try and extract the hidden message."

"I've already done that."

"You don't hang about, do you?"

"It was the only way to be sure that I'd found the right folio."

"Of course. Sorry, that's me being a bit slow."

"It's quite ironic that it's in the Royal collection, given that it was intended to undermine the legitimacy of the Hanoverian reign."

"So it is a Jacobite document then?"

"Yes. Well, I suppose strictly it's a Jacobean document that was then used to support the Jacobite cause."

"Okay. So, what does it say?"

"Well there's two separate texts. The first is the Jacobean document I mentioned, which is called *Confessio*."

"What, as in confession?"

"Exactly."

"Who's confessing to what?"

"I'll send you the full text in a minute so you can read it for yourself, but essentially it's Queen Anne confessing to an infidelity."

"Bandy-legs again?"

"No, her great-grandmother, Anne of Denmark the Queen Consort of James the First. It throws doubt on the legitimacy of her daughter Elizabeth and hence of the whole branch of the family tree that led to the House of Hanover. What's more it suggests consequent consanguinity which was much worse; if it had become public at the time it would almost certainly have completely destroyed any chance George had of retaining the throne."

"Wow. Powerful stuff. And she actually confessed this?"

"Yes. She was so appalled at what had happened that she couldn't keep the secret any longer. She was originally a Lutheran but eventually converted to Catholicism, much to the courtiers' dismay. So she made a confession and her priest advised her to write it down formally and send it to the Pope. The second text is a passage that includes notes and instructions for the recipient, which says that the confession was held in the personal papers of the Popes until 1742, when a cardinal who had been the personal assistant to Clement the Twelfth mentioned it to

King Louis. By then, of course, with the Act of Settlement and the accession of the Hanoverians to the British throne it had become a whole lot more significant. Louis clearly believed its publication could destabilise British society and unseat an already unpopular monarch and government. He knew how to use Leonardo's algorithm, which had been employed by the French kings since Leonardo had entrusted it to King François at *Amboise*. Louis also knew that the folio describing the algorithm was in the Royal Society, so he must have decided that it would be worth revealing the secret of how to apply it properly to an English Jacobite supporter if it meant that a friendly king would be installed in London as a result. The secret of making the algorithm work was hidden in two copies of Dryden's Works of Virgil."

"Two?"

"Yes. There's another copy somewhere that has the same amended illustrations and presumably the same binding. The *Confessio* was hidden in another text made to look like a genuine Leonardo folio. Actually this bit is quite appalling. According to the second passage, they took a real Leonardo folio and bleached the ink off, then employed a forger to write a new text on it in Leonardo's style."

"So they destroyed a real page of Leonardo's notes?"

"I'm afraid so. The plan was to send it, along with another genuine folio to add authenticity, to the Royal Society in London, meanwhile dispatching the Drydens to different Fellows so that hopefully at least one of them would be able to use the algorithm to extract the *Confessio* then print and publish it."

"Does it give any names?"

"It does. The courier was to be the Comte de Saint Germain."

"Bingo!"

"Oh don't start that again. There's no way he could be your Philus, you know."

"Okay. Does it name the Royal Society Fellows?"

"Only one. Samuel Johnson."

"What, of dictionary fame?"

"The very same."

"I didn't know he was a revolutionary. Mind you I don't really know much about him at all."

"It's now widely believed that he was a sympathiser, and I guess this confirms it. What's more he was a big fan of Dryden, so it's a good bet he'd already have an edition of the Virgil and could spot the differences in the pictures."

"Anyone else?"

"A couple of other names of contacts for further distribution, an Anton Deque in Northumbria and John Witherspoon in Scotland."

"Neither of them mean anything to me."

"Nor me. Although Witherspoon seems familiar."

"The pubs maybe?" I suggested.

"What pubs?"

"Oh no, that's Wetherspoon. But there's an American actress, Reece Witherspoon?"

"I don't think so. Maybe I'll look into him a bit more. Anyway, it seems like the bulk of our theory was right after all."

"Clever us."

"I'll send you the text of the *Confessio* to read."

"My Latin's not good enough."

"Don't worry I've already translated it for you." She laughed and continued, "I think I need to have a chat with someone who's a bit more clued up on British Constitution than me, so I can figure out what the real implications of this document were likely to have been. I may be over-estimating it."

"Fine. But, for now, don't give away any copies of the

text until we've decided what we should do."

"Like what?"

"Publish maybe? A learned history paper from you, a cryptography paper from me, even an article jointly for a popular history magazine?"

"Okay. I'll send you that email in a minute and call you again in a few days when I've done some more research."

Oxford

I read through the translation of the *Confessio* that Al had sent me. Although I had been quite busy I did manage to spend a few minutes reading up on the Act of Settlement and Anne of Denmark, but nothing I read was any more helpful than what Al had already told me.

When Al and I next spoke, she was calling to tell me she had decided to seek some advice from an old college-friend, now a researcher in Oxford, about the significance of the *Confessio*. Coincidentally I had been about to organise a visit to Oxford to meet a potential client, so we arranged to travel up together.

~

The 9:22 semi-fast train pulled out of Paddington, sufficiently late to negate its semi-fast label. Al sat gazing out at the strange extra platforms that seemed to sprout out of the station and extend along the tracks as if they had been added in an optimistic heyday to cater for super-length trains that had never arrived. They looked old and tatty. Al commented that she had never seen them anything other than deserted, whatever time of day she had travelled from this station. I noted the time with mild irritation arising from the realisation that, had we known the train would leave this late, we could have bought cheaper tickets.

Settling back in her seat Al took the opportunity to doze for a while, partly to recover some of the sleep she had foregone to be sure of getting to this train on time. The background hum of the motors and the repetitive dull clacking of the wheels on the track acted as a soporific so, after what seemed to her merely a couple of minutes, she was somewhat startled by an overly abrupt termination at Oxford. Blinking as she peered out of the window to get her bearings, she recognised what little we could see of the station; we stood up and gathered up our bags and Al retrieved the coat she had folded on the seat next to her.

Walking from the station towards the History faculty building where she had arranged to meet her friend Ethel, along familiar roads and past the occasional familiar landmark, Al remarked on the changes since she had first come here some thirty years ago. Far more vehicles everywhere, apart from bicycles, which seemed to be in decline. New buildings, some pleasantly blending with the variety of older buildings, seemed to have sprung up all over the place – the architecturally innovative being most obvious in their often incongruous juxtaposition with the neo-gothic. The city of dreaming spires seemed, in places, rather to be experiencing a nightmare. Still, some things had remained much the same. Although she was heading to a relatively new building for her meeting, it was in the heart of the city near her old favourites of the Bodleian Library, where she had apparently spent many a long day researching in the quiet dusty shelves, and the Sheldonian Theatre which holds a special place in the heart of most Oxford alumni. We walked past Trinity College heading towards the tourist's favourite Bridge of Sighs. Pausing to look at the misnamed bridge, Al said it immediately brought to mind moonlit strolls in Venice across the Rialto on which it was modelled. With a faint smile, she told me she also remembered escapades here from many years before that. She turned, kissed me on the cheek, said goodbye and, pushing open the unassuming doors of the Modern History department, disappeared inside. As the doors swung shut behind her I struck out on my own towards the office of the IT company I was visiting in the next street.

~

When Al met Ethel, it was the first time they'd seen each other in over a year. Much had been going on in Ethel's life that Al was keen to know about. Ethel had recently started to share a home with a partner and was now happy for the first time in years. Al had always been amazed at how much criticism and even outright abuse Ethel had to put up with, as a pre-op transsexual; it was about time Ethel had something going right for her.

Once Ethel had excitedly brought her up to date with all the news, including showing her photos of Dolores, the bricklayer with whom Ethel was now living, Al was keen to talk about the *Confessio*. Ethel immediately admitted that there was a much more suitable person to offer an opinion.

"I hope you don't mind, but I took the liberty of calling Professor Trubshawe. From what you told me on the phone it was obvious that he would be the best person for you to talk to. So I made you an appointment to see him this morning. Do you know him?"

"We have met a couple of times, but I don't really know him that well. You're not coming along?"

"No thanks. I don't want to cramp your style. Besides he's not very tolerant of, erm, well... let's just say 'people like me'. But a brilliant historian and expert in constitutional matters. Just what you need."

"Oh Ethel. Look, once I've spoken to him I'll come back and find you and we can have a late lunch. Deal?"

"Deal."

"Great, see you later. Now, where's the Prof's office?"

~

"Come in Dr. Mint. Or may I call you Alison?"

Manley Trubshawe stood as Al entered his cramped and untidy office.

"My friends call me Al. Thank you for agreeing to see me."

"No trouble at all. It's nice to see you again, it must be three years since we last met? I have to admit that the little your gruff friend told me on the phone rather intrigued me, so I have been eagerly anticipating your arrival all morning. The main upshot of which, in fact, is that I actually remembered to organise a pot of tea for us – which came as a surprise to Vanessa."

"Vanessa?" Al asked, puzzled.

"Vanessa. Oh yes, sorry, Vanessa's our secretary. She's used to me asking for tea at the last minute. I think she was a bit thrown when I mentioned you first thing this morning. She'll be along any minute."

Al was still standing just inside the door. She put her bag down by her feet, started to remove her coat and looked around for a coat-stand or a hook to hang it on. When she couldn't locate one, Al looked back at her host and raised a quizzical eyebrow. He stood watching her for a few seconds before realising what she had been seeking.

"Allow me." He held out his hand to take her coat and then unceremoniously dumped it over the back of a chair, the seat of which was covered in books. "Do sit down," he said, almost as an afterthought, indicating another chair that was clear of detritus. He shuffled back to his own revolving chair, sat down, spun round to the desk to retrieve his pince-nez glasses, and then turned back more slowly to face her.

As she settled herself on the rather uncomfortable

wooden chair, there was a creak in the floorboards behind her and a tall, slim, dark-haired girl walked past to deposit on the desk a tray with an elegant matching set of a tea-pot, two china cups and saucers, a milk jug and sugar bowl. She turned to leave without a word, smiling knowingly at Al as she left the room, pulling the door shut behind her. Al guessed that Vanessa could be no older than 21, younger than some of the undergraduates and all of the postgraduate students in the department, not to mention the academic staff.

"Absolute angel, our Vanessa. Don't know what we'd do without her. Did her degree here, then stayed on to do research. There was some sort of coup in her country, one of the West African states, and the government stopped paying her fees. So she's working as departmental secretary during the day to earn the money to live, eat and cover tuition. In the evening she's doing her research. She's got real strength of willpower, that girl."

"Can't she do some teaching to earn money?"

"She could, but frankly that would pay less. She seems to be happy. And she makes a jolly good pot of tea. Talking of which you're honoured because she's used the best china, normally only use that for important people."

Al smiled, not quite sure whether to acknowledge the back-handed compliment.

He smiled awkwardly, his mind having finally registered what his mouth had just said.

"Shall I be Mother?" he asked.

Not waiting for a reply he started pouring tea into both cups.

~

After the ritual tea pouring, polite sipping and a fruitless search for some edible biscuits, a long silence ensued. Finally Al placed her empty cup on the saucer and carefully deposited it on the edge of the desk nearest to her. She cleared her throat decisively.

"I think we should probably get down to the matter in hand," she said.

"Yes indeed. Your friend mentioned that you'd found a text whose content could have comprehensive constitutional consequences."

"Correct." Al smiled at his affected alliteration, wary lest the Professor prove to be a particularly pretentious pontificator.

"While I'm naturally keen to dive into the text itself, I suspect that it would be prudent to start with an understanding of its provenance and hence how much authority we can ascribe to it."

"Absolutely. It started because a friend of mine uncovered a steganographic technique invented by Leonardo."

"Leonardo?"

"Da Vinci."

"Ah, that Leonardo!"

"Exactly. We believed that some Leonardo folios that had previously been ignored as 'ramblings' were in fact the output of this technique. While looking for such folios I came across one that was indeed an encoded text. Applying Leonardo's technique in reverse resulted in the Latin text that I want you to examine. It was accompanied by a second text giving a brief history and instructions to the intended recipients. They claim it was hidden on the orders of Louis XV, to be sent to two Fellows of the Royal Society in London. The copy I found was to be delivered by the Comte de Saint Germain to Samuel Johnson. He was to decode it, ready for publication to support the Jacobite cause. He was also supposed to pass it on to an Anton Deque in Northumbria and John Witherspoon in Scotland, both of whom were Jacobite sympathisers who could arrange for its local publication and promulgation. It seems like this was the rumoured propaganda that never materialised, the firebrand that the French expected to ignite an uprising in London as well as the north."

"Where did you find it?"

"The Royal collection at Windsor."

"No!"

"Yes. But it had never reached Johnson. It seems like it was confiscated from the Comte by customs officials who then lost it for years until it was found and added to the King Charles collection."

"Unbelievable."

"Surprising, maybe, but the facts all fit so I think it is quite believable."

"Just so. Merely an expression, my dear. Do forgive me. Pray continue. Tell me about the text itself."

"The *Confessio*."

"Whose?"

"Anne of Denmark."

"Confessing what?"

Al reached into her bag and drew out an envelope. She removed three sheets of paper with neatly written text and passed them over to him.

"Here, read it for yourself."

Although the text that Al gave Trubshawe to read was the original Latin, her translation of it into modern English is included overleaf for the benefit of the reader.

175

Confessio

I Anne, daughter of Frederick the Second, King of Denmark and Norway, wife of His Serene Majesty James the Sixth of Scotland, the First of England and Ireland, Queen Consort of Scotland England and Ireland, mother of Princess Elizabeth and Prince Charles, do hereby CONFESS to almighty God, to blessed Mary ever Virgin, to blessed Michael the Archangel, to blessed John the Baptist, to the holy apostles Peter and Paul, and to you Most Holy Father that I have sinned exceedingly in thought, word, and deed, through my fault, through my fault, through my most grievous fault.

I was born in October of the year of Our Lord 1574 at Skanderborg Castle in Denmark, barely a year after my sister Elisabeth. My mother, the Queen Sophia, suffered long in her labour at my birth and before she had fully recovered her strength she was again with child, my brother Christian, whose birth was at last a great joy to my father. My mother seemed almost permanently confined until my ninth year. After that she and I spent some time together, but she preferred to spend her days with Christian, to ensure he was educated as befitted a future king. I, on the other hand, was given a queen's education by my mother's ladies. At fourteen I was married by proxy to a man eight years my senior, whom I had never met nor had any desire to marry. He was James, King of Scotland, a kingdom across the sea with which my father had long sought an alliance. In the drawn-out dowry negotiations, started by my father but concluded after his death by my mother, the loss of a few islands seemed to be of more concern than that of a daughter. I was despatched to a foreign land to join my new husband against my will, but God answered my prayers and intervened in the form of a terrible storm which forced my ship back to the Norwegian coast. I hoped this Divine Providence would save me from my fate, but James came to claim me in person. We were formally wed and I was bedded five weeks after my fifteenth birthday. We spent Christmas and the spring in Denmark, but eventually James took me back with him to Scotland and I was crowned Queen.

Although James was older than me, we had, to my surprise, become friends in Denmark and once back in Scotland I quickly came to love his land. However, I did not much care for many of his people, especially the so-called nobility. Growing up in my father's court I was accustomed to being surrounded by people of intellect and lively conversation. I had enjoyed having philosophical and theological discussions with my father's advisors as well as my own friends. At James' court I had no access to such intellectual exchange and it soon became clear that I was not expected to participate in the affairs of state. I was determined, however, that I should not become merely a breeding mare, as my poor mother had been.

Although I had been brought up following the teachings of Martin Luther, I had always felt that the austerity and joylessness of protestantism could not be God's real intention for His people. The Scottish Calvinists were yet worse. If I wore white-lead upon my face or dressed in fine satins or lace I was accused of vanity; I was criticised for singing or dancing, even when alone in my own chambers. I realised that God was calling me to his true church, the one he himself established, so, with the connivance of a few Catholic nobles to whom I had been introduced, I was secretly baptised into the Church of Rome by father Abercromby and took holy Communion whenever I could.

Despite his need for an heir, my husband had rarely visited my bedchamber since we had returned to Scotland, but instead spent most nights being visited himself by young boys. After four years, though, I did become pregnant and our son the Prince Henry was born. I had decided that I would not ignore my children as my own mother had done to me, but would spend my days with them to teach and watch over them. But, although James knew of my Catholicism and had not objected, many of the court were determined that I should not be allowed to exert any influence upon my own son. Their control over my husband proved greater than my own and my dear child was taken away from me and delivered into the poisonous grasp of two soulless, heartless, reactionaries to be brought up as an anti-Catholic protestant, with instructions that I was not to see him again until he had reached his eighteenth year. I could not bear to be separated from him, but all my attempts to see him were frustrated.

In despair I went to visit Anna, a cousin of one of my childhood friends who had now become Queen of Sweden and Poland, and who was suffering with a difficult pregnancy. Helping to ease her pain also helped me cope with my own. By the end of that year Anna was delivered of her son Wladislaus. There were to be great feasts to celebrate. Anna and Sigismund were Catholic, but when he had inherited the throne of Sweden Sigismund had agreed to protect Swedish Lutherans and so both Catholic and protestant nobility came to Krakow to celebrate with them. My husband, however, fearing that he should lose the loyalty of his realm were he to visit the court of a Catholic monarch, declined the invitation. I remained with Anna for the festivities. The Poles can always be relied upon to throw an extravagant feast. Wladislaus' birthday celebrations were no exception. Anna had arranged for a beautiful, bejewelled dress to be made for me, in thanks for helping her through her confinement. Forgive me for sounding vain, but I can truly say that I was the most beautifully dressed person there.

It was then that I met Frederick, Elector Palatinate of the Rhine. Although a Calvinist, he was in no wise dour like the people that had surrounded me in Edinburgh and were keeping Henry away from me in Stirling. Educated, erudite and intelligent he treated me as an equal and charmed me with his wit and humour. Although he had only intended to come for one feast he stayed at Sigismund's court for the whole Christmas period, and we spent much of the time in deep discussions of matters theological, philosophical and metaphysical. In those few days I had more discourse with Frederick than in a lifetime with James. Eventually the time came for us both to leave. On our last night I knew I would miss him for the rest of my life, but the result of what I did torments me to this day. I brought him to my chamber and let him know me, as a woman should only be known by her husband. We spent a most passionate night together, but in the morning we parted, as I knew we must. He returned to his pregnant wife Louise, I returned to Scotland. It is an irony to me that he was known widely as Frederick the Righteous; an epithet that now makes me both laugh and cry.

On my journey home I began to suspect that I might be

with child. By the time I reached Edinburgh I was quite sure and distraught that God should be punishing me so for one transgression. I was sore afraid that, were my husband the King to discover my sin, I should be tried for treason. However, when I arrived, James was having a squabble with his latest boy and, perhaps out of spite, welcomed me not only with open arms but also into his bed. I said nothing and I still do not know whether he ever suspected. When I gave birth to a daughter everyone was concerned that, apparently arriving a month early, she would be too weak to survive. But she was a hearty child and grew up to be not only strong but also the most beautiful woman in the court. I wanted to call her Frederica in honour of my father, but James insisted we name her Elizabeth, after his cousin the Queen of England with whom he wished to ingratiate himself. His daughter's birth seemed to re-kindle James' interest in me and I was soon heavy again with my second daughter the Princess Margaret. From this point on my worst fears were realised and I was almost permanently with child for the next eight years. My poor dear Margaret died at just a year old, shortly before I gave birth to her brother Charles, a small sickly child. Then another son, Robert, was born but died soon after. Once again I was sure that God was punishing me.

Meanwhile the dreadful aged queen in England died at last, leaving no heirs, and James hastened to London to claim her vacant throne. I took the opportunity to try to be re-united with my son Henry, but was firmly rebuffed and could not raise enough armed support to force my will on the evil countess who was keeping him from me. Although I was once again great with child and close to my confinement I was determined at least to see Henry. But I was again thwarted at every turn. I became furious and could not contain my anger, lashing out at everyone and everything around me. As a result I miscarried the child, a son that I would have called Frederick. James summoned me to London. Although Henry was also going to London, I was not permitted any time alone with him on the journey south. I took the coffin containing Frederick's tiny body with me so that I could show James the son he had lost through his intransigence. Charles remained behind, too weak to risk the journey. We arrived at Windsor where I was given possession of the old Queen's wardrobe of thousands of dresses. At least the English court seemed to be more lively than that in Edinburgh. James and I were crowned together in an anglican ceremony. I refused to take their communion which annoyed James and apparently caused quite a stir among the common folk. But, nonetheless, he still did nothing to stop me from attending Mass, receiving Holy Communion, or communicating with your predecessor, His Holiness Clement VIII.

In London there was more culture, entertainment and many more intellectuals. I was less constrained, free to enjoy lively debates and indulge my interests in the arts, as well as attending masques and other diversions. The anglicans were at least less prone to criticise me, having become used to the old queen who had been both vain and extravagant. But James still seemed to want me permanently pregnant. When my last daughter Sophia died a day after her birth I decided that I had had enough. I told James that we would now live apart and I was determined never to share his bed again. I moved into my own palace, which I named Denmark House.

By the time your Holiness was elected, life was becoming more difficult in England. There was widespread suspicion of Catholics and much hatred. Now that I was no longer in almost-permanent confinement, I had hoped to be able to spend time in more interesting pursuits, but the new political mood meant I was regarded with as much distrust in London as I had been in Edinburgh. My life was threatening to become rather mundane. But, although I needed to be more circumspect about theological and philosophical discussions, I was yet able to enjoy less controversial activities. I employed Mr Ben Jonson to write some fine dramatic entertainments to be produced and performed in my palace, engaging Mr Inigo Jones to design the sets. Mr Jones was a most artful and ingenious architect and his work impressed me such that I also employed him to redesign the palace itself, adding a new courtyard and renovating much of the older part of the building, as well as constructing for me a new palace at Greenwich. The King was forever complaining about the costs, but content that I was at least 'keeping out of trouble'.

Just as my life seemed to have become bearable again, two separate events conspired to break both my heart and soul for eternity. James was keen for Elizabeth to be married and become somebody else's responsibility. She and her brother Henry had become very close and, although he would miss her, as Prince of Wales he had helped choose her prospective husband. Now that Henry had reached eighteen I was able to see more of him, but he had been indoctrinated as a rabid protestant and had no sympathy for my religious convictions. It was he who told me of the choice for Elizabeth's spouse, the son of Frederick the Righteous; my Frederick. Frederick had now become the leader of the union of protestant German states, so an alliance through a marriage to his son seemed to James and Henry an ideal choice to dispel any suggestion of further creeping Catholicism. I was shocked and appalled. Elizabeth could not be allowed to marry her half-brother. But I was too scared of the repercussions for me if I told James, or even Elizabeth, the identity of her real father. I tried in vain over the next months to dissuade Elizabeth. I tried to persuade Henry that he would rather keep his beloved sister nearby than send her off to the Rhinelands. I think I might even have been close to swaying him when he developed a fever malign and died. Once again I was distraught. Having but recently had the opportunity to spend time with my son he had been cruelly snatched away from me. The whole nation mourned his loss so for once I had something in common with everybody else. Nevertheless, Elizabeth's wedding went ahead. Frederick's son, also called Frederick, came to London and they were married in the palace of Whitehall.

I was appalled. What had I done? What could I do? I finally realised that my only recourse was to make my confession and place myself in God's hands once again. My confessor persuaded me I should make this confession directly to you Holy Father.

All these occurrences I have here truly recorded, in the presence of my confessor, praying you to accept it for verity, the same being so true as cannot be reproved.

This confession I make of my own free will in the sight of God, to ask forgiveness and absolution for my sins.

Anne, Denmark House, London, April 1616.

Trubshawe plucked the glasses from his nose and carefully laid them on the papers covering the desk in front of him. Al had watched him quietly while he read Anne's confession, and now waited for his comments. He made some strange tutting noises as he rubbed his eyes, but finally he picked up his glasses again, re-perched them on his nose and turned to face her once more.

"Well, that's quite a story!" He seemed almost lost for words.

"Indeed. What do you think would have been the impact of this had it been published by Johnson?"

"Devastating I imagine. Obviously there would have been a rush by Government supporters to denounce it as lies, but I should think that was why Johnson was chosen to be the publisher – to add credibility, and because it would have been a very unpopular move to try and arrest him as a traitor. You know, the rebellion could have succeeded and things might have worked out very differently. America could still be a colony for heaven's sake!"

"What about now?"

"Now?"

"What will the impact be now, when this becomes public?"

"You'll want to authenticate it first."

"Obviously."

"That's going to be tricky if you haven't got the original."

"I know. It may still be in the Vatican archives, but even if it is I doubt they'd let me have access."

"So it's going to come down to textual analysis to verify that the grammar, spelling and style of the Latin are consistent with other known texts by Queen Anne. Very tricky. If you leave it with me I can make a start for you."

"Thanks for the offer, I may take you up on that later,

although at the moment this is my only copy so I want to hold on to it for now. But you didn't answer my question."

"Which one?"

"What impact will this have when we publish it?"

"Oh. That's hard to say. You'll obviously have a lot of opposition, accusations of forgery and so on. Both official, government-sponsored opposition and from various pressure groups, lobbies, political organisations. Expect some nutters too. But apart from that, if it gains acceptance as an honest account there'll be a huge debate about the validity of the Act of Settlement, probably stir things up about the consequent exclusion of all Catholics from the throne. There have been so many precedents set recently where past actions are publicly repudiated with apologies and even reparation. It's easy to see that there could be a lot of pressure for the same thing to happen here, which means, I imagine, that, in the extreme, it could destabilise the monarchy or even rewind the legitimate blood-line."

"And we finish up with a sheep-farmer from the Australian outback as king?"

"Actually I think you'll find that the European royal families are so inextricably interlinked by close-relative marriages that the true heirs are probably not far from the throne anyway. In fact I'm pretty sure that both the Duchess of York and the late Princess of Wales could trace their ancestry back to that passed-over royal bloodline. I'm sure there's a conspiracy theorist on the internet somewhere who is already using that to explain both of their unhappy tenures as members of the current royal family. But whoever the heirs turn out to be, it's also not totally far-fetched to believe it could bring down the government and quite possibly unleash anarchy in the UK."

"Sounds like the cue for a song." Al grinned.

"No, I'm quite serious!" Trubshawe scowled at her. "Things like this do matter, even in this day and age. Just look at the historical roots of the all-too recent turmoil in Northern Ireland if you don't believe me. No, you'll need to think carefully about the potential implications before you publish such explosive material willy-nilly."

"That's why I came to talk to you."

"And I'm glad you did. Have you told anyone else about this?"

"Not yet."

"I don't think you should mention this to other people for now. Concentrate on authentication before you even consider going public. When you're ready to publish I would suggest you choose a suitable peer-reviewed journal rather than a popular magazine, so that you can benefit from some further scrutiny. It will inevitably take longer and delay publication but after all these years a few more months isn't going to matter really."

"What about running it past some government legal people? To get their view on the constitutional implications."

"I wouldn't bother. That will just give them the chance to invent some ammunition to discredit you."

"But surely the peer-review process will do that too?"

"No-one should pass it on without asking you first. Especially if you make it clear to the editor that you're concerned about government intervention – but you ought to be able to expect them to work that out for themselves!" He raised an eyebrow briefly. Al couldn't decide if this was mere emphasis or to indicate his own meagre expectations of such editors.

After further discussion about appropriate journals and the likely reaction of other academics, it was time for Al to return to Ethel.

"I haven't eaten in the city centre for years, are there still any decent vegetarian or vegan restaurants here?" Al asked as she stood and reached for her coat.

Trubshawe looked a little flustered.

"You don't want to use words like that around the university these days. If the medical researchers hear you they'll have you arrested as an animal rights activist."

"You're not serious?"

"They're trying to get the whole city designated as an exclusion zone for anyone who expresses concern about animal welfare. I'm sure they'd include vegetarians in that. You might be better off going straight back to London."

"What a shame. Oxford used to be an important moral centre, seems like now it's gone the other way. I'll be in touch when I have a better idea of what I'm going to do next."

"Nice meeting you again. Do get back to me if you want help authenticating the confession."

"Thanks. Goodbye."

As Al was turning the door-handle, Trubshawe said "Good luck."

~

Back in Ethel's office, Al briefly outlined what the Professor had said. She finished with his warning about veggie restaurants.

"Phooey," said Ethel, "you just have to know where to go. Come on, I still know the best places."

"Is Dolores going to join us?"

"No, they don't get very flexible lunch-breaks. Next time maybe."

As the two of them were making their way out to the street, Ethel whispered "Did you get to see Vanessa?"

"Yes, she brought in some tea." Al replied, unsure why

they were whispering.

"That girl has a body to die for. I am soooo jealous."

And so, to lunch…

Cenobite

For once I had a quiet day planned. No pressing reports for clients; no meetings; this quarter's VAT return already done, so no bureaucracy to assuage. I had been promising myself a clear day to do some housekeeping on my server – clear out redundant files, archive old logs, that sort of thing. Yes, I know how to live life to the full!

I also allowed myself the luxury of a leisurely breakfast, listening to Radio 4's Today programme right up to the pips. It was a beautiful day with blue sky and occasional fluffy white clouds, too good to be true and definitely too good to be wasted, so I took my coffee outside to drink under the vine that sheltered the patio. Having experienced vines in the gardens of friends and relatives in Italy, and even in Toronto where a large contingent of my Italian relatives now live, I had always been keen to have the same at home. It was Al, in fact, who had helped me buy the right variety – ideally suited to the unreliable and short-lived summers perpetrated by the English weather. Over the last five years the vine had flourished and the yield had increased. Last year I even tried my hand at making wine, but obviously didn't sterilise the demijohn properly as I lost the whole batch to pernicious mould. This year grape juice, a much easier proposition – picked, washed, pressed, bottled and frozen all within a day. But the beauty of the vine is not really the harvest which, in many ways, is just an added bonus. Watching the leaves gradually change colour during the summer months from green through various shades of red until they are each a fractal masterpiece, is one of the main attractions. The immature grapes as they are developing, at first so

189

translucent that they seem to glow with the sun behind them, gradually becoming plumper and less ethereal, darkening to a delightful green, then showing a blush of purple, and finally exploding into that deep vibrant colour that makes your mouth water. The dusty bloom heightens the intrigue and by contrast emphasises the succulence of any grapes that have been carelessly touched or rained upon to reveal the shiny purple-black orb beneath. You may have guessed by now that I rather enjoy sitting under my vine.

As I was finishing the coffee (back to the decaf again!) and resigning myself to heading indoors to tackle the server, my phone lightly trilled. It was the tone that indicated an incoming call from one of a very select group of close friends. I picked it up to see that the screen was identifying Al. Surprisingly excited to have this opportunity to talk to her – and not just because it would allow me to stay a little longer under the vine – I pressed the answer button.

"Hi Al, how are you?"

"I'm okay. Have you got a minute?" She sounded rather worried, so I decided not to gloat about enjoying the sunshine and vine.

"Of course, what's up?"

"You know that firewall that you set up for me, that I thought was just you being paranoid? You said it would give me an alert if anyone tried to attack my computer, but I haven't heard a peep out of it in the eighteen months since you set it up."

"Yes?" I replied cautiously.

"Well it's just flashed up a whole series of messages saying I'm under attack. Is this one of your jokes?"

"Nothing to do with me. It could be a false alarm but I set it up to make sure you didn't get unnecessary alerts, so it's probably real. Let me get back indoors and then you

can give me the details of what the message actually says."
I was walking back into the house as I spoke.

"Which one? There's hundreds. But, actually, they all look much the same. Something about a port scan?"

Once I was settled in front of my Mac, Al read out the details from a couple of the alerts. It was indeed a port scan. I asked her to read me the IP address from which the scan was being launched. Each message showed the same address, very amateurish. I checked it out and traced it to a small service provider in Huntingdon.

"So what is a port scan?" Al asked while I was checking out the ISP's website.

"Computers communicate through ports."

"The sockets on the back?"

"Sort of, but these are virtual sockets rather than physical sockets. Each port has a number from 1 to 65 thousand. Some are used for specific purposes. So for example port 80 is used to get pages from a web server, and port 123 is used to get the time from a time server. That way, lots of different applications can be sharing one physical network connection and when any messages arrive the system knows which application is using which port and can give the message to the right one."

"Like a set of pigeonholes in a mail room?"

"Exactly. So if attackers want to try and find out about a computer that's connected to the internet at a particular IP address they send a short message to each port in turn to see if they get a response. Depending on which port and what response they get back, they can set up a connection which they may be able to exploit to attack the computer or they can find out information about the computer which may help them understand the best way to attack it."

"What, personal information?"

"No. If the computer responds to messages to certain

191

ports then, for example, they can deduce that it's likely to be a Windows machine and they can then launch Windows-specific attacks. Other ports might suggest a file server, a web server, or a mail server, each of which may be vulnerable to different types of attack. So seeing someone perform a port scan on your IP address is the first indication that they're trying to probe you for vulnerabilities to work out how best to attack."

"Will they have found anything?"

"Have you changed any of the firewall settings?"

"No. I wouldn't dare!" Although she still sounded worried I could hear her grin so I was hopeful that she was beginning to relax a little now.

"What about the firewall settings in System Preferences on your Mac?"

"No."

"Okay, in that case whoever launched the port scan has achieved nothing – not even confirmation that they're actually attacking a computer. I set your firewall into stealth mode so no-one can see you unless you actively respond."

"Which means?"

"Which means as far as the attacker is concerned he was trying to scan a black hole. That's why he gave up straight away."

"Gave up straight away? There were hundreds of messages."

"Yes but that was just the port scan – one for each port that he tried. When you read out the last alert to me that was the final port. He gave up because as far as he was concerned there was nothing connected – to all intents and purposes you're invisible."

"Okay, I see. I think. So who do you think tried to scan my ports? It's never happened before. Do you think it's something to do with the *Confessio*? Maybe someone's found out and wants to make sure we don't publish it. Could it be Special Branch or MI5?"

"No, it was far too amateur."

"Ahah. Double bluff?"

"Now who's being paranoid?" I laughed. "No, if the government wanted to know what was on your computer they wouldn't waste time like this, they would just kick down your door and confiscate the machine. This was definitely someone who hasn't really got a clue what they're doing. From a quick glance it doesn't even look like they tried to cover their tracks, so it may just have been a script kiddie. I'll look into that later and see if we can trace them back, but for now you should just take some basic precautions. Have you made a backup lately?"

"I always backup on Friday evenings, but I've done quite a bit of work since last Friday."

"Okay, it's probably worth making another backup today and take it home with you. In fact, just to be on the safe side make a copy of your backup CD and post it to my escrow agent. I'll find the address for you in a minute. First though, you could make an offsite backup right now. Look in your Utilities folder and you'll see a script called Critical Backup. Have you found it?"

I heard a few mouseclicks and then Al replied.

"Yes, found it."

"If you double-click it will connect you into the TOR network."

"The what?"

"TOR. It stands for The Onion Router. It's a way of establishing secure connections without eavesdroppers being able to tell where you're connecting from."

"Why Onion Router?"

"Because the way it works is to add layers of security, each one on top of the last. Like the layers of an onion."

"I know I'm going to regret asking this, but how?"

"Long answer or short answer?"

"I'll go with the short answer."

"Techie stuff!"

"That was a little shorter than I expected. How about a medium length answer." I definitely detected a smile in her voice now.

"Okay. You know in a spy film when the bad guy makes a phone call, the good guys can't trace it in time because it's been routed all round the world?"

"Yes. But isn't that just made up for dramatic effect?"

"Well this is real and it works just like that, creating secure connections around the world between a network of servers, most of which are run for free by volunteers contributing a little bit of their bandwidth and processing time. The connections keep changing, so if you connect through the network to a web server, say, and someone tries to trace where your connection is coming from, it looks to them like one of the machines in the TOR network, then a few seconds later it will change and look like a different machine, and so on. It's quite neat and very handy if you want to connect computers anonymously."

"So this is used by hackers to avoid detection?"

"Could be, although there are some limits in place to try and reduce the opportunities for mischief. But it can be used by anyone to avoid the prying eyes of oppressive regimes, nosey corporations and also to avoid being hacked. It's becoming quite popular, even among non-nerds!" I laughed. "It should have managed to set up your connection by now. Have any messages popped up?"

"Yes, one has just come up saying 'Al, you are now securely connected to PWConsulting.org. Welcome back'. PW Consulting? That's you I assume?"

"It's one of my servers, a semi-public one that runs as a

hidden server on the TOR network. On your desktop you should now be able to see the icon of a disc called 'AM on PWC'."

"Got it."

"Okay, that's some secure disk space I set aside for you on my server. If you just drag anything critical onto that icon it will be copied across the network. So include anything you normally back up, email folders, address book, any work files. It's all secure and private. Even I can't access it."

"But I didn't log in. How does it know it's me?"

"The password is stored in your keychain, which is only accessible when you're already logged into your Mac. To access it from anywhere else you would need to manually enter the password."

"Which is…?"

"I don't know. It's the emergency password I got you to create when I set up your machine. You said you'd remember it."

"Oops!"

"But just in case," I laughed again, "I made a copy of your keychain and lodged it with my escrow agent. So as long as you can remember your login password from eighteen months ago we can get access."

"I haven't changed it since then."

"Al, I'm shocked. I told you to change it regularly."

"I could change it now and then again in another eighteen months. That would be regular."

"I'm sure I actually said frequently too."

"Sorry."

"Well this port scan shows that I wasn't entirely unjustified in my concerns for your security."

"All right, I already said sorry."

"Don't worry. Anyway, copy the files over that you want backed up. When you've finished put the disc away.

You'll notice that Critical Backup is in your dock. If you quit that, it will disconnect you from TOR and reset everything back to your usual settings. Then you can do your normal backup to CD. Okay?"

"Okay."

I had been opening my Address Book while we were talking, so I could now tell Al the address of my escrow agent. Once she had copied it down and confirmed it back to me we said goodbye and I hung up. I went back to the web pages of the Huntingdon ISP that had been hosting the source of Al's attack. With hardly any effort at all I was able to access their customer server to try and track down more information on the user who had performed the port scan. Luckily they assign static IP addresses to their users so I could quickly identify the culprit, a user called cenobite. I sent a finger request and got back a profile of cenobite, whose name was apparently Cenobite Skrump! This sounded like a character from a Dickens story, but then I remembered that Huntingdon had been Cromwell's home town, and a centre for puritanism. Cenobite Skrump could easily be a puritan name. I searched the web and various newsgroups to see if the name showed up anywhere.

I eventually found him (I assumed it was a man) participating in some sectarian forums. Most of his posts were mindless diatribe and typical uninformed propaganda, not so different from the rubbish spouted by Cromwell and his cronies back in the 17th century, all quite intolerant and unpleasant. But then I found a posting in a thread that made me pay more attention. It was a recent discussion about a rumoured document challenging the Act of Settlement and capable of being used to re-establish the legitimacy of claims to the English throne by Catholic descendants of King James. While this document was neither named nor described in any detail, it seemed almost certain that it was Al's *Confessio* that was being discussed. The vile Skrump had posted a series of progressively more agitated messages, culminating in a pledge to remove the threat of any challenge to the protestant hegemony of the throne.

Although Al had not been personally identified in any of the messages in this thread, Skrump had obviously been able to track down her IP address to launch his port scan. I read backwards up the thread to see where this discussion had originated. The initial, almost tentative, posting had been by an Eleanor Trubshawe:

```
4 days ago
Eleanor Trubshawe (joined 12 Sep 2001)
Subject: Act of Settlement

Hi. Does anyone know what could happen if the
Act of Settlement was found to be illegitimate?
I'm American so I don't really understand the
whole monarchy thing, but I have heard that a
document has been found that would invalidate
the Act of Settlement.  Does this mean that
other people would have a better claim to the
throne of England than the present Queen?
```

Among the authors of follow-up messages, Skrump had been the most obviously affected:

```
4 days ago
Cenobite Skrump (joined 25 Apr 1999)
Subject: re: Act of Settlement

We must NOT let this happen.  We'd have foreign
scum on the throne.
```

Followed the next day with:

```
3 days ago
Cenobite Skrump (joined 25 Apr 1999)
Subject: re: Act of Settlement

We must keep the papists out.
```

There were a whole series of messages from Skrump, within the space of a couple of hours, all saying much the same thing. Then the day after:

```
2 days ago
Cenobite Skrump (joined 25 Apr 1999)
Subject: re: Act of Settlement

This so-called evidence must be fake.  We should
destroy it to stop it being used by the servants
of the whore of Babylon.
```

Finally yesterday:

```
1 day ago
Cenobite Skrump (joined 25 Apr 1999)
Subject: re: Act of Settlement

I won't let these scum destroy our country and
soil our throne.  I will remove this threat to
our way of life from the evil antichrist.  I
know who has made this false testimony and I
will destroy it.
```

Luckily this discussion forum had a button marked 'Report as offensive', so I clicked on it and got a response telling me that the thread would be removed while it was examined by a moderator. Within seconds the whole thread had disappeared from the postings list.

The tone of Skrump's messages was concerning, especially as he claimed to have identified the source. But how did he identify Al? More to the point how did this Trubshawe woman know about the *Confessio*? I decided to call Al back and give her an update.

~

"So this Skrump person is going to destroy the *Confessio*?"

"That's what he says."

"How did he find out about it?"

"The thread was started by someone called Eleanor Trubshawe."

"Trubshawe?"

"Yes. Why do you know her?"

"No. But the only person to whom I've spoken about the *Confessio* was Manley Trubshawe. I think his wife might be called Eleanor."

"Who's he?"

"Professor of political history at Oxford. When I went to see Ethel she suggested I talk to him and arranged a meeting for me. I've seen him a couple of times before at various events, conferences, that sort of thing. He briefly helped me with some research a couple of years back. So I asked his opinion on the likely impact of the *Confessio*. He promised he wouldn't tell anyone before we decided whether or not to publish anything. But I have no idea why his wife should be so interested. Not that I've ever met her, but he's never mentioned her as being involved in his work. Frankly I'm surprised, I wouldn't have expected him to break a confidence like that. Maybe he just told her casually and she's blabbed."

"Or maybe he doesn't keep his promises."

"It's very odd. I'm actually quite lost for words."

"Well the main thing is to keep you safe and secure. Keep an eye out for strangers taking too much interest in the shop."

"You think that this Krump…"

"Skrump."

"…Skrump, whoever, will come here to the shop?"

"I don't want to sound over-dramatic, but as his electronic attack has failed he's likely to try something a bit more direct."

"Ohh… Do you think I should close the shop for a while?"

"I don't know. How do you feel about it?"

"It seems a bit pathetic to run away and hide from some bogey man who might not even exist."

"He definitely exists, he tried the port scan remember. But you should do whatever you think is right. Just make sure you take care. And if anything else happens, call me. You can always come to sunny Kent for a while."

"That really would be running away."

"Just bear it in mind."

"Okay. Thanks. I'll talk to you tomorrow."

~

I didn't sleep well that night. I guess I was worried for Al. Worrying about this Skrump character. What he might do. How much he actually knew. I woke up much earlier than usual and spent the extra time freshening up the guest suite, just in case it would be needed soon.

Forum

2 hours ago
Cenobite Skrump (joined 25 Apr 1999)
Subject: Protecting our heritage (was re: Act of Settlement)

There comes a time when we need to take action.
We have to make sure that our heritage is
protected. We don't want the antichrist and his
minions in charge. We must make sure that we do
whatever is necessary to keep power out of their
hands.
----
1 hour ago
Barney (joined 1 Dec 2002)
Subject: Protecting our heritage

Isn't it a bit late? The power moved away from
the throne into the hands of the politicians
years ago. If you want to protect our heritage
then you should be more worried about the
liberties this government are taking.
----
30 minutes ago
FredF (joined 11 May 2001)
Subject: Protecting our heritage

That's right. What's the relevance of the Act
of Settlement anyway? Who cares which
descendants of some dead king are allowed to
wear the crown?

---

25 minutes ago
WARTS (joined 19 Jan 2002)
Subject: Protecting our heritage

It's about time we did away with the crown, the
throne and the monarch. It all started going
wrong when they re-instated the monarchy.
Cromwell had the right idea. We need a real
protector to run a proper republic, not a
tourist attraction for weak politicians to hide
behind.

---

20 minutes ago
Cenobite Skrump (joined 25 Apr 1999)
Subject: Protecting our heritage

You're all missing the point. If the Act of
Settlement goes, we don't get a republic; we
don't get a stronger government; we don't get a
fairer society. We get Rome's lackeys, here in
God's green and pleasant land. Before you know
it they'll be forcing us to live by their rules.
There'll be popish temples everywhere and we'll
be forced to drink blood. It'll be Bloody Mary
all over again. Well I, for one, won't stand
for it. I'm going to make sure these scum don't
get their way.

---

15 minutes ago
Barney (joined 1 Dec 2002)
Subject: Protecting our heritage

Mate. I think you're barking up the wrong tree.

```
------------------------------------
```
14 minutes ago
FredF (joined 11 May 2001)
Subject: Protecting our heritage

Or just barking!
```
------------------------------------
```
13 minutes ago
Barney (joined 1 Dec 2002)
Subject: Protecting our heritage

It's this fascist government that will be
controlling what you are allowed to think, say
and do, not some clown wearing a funny outfit in
a Palace.
```
------------------------------------
```
12 minutes ago
Dave the rave, Guest
Subject: Protecting our heritage

You mean Nigel Martyn?
```
------------------------------------
```
11 minutes ago
Barney (joined 1 Dec 2002)
Subject: Protecting our heritage

Not Crystal Palace, you muppet ;-)
```
------------------------------------
```
10 minutes ago
Cenobite Skrump (joined 25 Apr 1999)
Subject: Protecting our heritage

You think this is funny? Some kind of joke?
It's not. It's deadly serious. You'll see.
I'll get this document, this so called 'proof'
and destroy it. Then I'll destroy the woman
who's cooked it up.

```
-------------------------------------
7 minutes ago
Barney (joined 1 Dec 2002)
Subject: Protecting our heritage

You need to calm down mate.
-------------------------------------
3 minutes ago
Cenobite Skrump (joined 25 Apr 1999)
Subject: Protecting our heritage

No.  I need to take some action.  You lot are
all a bunch of liberal pansies.
-------------------------------------
2 minutes ago
WARTS (joined 19 Jan 2002)
Subject: Protecting our heritage

I can help.  Let's talk IRL about action.
-------------------------------------
1 minute ago
Cenobite Skrump (joined 25 Apr 1999)
Subject: Protecting our heritage

Okay. PM me.
-------------------------------------
```

Lynn

Al rang in the morning, somewhat sooner than I had expected. I was immediately concerned that something had already happened to worry her, but I was completely unprepared for what she had to say.

"I had a strange email this morning. Waiting for me when I arrived."

"What, from Skrump?"

"No, I don't think so. Well, actually I hadn't thought of that. I suppose it could be. Some sort of trick. It's from an email address that I don't recognise and when I tried to reply the server rejected it as an invalid address."

"What does it say?"

"It says 'Invalid email address'".

"No, the original email!"

"It says 'We need to meet' and 'You are in danger'. But there's no indication of who, when or where to meet."

"Are there any other clues in the header?"

"The what?"

"The header. Where details like from, to, date, and routing information are recorded."

"I don't know. What should I look for."

"Look at the message-id, or the X-mailer."

"I don't really know what I'm looking at or for. Can I forward it to you to check out?"

"Sure. But don't forward it, that will lose some of the details. Save it as a text file and send that to me."

After a few seconds she said "Okay, on its way" and seconds later it arrived in my inbox.

```
Return-Path: <whom@sweet.whom>
Received: from mail.mintbooks.co.uk
  by mailstore for Al@mintbooks.co.uk
  id 1FpASd-3eJknw-02-DlQ;
  08:53:35 +0000
Received: from [66.69.78.32]
  (helo=[77.73.78.84])
  by whom.sweet.whom
  with esmtp (Exim 4.32)
  id 1FpASd-0005vB-1q
  for Al@mintbooks.co.uk;
  08:53:35 +0000
To: Al Mint <Al@mintbooks.co.uk>
Content-Type: text/plain;
  charset=UK-ASCII; format=flowed
X-Mailer: Whom Mail
From: <whom@sweet.whom>
Subject: We need to meet
Message-ID:
<F21B719FAD7EE9C94156@whom.sweet.whom>
Date: 15:30:00 +0000

You are in danger
```

I looked at the email and the first thing I noticed was that it had apparently been sent 6 hours in the future, but not due to some time zone effect as it claimed to have been sent at 15:30 GMT. Although this could mean that the sender had an inaccurately set system clock on their computer I thought it might be a deliberate means of indicating the proposed meeting time.

"I think I know when you're supposed to meet."

"When?"

"Half past three this afternoon."

"Okay. But I still don't know where or who I'm meeting."

"As you discovered, the sender's supposed email address is invalid, or incomplete. There's no top level domain."

"What?"

"You know, like .com or .net or .co.uk"

"Oh, right."

"Whom at sweet dot whom. Hmm. Whom sweet whom."

"What did you say?"

"Whom sweet whom. Why? Does it mean something to you?"

"Yes. It was something my dad always used to say. His Scottish relatives pronounced 'Home' as 'Whom'. It's Lallans."

"Lallans?"

"The language of the Scots."

"I thought that was Gaelic?"

"Gaelic is the highlanders', Lallans is lowlands Scots. Anyway, he often said 'Whom Sweet Whom' when we got back home after a long day out. It was a bit of a family joke. But I didn't even notice that it was the sender's address until you read it out."

"So this email may be from someone who was close enough to your family to be aware of the joke. Maybe they're trying to re-assure you that they are friendly."

"But we still don't know who THEY are."

While we had been talking I had been manipulating the text of the email in an editing and analysis tool. Just then one of the transformations I had performed had extracted the IP addresses from the email header in order to validate them with a whois service. While one was genuine, the other was unassigned, so it was clear that the whole line in the header must have been spoofed. Reasoning that it too may have been faked to provide rather than hide information, I examined the addresses more carefully. That's when I realised that each IP address was actually a string of ascii values of 4 characters.

"The IP addresses in one of the header lines is an encoding of eight characters."

"In English please." Al replied.

"You know what an IP address is?"

"Yes. You explained that to me yesterday, four numbers separated by dots. So I can see that this has an address of 66 dot 69 dot 78 dot 32. Oh and another one of 77 dot 73 dot 78 dot 84."

"Right, those two IP addresses aren't real addresses. Each of the four numbers can also be interpreted as the ascii code that represents a character."

"What characters?"

"Hang on let's see. B. E. N. space. M. I. N. T"

"My dad? He can't have sent it. He wouldn't know where to begin. He's hardly even got the hang of switching his computer on."

"Okay. Maybe this is meant to be the re-assurance."

"So what was Whom Sweet Whom for?"

"I don't know. Perhaps … location? Maybe you're supposed to meet at the family home which your Dad called Whom Sweet Whom?"

"What, Priestley Avenue?"

"Why not? Do your parents still live there?"

"No. Not for years."

"Can you get there by half three?"

"Of course. It's only in Hampstead."

"Well then. I think this email is telling you to meet someone – I still don't know who – at your parents' old house in Priestley Avenue at three thirty this afternoon. It's probably from someone who knew your family when you were living there."

"Do you think I should go?"

"Yes, I think so. But you should be careful how you get there. Make sure you're not followed."

"Isn't that a bit melodramatic?"

"Why would your mystery correspondent go to such trouble to conceal the details of your assignation unless they thought that your email might be intercepted? Or theirs?"

"But how could they be sure I'd understand the message? You're the one who figured it out."

"You're a smart cookie. You'd have worked it out yourself."

"Not necessarily in time though. Maybe they knew I'd have your help."

"I think you're selling yourself short, as usual. Anyway, are you going to go?"

"Will you come along?"

"If you want, but that might scare off whoever wants to meet you."

"I'd rather take that risk, than risk going alone."

"Okay, I'll meet you there."

"Thanks."

"No problem. See you later. Bye."

I re-arranged my schedule so I could head up to London at lunchtime to keep Al company at this mysterious meeting.

~

Just before half past three I was standing at the end of Priestley Avenue, keeping an eye out for Al. A taxi pulled up next to me, the door opened and she stepped out. After paying the driver, she led me along the pavement until we were standing outside an imposing Edwardian town house. Al was obviously quite nervous and was constantly looking around. I suggested she calm down a little and stop worrying, or she'd be more likely to attract attention, especially as this was probably an ardent Neighbourhood Watch area and I had already seen some net curtains twitching. Telling Al to calm down proved to be a bad move, rather like dousing a fire with petrol. So I tried to help her relax by telling her some of my best jokes! Within a couple of minutes she was laughing, if a little nervously.

An elegant woman was walking along the street towards us and as she drew parallel she stopped and asked us the time. Al checked her watch.

"Just gone half past three."

"Thanks Alison," the woman replied. Al looked at her in surprise.

"Do I know you?" she asked.

"You did, but you've obviously forgotten me. It's not surprising really, I haven't seen you for over thirty years. My name's Lynn Dentry, I'm your…"

"Godmother," Al interrupted, "I do remember you now. I haven't seen you since we moved away from Hampstead."

"I'm afraid my work took me abroad for a few years and since I returned it's been difficult to get back in touch with old friends."

"So what prompted this meeting? And why the cloak and dagger stuff? I assume this isn't a coincidence? It was you that sent me that cryptic email?"

"It was, and I'm glad you managed to decode it."

"Actually it was Peter. Oh, I'm sorry, let me introduce you. This is Peter White. Peter, this is my Godmother."

"We've met before, in fact." I said. "At a crypto conference last year. We were both presenting papers. Yours was better received than mine if I recall."

"That was only because yours was very technical while mine was more philosophical. Hello again. I expected Alison to enlist your help with my message."

"Why?"

"Known associate!" she grinned.

"Anyway, about that email," interrupted Al, "why am I in danger exactly? How do you know?"

"Did your Dad ever tell you what I do?"

"It was always understood that you were some sort of

diplomat. I think he said you'd gone abroad to be a cultural attaché in an embassy somewhere."

At that point I must admit I laughed. Lynn scowled at me while Al looked confused.

"What's funny?" she asked.

"Cultural attaché. It's a bit of a clichéd euphemism."

"For what?" Sometimes Al can be quite naïve.

"Spook."

"Intelligence officer, if you don't mind," interrupted Lynn.

"Spy?" Al looked surprised.

"Actually I've been promoted now. More admin unfortunately, less field work."

"And a much shorter job title!" I grinned. Lynn scowled at me again and Al looked even more confused. "Monogram," I whispered to her. She raised an eyebrow.

"What, like M and Q in James Bond films?" she whispered back. I nodded.

"When you two have quite finished whispering, I came here to talk about YOU not me."

"Right," said Al, "but like I said, why am I in danger? Who from? Is it Cenobite Krump?"

"Skrump," I corrected her.

"Skrump," she repeated.

"Who?" Now it was Lynn's turn to look confused. "No, the Americans."

"Americans?" both Al and I echoed.

"Yes, the CIA have identified you, Alison, as a terrorist engaged in anti-American activities. They requested assistance from our colleagues in the Security Service to facilitate extraordinary rendition of an Islamist terrorist called Ali ben Mint. We were asked to confirm the US intel, but when we did some very basic checks of the information they'd supplied we realised that their sources were spurious at best, or possibly deliberately distorted.

They'd used the fact that some people shorten your name to Ali, combining that with your Dad's name, to come up with a plausibly Arab-sounding alias. But once we'd untangled it and tracked it back to you, we advised them to refuse the American request. We confirmed that you're a UK citizen of impeccable character and that we have used your help in some of our own research…"

"What? I've never worked for MI5." Al was looking a little shocked.

"6 actually!"

"Whatever. I've never worked for any secret service."

"Not directly, maybe. But some of the academics that you've worked with, have. They used your work to complete research for us, so it was only a slight stretch of the truth. Anyway the Security Service told the CIA to back off and check their facts, but that may only delay them. If they've decided they're going to extract you then our objections may not stop them for long. I'm afraid they think they have free rein anywhere in the world. I recommend you lay low for a while."

Al was obviously shaken. "Is this serious? Not some kind of joke?" She looked at me. "Have you set this up?"

I put my hands up and shook my head.

Lynn said, "Believe me, this is completely serious I'm afraid."

"But what am I supposed to have done?"

"Does it matter?"

"Well, yes!"

"Okay. Once we'd worked out that it was you they were targeting, I arranged a little distraction and hacked into their field system."

"What, you hacked the CIA?"

"Of course, it's easy. They're arrogant and that makes them so careless that they don't take even the simplest precautions. Everyone takes a little peek into their systems: us, the French of course, Israelis, Russians, oh and the Australians and Canadians have great fun circulating the latest amusing titbits that they've extracted. We hack the US systems all the time. It's much cheaper than setting up our own," she grinned, "but usually not this inaccurate. Anyway, it seems that the Mothers have accused you of fabricating a scandal to besmirch one of the founding fathers."

"The Mothers?"

"Yes. I take it you've heard of the Daughters of the American Revolution?"

"I think so. Aren't they a sort of Women's Institute for well-to-do families in New England."

"Something like that." Lynn nodded. "Way back, when they were founded, they were rather more militant, but in recent years they've become something of a joke to most Americans. However since September the 11th, a faction has formed that is taking a much more pro-active rôle in addressing what they see as anti-American activities. Rather than being merely militant it seems they've become downright militaristic. In fact, even the American agencies are becoming concerned, they see them as interfering, trouble-making amateurs. They were laughingly christened the 'Mothers of the Revolution' in the Intelligence community because they were something of a joke at first, but no-one's laughing any more. They have tight family connections in Washington, on Capitol Hill, in the Pentagon, the State Department and most of the other significant agencies. You cross them at your peril."

"But what have I done to upset them?"

"I don't know, but whatever it is has offended them enough to want to stop you. Most of the US agencies are pretty much running rogue at the moment, they have been ever since September the 11th, and the White House clearly has no intention of reining them in until it's forced to."

"I still don't understand why the Americans are targeting me. It must be a mistake."

"Obviously they are barking up entirely the wrong tree here, but they may take a great deal of convincing and that could take some time. Once the field agents are on the case these things tend to take on a life of their own. For now I strongly recommend you disappear for a while – till it blows over."

Al opened her mouth to start to protest but then obviously thought better of it. She said nothing.

"Peter," Lynn looked at me, "can you hide Alison away somewhere? They do mean business. The bureau chief here in London, Bob Lord, has apparently taken a personal interest. We know he's been responsible for snatching various European citizens elsewhere, but he's never been successfully prosecuted because he has diplomatic immunity. He just gets moved on to another embassy in a different country. I don't trust him one little bit. Here," she took a photograph out of her pocket and handed it to me, "this is him. I think he misses his field days because he likes to lead snatches in person. Keep a look out, but most of all take Alison somewhere safe and keep her there."

"I had a strange visitor the other day, an American." Al now spoke up, as she looked at the photograph. "But it wasn't this guy. He said his boss wanted to talk to me about some work I was doing. I told him it was confidential and I couldn't discuss it, but he insisted I at least meet his boss. In fact, he's supposed to be coming to the shop tomorrow. He didn't give me his name, or his boss's name."

"Don't meet him, just in case," Lynn said forcefully.

Al was somewhat dazed by the news that the CIA were

gunning for her. Hopefully not literally. She still couldn't believe what she was being told.

"Do you know what Alison has done to attract so much attention from the Americans?" Lynn asked me.

"As far as I know, the only thing that's even vaguely controversial is something she's doing for me. She found a document that casts doubt on the legitimacy of the Act of Settlement and hence the validity of the reign of every British monarch since George the First. But I would have thought that Americans would applaud that. It certainly doesn't 'besmirch' any American founding fathers, as far as we know."

"I'll see if I can find more details about what has got them so riled. I'll let you know if I come up with anything – I've written my private Skype address on the back of that photo, but wait for me to call you. Meanwhile, you just spirit her away. She's my God-daughter, I'm relying on you to keep her safe."

"But will she be safe with me? Like you said, I'm a known associate, so surely they'll come looking for Al at my place sooner or later?"

"Known by us, not necessarily by them. I try to make sure that we don't share anything that we don't have to."

"Okay." I looked at Al. "Come on Al, Lynn's right. It's probably best if you come home with me."

When I turned back, Lynn had already walked away and was soon out of sight. Al was still very subdued. I hailed a passing taxi, gave the driver directions to take us to my house (it took some persuading to get him to go south of the river, even though it was only the middle of the afternoon), then settled back into the seat wondering what on earth was going on.

On the journey, Al phoned her friend Sarah who could always be relied on to mind the shop for a while. Al told her that she had to go away for a few days unexpectedly, but I had insisted that she didn't mention where. Sarah agreed to open up in the morning, check the post and generally keep an eye on things. Once she had finished the call, Al relaxed into her seat, resting her head on my shoulder.

After a while I asked her about the visitor she had mentioned to Lynn.

"Was it the *Confessio* that he wanted to talk about?"

"No, that's what's weird. He seemed to know about the folios we found in Vinci and said he wanted to talk about the text hidden in them. I don't think he knew about the *Confessio* at all."

"Why would the CIA be interested in Leonardo's robots?" I wondered.

We were both baffled and hardly spoke at all for the rest of the journey back to Kent.

Attack

The following transcript of a suspect statement given to the Metropolitan Police was provided as a result of a request under the Freedom of Information Act 2000.

Statement provided by John Bradshaw:
"Accompanied by Thomas Harrison, I disabled the alarm and forced the lock on the front door of the bookshop. Once inside the premises we searched for the document as instructed. Thomas wanted to take some of the books as a bonus, he said that there were bound to be some very valuable ones on the shelves. But we had been told not to touch anything else, which I reminded him.

On the desk towards the back of the shop we found the document we had come for, I folded it and placed it in the inside pocket of my jacket. While looking for the document I had moved the telephone that was sitting on the desk, which would be why my fingerprints were found on it. At no time did we interfere with the telephone and I have no knowledge of the device that I have been accused of attaching to the phone.

We had also been told to delete the document files on the computer, but the computer was an Apple and neither of us knew how to use it, so we left it well alone.

We then left by the front door. We were in the shop for a total of five minutes. Thomas and I split up and took different routes back to headquarters. Once there I handed the document we had obtained from the shop to a colleague. I did not read the document, nor did Harrison. I do not know what happened to the document. I had never previously visited the shop and I have not visited it since."

Crypto Da Vinci

Attacked

In the morning, after some strong coffee (my initial response to most of life's problems) and a simple breakfast of toast and marmite, Al was sitting in the lounge watching the BBC breakfast news when Sarah phoned.

"Al," she said, "sorry to call you so early but when I got here I found that the shop had been broken into."

"What? Are you ok?" Al went rigid.

"Yeah, yeah, I'm fine. Whoever it was, they were long gone."

"Oh thank God. Is anything missing?"

"I don't think so. When I arrived I could see that the door had been forced, but as far as I can tell your safe is untouched and all the books seem to be on the shelves. The papers on your desk are all over the place though, but otherwise I can't see anything obviously missing. Were there any especially valuable volumes hidden away anywhere?"

"No, nothing."

"Then I don't understand. It doesn't make sense. Why break in and not steal anything?"

"Did you call the Police yet?"

"Yes. I phoned them before calling you. They said they couldn't really do anything if nothing appears to have been taken, so they've just given me an incident number for insurance purposes."

"That's just great. Oh, what happened to the alarm?"

"I don't know. The phone line is still working, and there's power, so they must have disabled the system – or known the code. Do you want me to call the alarm people to come and check?"

"If you wouldn't mind. Sarah you're a gem. Oh, what about the door, you said it had been forced. Is it still lockable?"

"I think it'll be okay. Chris isn't busy today, I'll get him to come over and have a look to see if it needs reinforcements or anything."

"Thanks. Sorry you're stuck with all this hassle."

"Don't worry about it. That's what friends are for. I'll call you again after the alarm guy has been."

"Okay. One more thing. You said the papers on my desk are all messed up?"

"Yeah. Knowing how tidy you usually are, I'm sure the desk was disturbed, but only the desk. Like they were looking for something specific there."

"Can you see a large brown envelope with the word *Confessio* on the outside?"

"Hang on." There was a rustling noise as various papers were re-shuffled.

"Nope, not that I can see. Was it important? Or valuable? Is that what they were looking for?"

"If it's missing I guess so. It's not valuable but might be important to some people. Is my Mac okay?"

"Looks okay to me. Do you want me to switch it on and check?"

"No don't bother. I'll do that when I eventually get back."

"What about your email? Should I do anything in case there are some orders, or can you check it from where you are?"

"Yes, I'm sure we can sort something out."

"How long are you going to be away? Do you know yet?"

"I was hoping just a day or two, but this makes me think it may be longer. Listen Sarah, once Chris has secured the door and the alarm is working again, just lock up and go home. Don't bother opening up again, I don't want you to be there if someone comes back."

"Do you think they might?"

"I hope not. But just in case, I don't think you should hang around any longer than necessary. I'm really sorry I asked you to watch the shop and got you involved in all this."

"Don't be silly. I'm fine. I'm sure everything will work out. I'll call you later."

"Okay. Bye Sarah, thanks again. And thank Chris for me too will you."

"Will do. Now don't worry about it Al. Bye."

As soon as she'd put the phone down, Al looked at me with a worried expression.

"I guess Lynn wasn't kidding," she said. "The shop's been broken into and the only thing taken seems to be my copy of the *Confessio.*"

"How did they get in?"

"Forced the door. I don't know why the alarm didn't trigger though."

"Sounds a bit amateurish for spooks, even the CIA…"

"Maybe they want it to look amateur to distract attention?"

"You really are beginning to sound as paranoid as me." I laughed. "But if you're right, it would be to cover up something else. They knew you weren't there, but they probably don't know that Lynn has tipped you off to their interest. If they aren't getting support from MI5 they've got to be a little more cautious. They've probably got the shop under surveillance."

"What? But Sarah's there. I'll call her and tell her to leave straight away." She picked up the phone.

"Ask her to look out of the window and see if there's anyone suspicious hanging around."

Al called Sarah, who soon spotted a man in an overcoat and sunglasses standing across the street from the shop.

"Very clichéd! Almost a caricature. As if it's just for effect, like you suggested."

I smiled. "Get Sarah to call the police and tell them that she's seen someone loitering outside and is scared that the person who broke in has come back. If she can manage to sound wimpy and scared enough they'll send someone round."

After a while Sarah rang back to say that a police car had arrived and they were now talking to the man. We told her to leave straight away and go home by an indirect route, ideally changing taxis. Sarah had used her phone to take a photo of the man, when he was being questioned by the police. They had made him remove his shades. She sent the image to Al. We could immediately see that it was the man in the photo Lynn had given us.

~

Only a few minutes later Al got another call from Sarah. She sounded breathless.

"You know you told me to change taxis?"

"Yeah. It's probably just me worrying too much."

"It isn't. I think I'm being followed."

"What? By whom?"

"I don't know. There was a guy walking down the road as I left the shop. I locked up and headed towards New Oxford Street, I thought that would be the easiest place to get a cab. Then I heard someone shouting behind me. I glanced back and it was the same guy, he was standing outside the shop and calling out your name. After what you'd said, I ignored him and carried on. I heard him running but by then I'd got to the end of the road and managed to flag down a cab straight away – pretty amazing, actually. Anyway as we drove off, the man came flying out of the end of Coptic Street and got into another cab, and now his cab is following my cab. It's like a cheap film, 'follow that cab!' Only it's not funny. To be honest I'm a bit scared. And I haven't got a clue how to 'lose him' – that's the right phrase isn't it?"

"Hang on, I'll see what Peter suggests."

"Hi Sarah. Where are you?" I asked.

"Just going over Holborn Viaduct. We're heading for Liverpool Street."

"Okay. How well do you know the area?"

"Reasonably."

"What about Bank tube?"

"It's a bit of a rabbit warren – lots of different exits."

"Absolutely. With a bit of luck your tail won't be familiar with it, so you can lose him down there. When you get to Poultry, ask your cabbie to drop you as near to the tube entrance on the corner with Princes Street as he can, then go down to the station and around to the Lombard Street exit."

"Isn't that closed at the moment?"

"Damn. Okay, come out at King William Street and leg it down St Swithin's Lane. You should be able to pick up another cab in Cannon Street, then head back to Blackfriars. It's easy to get back home from there isn't it?"

"No problem. Okay I'll call you again if I get stuck. Thanks."

"Let me know when you're home safely," added Al.

~

We spent the next hour and a half nervously watching the phone, waiting for Sarah to let us know she was safe. Eventually it rang, and Al snatched it up.

"Sarah?"

"Yeah, I'm home now. Safe and sound. I lost the guy at Bank as Peter suggested. That was exhilarating and scary at the same time. What's going on Al? Who are these people watching the shop and chasing me – or you, I presume he thought I was you?"

"We don't really know. We have our suspicions."

"Are you going to let me in on the secret?"

"It's probably safer if we don't."

"I'd say it's a bit late for that, wouldn't you? I've just been chased halfway round London. Halfway through London, in fact. Okay, maybe not half, perhaps more like an eighth. An eighthway through London? That doesn't sound right. How about partway through London. Partway through the centre of London. Well, through the City at least…"

"Sarah?"

"What? Oh sorry. But the point is that I think I've earned the right to know why."

"We really don't know what's going on. We found something hidden in some pages of Leonardo's notes. We decoded it and translated it and now it seems like the CIA wants to stop us."

"Oh my God. The CIA. What on earth did you find? President Bush's nuclear launch codes?"

"What, hidden in Leonardo's notes? That would be pretty amazing wouldn't it! No. Hang on."

Al looked at me and I nodded.

"Okay. We've found two different things. One is a document which suggests that none of the kings and queens of Britain since George I were actually legitimate. That was the piece of paper that was missing from my desk, which is why we think it might be what they're interested in."

"I can see that that might be political dynamite here, but

not for the CIA surely?"

"Exactly," Al replied, "which is why we don't understand what's going on."

"You said you found two things. What's the other? Might the CIA be interested in that?"

"It's a set of notes by Leonardo about a commission to build a humanoid robot. But he didn't finish the project and then destroyed all the evidence."

"Except the notes presumably?"

"Which he hid using a code."

"Not of much interest to the CIA either, then?"

"You see our confusion."

"You're sure that's all?"

"Yes. Nothing else."

"So what makes you think it's the CIA. Maybe it's someone else with a genuine interest in one of these documents. Surely MI5 or, I don't know, Special Branch, would be worried about your king-denying text? I mean, if they bumped off Diana to keep the throne safe, surely they'd be more than keen to stop this becoming public?"

"It was MI5 who told us it was the CIA." Al replied.

"Actually it was MI6." I pointed out.

"Pedant," muttered Al.

"Ha! Misdirection!" Sarah almost spat the words out. "They warn you about the CIA so you don't realise they themselves are actually the enemy."

"You're sounding as paranoid as Peter."

"I've just been chased around half of London."

"Don't start that again!" Al laughed.

"So I have the right to be paranoid," Sarah continued, "it's my problem too now."

"Well," I interrupted, "it seems like they lost you and hopefully they have no idea who you are. Don't go back to the shop until this is all sorted out and you should be able to keep clear of them. I'm sure you won't be bothered again."

Sounding a bit more relieved, but not entirely convinced, Sarah said goodbye and Al put the phone down.

"Well I'm glad that's over," she sighed.

"*Au contraire*. It seems like it's only just starting..." I, too, sighed.

Kent

Al was looking concerned.

"If Lynn was right, what am I going to do?" she mused.

"Well, at least you're safe here. Which gives us time to deal with them."

"Deal with them? How? If it really is the CIA how am I going to deal with them?"

"You're not dealing with them alone. I'm here."

"Oh that makes all the difference!"

"Your belief in me is touching."

I tried to look as if I was offended.

"You know I didn't mean it like that. But what can WE do against the might of the CIA?"

"For a start, you have to stop believing their propaganda. What you call their 'might' is based on two perceived strengths. Information – which they laughably call 'intelligence', although you and I both know there is a big difference between the two – and what I call stompability."

Al momentarily winced as her innate love affair with the English language reeled from such an unexpected affront.

"Stompability?"

She had managed to turn her wince into an incredulous grin, complete with raised eyebrows. It was the first time she had smiled all day.

"Yes, of course. Usually they get to charge in somewhere and stomp all over the local citizens, law enforcement, even military – thanks to the collusion of weak indigenous governments who don't want to take the risk of standing up to the world's biggest bully."

"So what's different now?"

"Thanks to Lynn, the British intelligence service have already blocked them in your case. Given the so-called 'special relationship' and the American government's need for UK support elsewhere they are extremely unlikely to stomp around here at the moment. More likely to pussy foot!"

"But how is that better? Surely that just means that they'll operate surreptitiously, outside the law?"

"Exactly, which means we can use the law to our benefit. But first we need to find out what they're up to."

"How?"

"Leave that to me."

~

Some years ago, when I was working as a security consultant for a large retail bank, I had worked with an ex-policeman called Barry Barnes. Like many organisations, the bank had distinguished between physical security and information security, but unlike most there had been one department handling both, ensuring a complementary set of policies – as a result they had a much better record of preventing criminal attack. Barry had been responsible for physical security, which encompassed everything from security guards to CCTV and explosive dye packs. He was an expert at surveillance techniques as well as deploying deterrents. Subsequently, he left the bank during a particularly demoralising re-organisation and set up his own consultancy offering private investigation services. Although he occasionally had to follow faithless husbands or wayward wives to obtain evidence for divorce proceedings, most of his work was corporate surveillance or undercover infiltration to investigate fraud or theft. We had kept in touch and he had asked me to help with computer forensics on a couple of cases. This time he could return the favour. I called and asked him to put teams in place for a couple of days to keep an eye on both Al's home in Dulwich and the shop in Coptic Street.

~

Before I went back to join Al in the lounge I checked my emails. There was one waiting for me from Lucia. She apologised for disturbing me but asked whether I could send her another set of copies of the decoded texts that we had asked her to translate. She had been away for a few days and when she got back to her office at the University it had been ransacked. Luckily, she said, very little damage had been done, but some of her papers had been taken including the Mechanicant texts. She said that a few of her students' recent assignments had also gone missing, so she suspected that it was perpetrated by an undergraduate trying to cover the fact that they had failed to submit their work on time. She didn't think it was anything to worry about, in fact she thought it was likely that the Mechanicant texts had just been thrown away by the culprit. But she promised to keep them locked in her cupboard from now on.

If this had happened in isolation I would probably have agreed with Lucia's assessment. But in the context of the earlier message from Simonetta, and Sarah's recent chase halfway around London, I wasn't so sure. But, of course, I sent the decoded texts to Lucia – at least now she had them electronically rather than just the handwritten versions we had left with her in Florence. I decided not to worry her unduly so I assured her that I was not concerned at their accidental loss. I didn't mention Simonetta's warning or Al's recent visitors.

Now Al and I had to consider this latest event. Why

were we attracting so much attention, and should we continue with our investigations now that it was starting to affect our friends?

Retrieval

The following email was intercepted and subsequently (long after the event) made available to Peter. It is included here in the correct chronological context for the convenience of the reader.

```
To: Field Ops
From: M
Subject: URGENT operation required

            ----- Original Message -----
            To: Field Ops
            From: M
            Subject: New operation

            There is a document that reveals an
            indiscretion between Anne of Denmark
            and Frederick the Righteous.  It is
            apparently hidden in one of the
            Leonardo da Vinci folios in Windsor.
            We need to find it, destroy it and
            remove any copies, images or other
            evidence of it.  I don't know which
            folio, but it has recently been the
            subject of attention by Dr. Alison
            Mint.  First, find out from Windsor
            which folio she has been consulting.
            Then get rid of it.

            ----- Original Message -----
            To: M
            From: Field Ops
            Subject: Re: New operation

            Why?  What's the big deal?  I can't
            see the problem here.
```

----- Original Message -----
To: Field Ops
From: M
Subject: Re[1]: New operation

Fortunately that's not your job, it's
mine. I wasn't asking for your opinion,
I was giving you an instruction.

----- Original Message -----
To: M
From: Field Ops
Subject: Re[2]: New operation

As you are aware, I have limited
resources. I have to prioritise how I
use them. If you don't give me more to
go on I'll be concentrating on other
operations that have demonstrable value.

----- Original Message -----
To: Field Ops
From: M
Subject: Re[3]: New operation

Fine. Anne was married to James I of
England and was the mother of Elizabeth,
who married Frederick V, son of Frederick
the Righteous. But according to Anne's
documented confession, Frederick the
Righteous was actually Elizabeth's father
not James. This means that:
- not only was Anne unfaithful;
- her daughter Elizabeth was illegitimate,
with no rightful claim to the throne;
- and Elizabeth married her own half-
brother, (which, if it had become public
knowledge, would have made her an
abomination in the eyes of most people at
the time);
- therefore, Elizabeth's daughter Sophia
had no rightful claim to the British
throne, and hence neither did George I;

If this becomes public, even now, the Act
of Settlement would be rendered impotent,
resulting in the strong possibility of a
legal challenge to our present Queen and

her removal from the throne. In which case
there is a distinct likelihood that the
monarchy would be dissolved rather than
placed in the hands of an unsuitable
(albeit legitimate) claimant.

Does that answer your question? Do you
have enough to prioritise?

----- Original Message -----
To: M
From: Field Ops
Subject: Re[4]: New operation

Thank you for the background. I see the
reasons why you wish it prioritised above
average. I will get back to you.

----- Original Message -----
To: Field Ops
From: M
Subject: Urgent new operation (was: New
operation)

I don't want it prioritised above average, I
want it prioritised as urgent. Do you
understand?

----- Original Message -----
To: M
From: Field Ops
Subject: Re[1]: Urgent new operation

As I said before I have limited field resources
- we're not the CIA you know! I can probably
get the original out of Windsor, but there are
likely to be copies and images all over the
place - especially on various servers around
the internet. I don't have the resources to
track all of those down and retrieve them.

----- New Message -----

In that case, I'm sure our German friends can
help. They have a common interest in protecting
the reputation of both Fredericks.

Missing

Later that day I was setting up an old Mac in the guest room so Al could check her email and get on with her work when she was ready. As I was adding bookmarks to the web browser I went to the Royal Windsor website to find the page with the image of the folio that had contained the *Confessio*, but it was nowhere to be found. From their home page I checked the news and found a short item noting that a folio that had previously been attributed to Leonardo had just been identified as a forgery and had been removed from the collection. I called down the stairs to Al to tell her.

After reading the news item and quickly searching through the website to check that the image really had gone, Al called Cecil, the curator of the Leonardo collection, to find out exactly what had happened. He confirmed that the folio had been removed after they had received a report from a 'government scientist' that categorically demonstrated that the folio was not contemporary with Leonardo. Although Cecil had argued for a wider discussion and peer review of the report, pressure had been brought to bear on his superiors and he had been instructed to remove the folio and pass it to the forensics department at the British Library. Al asked him for the name of the person who would now be responsible for the folio so she could arrange to examine it again herself, but Cecil admitted that it would be impossible. Apparently there had been an accident in the forensics lab and the folio had been destroyed by spilt solvent from a broken beaker. Cecil also warned Al that there had been instructions against talking to anyone about the folio, with a specific reference to her – which he was choosing to ignore as they had know each other for such a long time. He said that he had never known a situation like it, where political pressure was so intense on what he regarded as a purely academic issue and where such unprecedented action had been taken so abruptly and without any due consideration. He added that he was concerned about the implications of such interference in the collection.

"It has even been removed from our image library, not just from the website, so I checked the archived copies and they've been removed too," he sounded shocked, "I don't understand what's going on my dear. Do you? It's not even a particularly significant folio."

"Cecil, you were right when you said that this is political not academic. If I tell you what I know you must promise not to tell anyone else, it could be dangerous if you do."

Cecil hesitated.

"You make this sound very secret squirrel. Do I really want to know?"

"I don't know. Do you?"

There was a pause and Al could hear him breathe deeply before speaking.

"Oh, go on then. What harm can it do?"

"Knowledge is power, Cecil."

"My dear, don't you start with those clichés," he laughed nervously, "one of the reasons I love you is because you're above all that."

"Okay, sorry. The folio was a palimpsest."

"I know that. I realised years ago. But I've never had the time to examine it closely enough to try and determine what the lost text was."

"It's a hidden text that's important, but not a lost one. The folio itself was genuine, from one of the notebooks that was owned by Louis the Fifteenth. He had the original text erased and replaced with a text that had been enciphered using a code invented by Leonardo, and written in Leonardo's own style so it would look genuine if it was examined by the excise when it was brought into London."

"I've looked at that folio so many times my dear. It wasn't particularly well composed, almost incoherent. Like random jottings. But it didn't look like it was in code."

"It's a very clever code designed to make the result look like genuine text, albeit not very meaningful. But certainly good enough to avoid detection by the Excise."

"Mmm, and me too, obviously!" he sighed.

"Don't feel bad, Cecil. No-one else had even realised that the code existed until now. So you mustn't be too hard on yourself."

"Well... Alright then, but what was the text that had been coded?"

"A confession by Queen Anne of a brief affair."

"Anne?"

"Wife of James the First."

"Ooh. Delicious, but hardly earth-shattering dear, even for a Queen, especially after all these years?"

"The result of the affair was her daughter Elizabeth."

"And?"

"The affair was with Frederick the Righteous."

"Never heard of him."

"Elizabeth then married the son of Frederick the Righteous."

"You don't mean her half-brother?"

"Exactly."

"Oh my dear. That IS rather more salacious. Genetically unwise too I'm sure, which probably explains a lot about the royal family. But I thought they were rife with inbreeding anyway?"

"Cousins, not siblings. In the 18th century the revelation would have been enough to invalidate the Act of Settlement. Maybe it still would. Which could completely destabilise or even destroy the British monarchy."

"Ah! So you are an anarchist after all?"

"Cecil, I'm hurt that you could think that. I'm interested in this from a purely academic perspective, but there are others who are concerned to protect the establishment. Now, of course, they've destroyed the evidence so the whole thing is academic anyway, if you'll pardon the pun."

"Oh very good!" he paused. "If everything's been destroyed then there's nothing I can do, is there?" Then as an afterthought he added, "Am I an accessory now?"

"No Cecil. We haven't done anything wrong so you can't be an accessory."

"Well, to be honest, that doesn't seem to make any difference these days, does it?"

"Now who's the anarchist?"

"When you've been living in a world that has it in for you as long as I have, you'll recognise it as realism not anarchy my dear."

"Oh Cecil. Really there isn't anything to worry about. Has someone suggested otherwise?"

"Well, although nothing was actually explicit, there was a hint that we shouldn't talk to anyone about the folio because of an ongoing 'anti-terrorist' investigation. Then they mentioned you my dear. They didn't actually accuse you of anything specific, but the implication was certainly there."

"I guess that if revealing the truth undermines the establishment, then they might want to label it as terrorism."

"You'd better be careful, you have your reputation to think of. But don't worry about me, my dear. I won't talk to anyone."

"Thanks."

"You know," he added, "I've just realised that I may be able to help after all. When we were scanning the folios originally to put them online I had copies of all of the high resolution scan files in my private area. They should have been automatically backed up. I can get the IT people to recover the scan file for the folio. Mmm, I'm sure that nice Darren would do it for me – such an accommodating young lad. Tell you what my dear, I'll see what I can do. Call me again in a day or two."

"Okay, thanks Cecil. If you can find that scan it would be great. I really appreciate the offer."

"It's fine. Mind you, I just hope this phone's not bugged," he laughed.

"Oh, I hadn't thought of that. Crikey, I hope not for your sake. I'd hate to get you into trouble. Thanks for being so candid and for trusting me."

"Always, my dear. When this has all blown over you can buy me a nice big drink. I know this wicked bar in one of the seedier streets in Soho…"

"Cecil, I'm shocked. But it's a deal. Thanks again, bye."

As Al put down the phone her hand was shaking. I had heard her side of the conversation and could guess at most of what Cecil had been saying. Al sat very still for a moment and then she looked at me with her big brown eyes.

"I'm really scared now. When it was just some nutter in Huntingdon it was a bit of a worry but seemed almost laughable. Then when Lynn said it was the CIA it became more scary, but at least she seemed to be trying to look after us. But now it seems like the government is trying to remove all traces of the *Confessio*. What will they do with us?"

"If we go ahead and publish what we know, then it will be more difficult to do anything to us without attracting attention."

"But the evidence is all gone now. They can just deny it and we won't be able to prove a thing."

"Not all the evidence is gone. If Cecil can recover that scan we'll have an image of the folio."

"I don't think that will carry anywhere near as much weight as the actual folio."

She was, of course, right.

Witherspoon

By the afternoon, Barry Barnes' security teams had confirmed that both Al's house and shop were under surveillance. His people had apparently remained undetected themselves but were keeping track of what they said looked like professionals. I advised him that they were probably from a US agency but re-assured him that Al was completely innocent of anything that the Americans might claim. He didn't take much convincing as he had met Al a couple of times and knew her to be a decent person. What's more, he had become disinclined to trust the CIA since his girlfriend had been injured when she was caught in the crossfire of an abortive CIA operation in London and the agents concerned had been spirited out of the country avoiding prosecution. I outlined a plan to deal with Al's unwanted stalkers and he readily agreed to help, suggesting some very neat improvements to increase the likelihood of success.

After my conversation with Barry, I left Al checking her emails and went to pick up some provisions. I also bought a cheap pay-as-you-go phone which Al could use without fear of being traced. When I got back she was still busy surfing the Internet, so I disappeared off to the kitchen to make us a meal. I promised to call her when the food was ready but, after a few minutes, Al appeared in the kitchen asking to help. I put her in charge of the potatoes.

In my experience some nice rosemary-roasted red potatoes will always lift the spirit. Meanwhile I had rustled up my standby nut roast recipe (cashew nuts, breadcrumbs, garlic, fried onion and a dash of passata) and, while waiting for the oven to heat up, I made a simple tomato sauce to go with it. Al had peeled and cut the potatoes and was parboiling them. This was the first time we had ever cooked a meal together and, despite the worrying circumstances it was fun.

As we worked Al told me that she had been catching up not only on her emails but also on some of the various fora and newsgroups that she had been monitoring lately. One of these, a Leonardo forum usually frequented by serious academics and art historians had, over the last couple of days, been a hotbed of discussion about robots. One member, using the unlikely pseudonym of Jim Morrison, had asked if anyone else had heard about some new research being done into Leonardo's robot projects – this had unleashed a myriad of contributions fomenting rumours and speculation suggesting the possibility of a forthcoming book about Leonardo's lost robots. Al had become quite concerned that our Mechanicant notes seemed to have been leaked, perhaps it was the papers taken from Lucia's office that were fuelling at least part of this debate. But as she read more and more of the responses, Al had realised that no-one had even an inkling of the nature or scale of the Mechanicant project. Finally she was reasonably happy that this putative book was not related to our own publication plans at all.

By this time the oven was hot enough for the potatoes which had been lightly coated in olive oil and had fresh rosemary sprigs from the garden tossed on them with abandon. They were now ready to roast. Soon the nut roast joined them, and finally some broccoli was zapped in the microwave. Twenty minutes later we were sitting down to eat.

"What I don't understand…" I started, between mouthfuls, "is why the Americans would be interested in the *Confessio*. Especially these so-called Mothers of the

Revolution."

"No, nor do I," agreed Al. "The publication of Anne's confession would have had no detrimental impact on American Independence. In fact, quite the reverse I imagine. It could have strengthened their justification for waging war against King George, whom they could have portrayed as an illegitimate monarch with no right to rule over Britain, let alone the colonies."

"So it must be something else then."

"But what?"

I took a sip of my Frascati.

"If we're still clear-headed enough after dinner, we can have another look at the *Confessio* and the instructions for Johnson, and see if we can find any clues. Mind you, this Frascati is deliciously fresh, so it might have to wait until tomorrow. In the meantime, eat drink and be merry..."

"For tomorrow we die?"

"No! For tomorrow is another day and we may be closer to understanding what is going on."

Feeling a bit lazy I had bought a ready-made cheesecake for dessert. After we had indulged ourselves, Al made some coffee while I filled the dishwasher. Then, as we sat down to drink our espresso and re-read Al's decoded text, this picture of domestic banality slowly transformed back into one of intrigue.

As she read through the instructions to Johnson for a third time, Al stopped and looked at me, wide-eyed.

"I might have something here," she spoke quietly, almost in a whisper as if scared of committing herself.

"Really? What?"

"You remember Lynn said the Mothers were accusing me of besmirching one of the founding fathers."

"Yeah. I must admit I'd ignored that, as it seemed spurious and irrelevant."

"Me too. But now I've re-read this I'm beginning to

think I know what it was based on. Give me five minutes to do a quick search on the web to refresh my memory and I'll fill you in. Tell you what, while I'm doing that, could you make some more coffee?"

"Okay. But hurry back, I'm intrigued..."

~

When we sat down together again a few minutes later, Al had a look of triumph on her face – which made a nice change from the anxious frown she had been wearing most of the day. I waited while she had a sip of her coffee.

"Well?" I asked, desperate to find out what she had discovered.

"Very nice coffee, thank you," she teased, grinning.

I raised an eyebrow.

"Okay," she placed the cup back on the saucer. "You remember when we first found the text, I said that I thought the name of Johnson's contact in Scotland seemed familiar?"

"Er... Witherspoon?"

"That's right. You thought of the pubs..."

"... and the actress." I added.

"Oh yes." She fixed me with a look that could have withered poison ivy. "Well, I had intended to check the name out but what with everything else that's been happening I never got round to it. Until now."

"So?"

"John Witherspoon was about 23 at the time of the uprising, and had been a Presbyterian minister for two years."

"Hardly likely to support the Jacobites then?"

"That's not an entirely valid assumption. Their support was no longer exclusively among Catholics. In fact, by the time of the '45 it wasn't so much religious as political, because there were plenty of factions other than the Catholics who were just as keen to get rid of the Hanoverians."

"So he was a supporter?"

"Apart from our new text there is very little hard evidence to go on. There have been various groups who have claimed that John Witherspoon was a Jacobite supporter; others maintain he was opposed to the rebels; some think he was a renegade militia leader."

"What do you think?"

"It's hard to say. There is one surviving contemporaneous account from the Battle of Falkirk that tells a strange tale that is generally taken to support the view that he was an innocent bystander who had turned up at the battle as a spectator."

"A spectator? At a battle? How weird is that?"

"Not unheard of, actually. Perhaps he felt he needed to see the horror of war for himself so he could talk about it more credibly from his pulpit? Who knows?"

"So what's this strange tale then?"

"The Jacobite army, under Bonnie Prince Charlie, had taken possession of Castle Doune and were using it as a prison."

"Castle Doune. That sounds familiar."

"Monty Python and the Holy Grail. They used it as the location for almost all the castles in the film."

"Oh that's right. My friend Richard lives near it. He says visitors to the castle are given coconut shells so they can impersonate Patsy."

"Well, a couple of hundred years before the Pythons, in 1746 to be precise, Bonnie Prince Charlie and his men used the castle as a prison to hold the government troops they'd captured during the Battle of Falkirk. There is an account by a small group of volunteers from Edinburgh who were captured along with two of their officers and imprisoned in the castle. As well as about 150 troops being held, there were also two spies from Aberdeen and one John Witherspoon, who said he was among those rounded up by the rebels while he was watching the battle. The castle was already in ruins, so the men were not being held in dungeons or any particularly secure area, but in a large room that led onto the battlements, from which it was a seventy foot drop. During the night the Edinburgh volunteers made a rope out of the blankets they had been given to sleep under. They were intending to let themselves down from the battlements in order to escape. Four of the prisoners – one of the volunteers, the two officers, and one of the spies – successfully made it down the rope. A fifth man, the other spy, was rather heavy and caused the rope to break just as he reached the ground. Although the last twenty feet of the rope was now missing, another of the volunteers tried to climb down but fell and broke an ankle and some ribs. The last of the captured volunteers pulled up the rope and attached more blankets to it. But when he tried to climb down he lost his grip and was fatally wounded. John Witherspoon had been watching from the battlements awaiting his turn but decided not to risk the same fate. The escaped officers and volunteers made their way back to the government troops, where they recounted the details of their capture and escape. Meanwhile, back at the castle, John Witherspoon was charged with attempting to escape, but he was released and returned to his ministry."

"So he was watching the battle, got rounded up by the rebels and then let go?"

"That's the generally accepted interpretation."

"Except…"

"Except, we have these instructions for Johnson that identify John Witherspoon as the person in Scotland who would disseminate the *Confessio*. So it's possible that Witherspoon had been at the Castle to confer with the Prince but, when the spies and the volunteers turned up, he needed an alibi and so was treated as if he had been captured. Which also neatly explains why he was quickly released unharmed despite supposedly being charged with attempting to escape."

"Okay. But I still don't understand the significance of this to the Americans."

"Twenty years later, our friend Witherspoon goes to America to become president of a college that would eventually become Princeton."

"Even so…?"

"He also became a congressman and ten years after that he was one of the signatories of the Declaration of Independence."

"A founding father."

"Precisely."

"But, even we didn't know until just now that we were potentially 'besmirching' a founding father, so how did the Mothers?"

"I don't know. Unless I mentioned Witherspoon to Trubshawe…"

"…and he mentioned it to his wife Eleanor who recognised the name."

Crypto Da Vinci

Republicans

In the morning Al decided to see what she could find out about Eleanor Trubshawe, or ET as we now called her, while I planned to further investigate Mr. Skrump.

Between our breakfast espresso (recent events having consigned the 'doctor's orders decaf' to the back of the larder), and the elevenses cafetière of Guatemalan Arabica, we both scoured every relevant source we could dig up online. As we relaxed under the vine after our efforts and savoured the richness of the coffee, a nearby cockerel crew. Alison looked surprised.

"I hadn't realised quite how bucolic this place is. Is there a farm nearby?"

"The village is surrounded by farmland, but that little ray of sunshine belongs to a neighbour. One of the nice things about living out here in the countryside is the peace and quiet, interrupted by the occasional dog or chattering bird."

"I'm amazed how many different types of bird seem to live in the trees in your garden."

"Sometimes you can just sit here and watch them in the tree. Magpies, blackbirds, wrens, robins, doves, sparrows all seem to have their own level. It's like an avian tenement block!" I grinned. "Then there are parakeets in that big silver birch in Ernie's garden, swallows and swifts swooping around on fine days. Even eagles sometimes."

"I don't believe you."

"There's a birds of prey centre further along the valley and they have to keep them exercised. Sometimes they venture this far."

"It's hard to believe we're only twenty miles out from

the centre of London. It's so quiet."

"If the wind's blowing in the wrong direction you can hear a bit of traffic noise from the motorway down there in the valley, but usually even that is muted. In fact the loudest thing around here is probably that cockerel. I have nothing against it announcing that the sun is in the sky. But I don't understand why it needs to remind us every two minutes." I shrugged. "But apart from that you're right it is really nice and quiet here."

As if to contradict me, the phone rang at that moment causing the entire resident population of the large plum tree in the middle of the garden immediately to take flight in panic. It was Barry calling to confirm that everything was ready for our planned counter-offensive against Bob Lord and his CIA cronies. Al used her new untraceable mobile phone to pick up messages from both her shop and home answer-phones. Finally, when peace had returned to the garden, I asked Al if she had made any progress.

"There wasn't a lot about ET herself on the net, but there was quite a bit of material that she had written. Things like postings on message boards, comments on blogs, polemics on right wing websites. What I did find out fits in with what we suspected, and combined with her views it suggests a very opinionated, affirmative, type person. She comes from a reasonably well-heeled family from Boston – they also have an apartment in New York on 5th Avenue, and a house in the Hamptons. She had the education to go with it, private schooling followed by a liberal arts degree at Amherst College, then a Masters at Princeton. While she was there she met Manley Trubshawe who was on a year's exchange from Oxford. After Princeton she came over to do the modern equivalent of the Grand Tour of Europe and on the way back she met up with Manley again. As a result she never went home. They've been married for years but have no kids. She seems to be the main driving force in the Oxford chapter of the Daughters of the American Revolution, the largest in Europe apart from London. They're very active. She hosts lots of events that try to bridge the Atlantic and foster the 'special relationship', and she takes a personal interest in US students who are on exchanges at the university."

"So if Trubshawe had told her about your visit, especially if he said you'd referred to Witherspoon she would have recognised the name?"

"Of course, Witherspoon was a past president of Princeton. Manley would have recognised his name too, as he'd spent a year there. In fact, I'm sure that's why he would have mentioned it to her in the first place."

"Okay, so you've found out how the cat got out of the bag. What's left is to work out who set it amongst the pigeons. I've been trying to track down Mister Skrump."

"Any luck?"

"Not as much as you've had with ET. For a start, Cenobite Skrump probably isn't his real name, but his online persona."

"You don't say?" Al interjected in mock surprise.

"Don't laugh, I lived near Huntingdon for a while," I said, slightly hurt, "and there were people there with names like that. But in this case I think it's an alias. But he..."

"Are you sure it's a man?"

"Not entirely, but it seems most likely from the language he uses. Anyway, assuming it's a man, he uses the name for everything, even his broadband account. Maybe the bank account to pay for it too, although I haven't checked that out... yet."

"There are some similarities with ET," I continued, "but also some very big differences. His politics are extreme, slightly to the right of Attila the Hun. He appears to idolise Oliver Cromwell and harks back to 'the good old days', although in his terms that means 1653."

"Oh! Not a royalist then?"

"Not at all. Quite the opposite."

"Then why is he so concerned about keeping the monarchy from being damaged by the *Confessio*?" asked Al.

"Aha, that's the £64,000 question!"

"And the answer is…?"

"Er… can I phone a friend?"

Al laughed.

"It doesn't make sense." Al said. "Okay so he's a republican, like ET, but that shared label hides a whole different philosophy and set of values. She's unlikely to care about who's on the throne here, and seems to be more agitated about the possibility that her beloved Witherspoon is tainted by scandal. Skrump's worried that a Catholic might take over the throne, whereas you'd expect him to welcome the chance to undermine the monarchy. He and his fellow republicans could use it as leverage to do away with the throne completely. I just don't see any mutual interest."

"One thing that is clear about Skrump, is that he's not particularly bright nor is he well educated. His vocabulary is limited and his grasp of grammar is tenuous. I'd guess he's probably in his fifties or sixties, left school quite young with no qualifications and has probably worked as a labourer ever since."

"That's rather patronising…"

"Not at all. He frequently uses words that suggests he works on the land, his posts are invariably censored by the moderators to remove swear words, and many of his phrases are pretty old-fashioned – even for Huntingdonshire."

"Isn't it Cambridgeshire – I thought they got rid of Huntingdonshire years ago?"

"You try telling that to the people who live there. The local paper is still called the Hunts Post. They were very unimpressed when they were assigned post codes starting with PE for Peterborough. The years pass more slowly in some parts of Huntingdonshire! But anyway, the point is that he's no intellectual. Unlike ET. He's unlikely to consider all the consequences of his, or anyone else's, actions. In fact, I suspect he's easily manipulated by others who want to use him as their attack dog, while remaining at a safe distance themselves. He often repeats phrases with no regard for context; as if he's been fed various arguments to use and just reproduces them parrot fashion."

"I came to the conclusion that ET could be quite Machiavellian, so she would fit that rôle."

"Right. So the scenario is this. You told Trubshawe about the *Confessio*, and implicated Witherspoon in the Jacobite uprising. He tells 'her indoors'…" Al raised an eyebrow but said nothing, "… who is worried that you're going to damage the reputation of one of her heroes. So she winds up Skrump with suggestions that the *Confessio* will allow a dirty foreign Papist to take over as King of England. His hatred of Catholics is even stronger than his hatred of the throne, so he reacts predictably, by trying to stop you publishing. But he has limited resources and experience so his attempt is bungled. As a result, or maybe as insurance, ET uses her contacts through the Mothers to present a distorted version of the facts in Washington that will provoke the Agency into action. They, in their turn, try to get the cooperation of MI5, who then ask MI6 for confirmation of the American intel. Luckily, Lynn sees the request and puts the kibosh on it, leaving the Yanks to act alone and outside the law. They break in to your shop, take the *Confessio* and undoubtedly plant a bug in the phone. Barry says they're watching your home too; they've probably planted a bug there as well. I think that brings us up to date?"

"Apart from your cunning plan to foil the CIA, my new phone, and the messages on the answerphones."

"Yes indeed. I must say, I'm almost looking forward to tomorrow."

~

The next day, however, got off to a very bad start. Impatient for news, Al called Cecil to see if he was having any luck recovering the scan of the folio. Five minutes later she came to find me, all the colour drained from her face.

"What's the matter?" I asked, concerned at how pale she was looking.

"He's dead," she mumbled.

"Who?"

"Cecil."

"What? How?"

"They wouldn't give me any details. I asked to talk to Cecil and they said he was unavailable and put me though to his assistant Lewis." She sniffed. "I've met Lewis a few times, I think I can trust him. He obviously didn't recognise my voice though. When I told him who I was he said that Cecil was dead. Killed yesterday evening on his way home."

"Killed?"

"That's what he said. The exact word. Not died, but killed. I asked him what had happened but he said he couldn't tell me."

"Couldn't or wouldn't?"

"I don't know. I guess it's too soon for anyone to know

more details. But he definitely said killed."

"Okay, let's not jump to conclusions too fast. While killed could mean deliberately…"

Alison moaned.

"…it could also mean a car accident or even an act of God."

"It's a bit too much of a coincidence don't you think? With everything else going on: people asking about us in Vinci; ransacking Lucia's office; hacking my computer; breaking into my shop. Now Cecil's dead. He was the only other person I've told what we're doing." She was biting her lower lip so hard I was worried she would draw blood. There were tears gently running down her cheeks.

"You were lecturing me the other day about scientific objectivity and sticking to the facts."

"Don't start on about Carter Philus again. Not now."

"I'm not. I'm just saying let's wait for the facts."

"Well. I'm going to wait in my room then." She walked off. It was obvious that I hadn't handled things as well as I could.

For the rest of the day we kept ourselves to ourselves. By the time the evening's adventure was due to start Al was calm, cool and collected, but very quiet.

Crypto Da Vinci

Refuge

The following redacted document was obtained as the result of a Freedom Of Information Request from the CIA.

INCIDENT REPORT

Incident ref: SN/AFU 007
Filed by: ███████, London (RL)
Arena: London, UK
Period: 8-11 ███ber 200█
Subject: Ali Ben Mint, UK Citizen, religious fundamentalist, suspected anarcho-syndicalist, wanted for anti-American activities.

Background: Surveillance operation on subject. Requested support for rendition from British Security Service denied. Surveillance teams installed at known lairs.

Locations:
A: ██████████ Avenue, Dulwich, England
    (known operational base in London suburb)
B: ██████ Book Shop,
    ██████ Street, London, England
    (neo-revolutionary bookshop in liberal quarter of London)
C: ██████████ Road, London, England
    (suspected safe house in downtown London)

Agency personnel:
D1	Coyote	Operatives: #225,#261
		Team Leader: #129
D2	Roadrunner	Operatives: #233,#254
		Team Leader: #109
AIC		RL (#079)

<u>Event Log</u>:
All timestamps are local (London) time:
8 ██████ber
20:00	Team Delta1 Coyote deployed at location A
20:00	Team Delta2 Roadrunner deployed at location B
22:00	Unknown males (U1,U2) observed disabling the alarm at B and effecting entry
22:06	U1 and U2 exited B and departed separately in different directions
22:30	Taking advantage of disabled alarm, #109 entered B, installed μFM transmitter in landline

9 ██████ber
08:30	Unknown female (U3) arrived at B
09:00	AIC arrived at B
09:15	Local uniforms (Met) arrived at B to investigate AIC, apparently at request of U3
09:20	U3 exited B while AIC detained, Roadrunner remained in situ, U3 departed. Unknown male (subsequent identification confirmed as Larry Doors, prominent US citizen) arrived at B and immediately departed pursuing U3.

10 ██████ber
09:23	Unknown male (U4) left message on answering machine at B, transcript follows: "Hi, it's Hugh, long time no see. Hope you're keeping well. Sorry to be abrupt, but we need to meet. I have some important information for you. Can't leave it in a message, must tell you in person. I'll try you at home."

09:47   Coyote confirmed that call had also
          been received at A. There being no
          indication of occupants at A, #261
          effected entry and installed µFM
          transmitter in landline. Listened
          to message from unknown male (U5) on
          answering machine, transcript
          follows:
          "I'm calling on behalf of Mr. Jahse.
          He needs to see you and has asked me
          to tell you to meet him tomorrow.
          He's currently staying in the safe
          house at ██ ███████ Road in
          ██████. Please be there at 9
          o'clock tomorrow evening. He asked
          me to impress on you that this is
      .   important. He also told me something
          else, what was it? Er... Oh yeah.
          Not to leave the address in an
          answerphone message. Damn!... Sorry"
11:45   Landline at B received call from a
          cellphone [subsequent investigation
          showed the cellular number to be
          non-contract (UK pay-as-you-go) and
          hence not traceable to an
          individual], used code to retrieve
          messages including that from U4.
          Landline at A immediately received a
          call from the same cellphone to
          retrieve messages including that
          from U5. AIC concluded that
          cellphone was being used by subject
          to obtain and erase messages
          remotely.

11 ████ber
19:45   Coyote and Roadrunner deployed at
          location C, safe house address given
          in U5 message.
21:00   Taxi arrived at location C. Female
          in heavy coat, hat and dark glasses
          exited taxi and approached door of

safe house. Rang bell and was
admitted. Believing her to be the
subject, AIC confirmed go for
extraction operation.

21:02   Coyote and AIC approached safe house
front entrance. Roadrunner
approached safe house rear entrance.
Coyote attempted to effect entry.
Safe house commandant apparently
triggered silent alarm connected to
local Law Enforcement office. The
doors being reinforced with steel
plates and frames, and having burst-
proof locks, resisted all attempts
at ingress.

21:06   Three Met patrol vehicles arrived.
A uniform ordered operatives to drop
to the ground. AIC reached inside
jacket to retrieve ID, in order to
stop Met interference, but one of
the uniforms shot AIC in the knee.
AIC fell and remaining operatives
immediately surrendered. Met
officers removed all operatives to
local Met headquarters.

22:45   After initial processing and
separation into isolated cells, AIC
was identified as leader and
questioned. As per standing
instructions, AIC did not admit to
unauthorised entry into A and B, or
installing unauthorised transmitters
on landlines at A and B. AIC used
previously agreed cover designed to
minimise obstruction from local Law
Enforcement. Informed interrogating
officers that CIA was acting on a
tip-off that the terrorist Ali ben
Mint, wanted by the US government,
was meeting a contact, Hugh Jahse,
at a safe house in London.
Interrogating officers immediately

adopted an antagonistic attitude,
accusing AIC of "aving a larff" (?).
AIC suggested officers check facts
with British Intelligence Service.
An officer contacted Security
Service and eventually spoke with a
senior official who denied existence
of Ali ben Mint. AIC was informed
of British Intelligence belief that
"US Agencies had concocted
allegations against an innocent
British citizen, Alison Mint, for
their own political purposes",
further it was alleged that US
agencies were "now trying to
manipulate British Intelligence and
Police Services for their own ends".
Officers then determined that AIC
had been questioned two days earlier
outside location B. AIC was charged
with "conspiracy to pervert the
course of justice", Met officers
repeatedly ignored rights to
Diplomatic Immunity. AIC and all
other operatives were denied the
right to a phone call, on the
grounds that they were "foreign
spies on British soil at a time of
conflict", and told that further
actions were to be determined by the
Met Commissioner in the morning.
All operatives were kept overnight
in individual police cells.

12 ███ber
07:45   Following loss of contact with
operatives for 12 hours, local
Agency staff followed standard
procedure and requested information
from Scotland Yard. Once appraised
of the situation, Agency staff

	contacted the Ambassador's residence.
08:45	Ambassador contacted British Home Secretary to demand release of US citizens. British Home Office agreed on condition they be immediately repatriated to the US and not permitted to return.
11:30	AIC and other operatives transported to London City airport to join waiting Agency aircraft.
11:55	Aircraft airborne, en route to Langley.

The following extract from the Metropolitan Police report
of the incident was provided by Lynn Dentry.

```
Incident report AF192765-43
Incident:
```

At 21:02 on the 11th, a silent alarm was sounded at
the Willoughby House refuge for battered women.
The two nearest units and an Armed Response Unit
were immediately dispatched, arriving at 21:06.
Officers observed a group of four men attempting to
gain forced entry to the premises via the front
door - while a second group of three men were
attempting the same at the rear entrance to the
premises. On being cautioned one of the larger
group reached inside his jacket. Fearing that the
suspect was attempting to draw a weapon, the senior
firearms officer incapacitated said suspect with a
shot to the knee causing him to fall to the ground.
The other suspects immediately lay down to await
further instructions. From an initial examination
it was clear that the wounded suspect was not in a
life-threatening condition but had passed out,
consequently he was bandaged and given a pain-
killer. All the suspects remained silent, refusing
to answer questions, appearing to be of foreign
extraction and limited understanding and were
discovered to be armed with handguns from which the
serial numbers had been removed. Concluding that
the suspects were dangerous and likely terrorists,
officers informed them of their rights and removed
them to Paddington Green police station for further
questioning. During transportation the wounded
suspect remained unconscious and none of the others
attempted to communicate.

Once the suspects had been secured in holding
cells, the wounded individual was revived and I
determined that he was the ring-leader. I decided
to question him immediately. It was at this point
that he first claimed to be one Robert Lord, an
intelligence officer of the United States' Central
Intelligence Agency. Although he was apparently in
possession of an ID to this effect, it could not be
confirmed by myself or anyone else present whether
this ID was genuine. He further claimed that a

known terrorist, one Ali ben Mint, was meeting with
a male contact residing at the premises where he
and his team had been apprehended.   He was
unwilling to reveal how he had acquired this
information, or how he knew the details of the
purported meeting.   The name he provided for the
supposed contact, Hugh Jarse, was clearly a joke.
He was assured that this was no laughing matter.

The suspect claiming to be Robert Lord confirmed
that he knew that the premises at which he had been
apprehended was a safe house, but then expressed
surprise when asked why he had therefore expected a
man to be living there.   He subsequently claimed
that he did not know it was a battered women's
refuge, believing it to be a safe house used by
terrorist organisations and unaware that it was
connected by priority alarm directly to the
Metropolitan Police control centre.   I was
disinclined to accept his story, but after his
repeated insistence that I check with the Security
Service, I asked Special Branch to make enquiries.

Not long afterwards I received a call from a senior
officer within the Secret Intelligence Service.
She assured me that 'Ali ben Mint' was a persona
invented by the CIA in a bid to try and concoct
allegations against a UK citizen, one Dr. Alison
Mint, a highly respected scholar and book dealer.
She said that the CIA had already attempted to
obtain Security Service support for an illegal
rendition operation against Dr. Mint but that
support had been denied.   She intimated that the
CIA was trying to manipulate the UK's Security and
Police services to serve American political ends.
She suggested that I check with the Savile Row
station about recent incidents at Dr. Mint's
bookshop in Coptic Street; she also indicated that
we would find that the detained agents had
installed illegal bugging devices in both Dr.
Mint's shop and home.   She added that she would
personally vouch for Dr. Mint whose safety was a
matter for national security, although she wouldn't
elaborate on the last point for obvious reasons.
Acting upon this information I was able to confirm
that intruders had been reported at Dr. Mint's

bookshop two days previously and that officers attending the scene had cautioned a suspicious character who had been reported to be watching the premises after the break-in had been discovered, and who had been identified as one and the same Robert Lord as we now had in custody. Special Branch contacted the secondary keyholder for Dr. Mint's Coptic Street bookshop and a sweep of the premises turned up a transmitting device attached to the telephone.

Fingerprints found on the phone were identified as belonging to one John Bradshaw, a known felon, who was subsequently detained but denied all knowledge of the bugging equipment. We were unable to contact Ms. Mint herself, or gain access to her home in Dulwich to ascertain whether a similar device had indeed also been planted there. However, we considered that there was now sufficient evidence to charge the suspects and keep them in custody. When charged, Mr Lord claimed diplomatic immunity and demanded to be freed. We declined his request, observing that as he and his associates were being charged under anti-terrorism legislation, the right to 'habeas corpus' did not apply. At this point, Mr. Lord became abusive and violent and demanded the return of his cellphone in order to call the US embassy. In my considered opinion, it was quite possible that the mobile phone in question was also capable of use as a weapon, so this request was denied. As he continued to be abusive and violent towards officers, including making offensive remarks of a racial and sexual nature, it was decided to allow him a cooling-off period in a separate holding cell from the other suspects, before taking any further action.

The following morning I contacted Commander Stock to inform her that we had charged some suspected terrorists who were claiming diplomatic immunity. Subsequently, as a result of discussions between the Home Office and the US State Department, Mr. Lord and his associates were conducted to London City airport where they were transferred into the custody of a US Marshal. All charges have been retained on file and all seven persons declared *persona non grata* and added to the Border Control Watch List.

HoHO

We were having breakfast when I received a text message from a number I didn't recognise. It simply said 'Skype'. Grabbing my coffee cup I trotted into the Office, Al close behind me. I clicked the Skype icon and within a few seconds was logged in. Almost immediately a call was flagged up. It was, of course, Lynn.

"Hi Peter, is Alison with you?"

"We're both here," I answered.

"Hello Lynn," added Al.

"I've been doing more digging and have some interesting information for you. But first, you might like to know that the immediate threat from Bob Lord has been dealt with."

"Thank you."

"Nothing to do with me. In fact, I was rather expecting you to explain."

"Really? Why what happened?"

"Apparently he and six of his agents were arrested last night when they tried to break in to a battered women's refuge in London. He claimed that there was a terrorist cell meeting there. He seemed to be expecting to find Ali ben Mint there too. Any idea why?"

"Why would I know?" Al replied, grinning. "I was here all last night. I haven't been back to London since we met you in Hampstead. What's going to happen to him, I thought he had diplomatic immunity?"

"The Met refused to recognise his credentials when he was arrested. He and his men were kept in custody as suspected terrorists. But this morning the US embassy has been bending the ear of the Home Secretary. So, even as we speak, Lord and his agents are being deported and will not be allowed back into the country. In fact, I don't think there are many European countries where he is welcome any more, and he certainly wouldn't be safe in the middle east, so he'll probably end up posted to South America. Shame!"

"That's a huge relief. Do you think it's safe for me to go home?"

"Leave it a couple more days just to be sure, but I think it's probably okay now. Especially as your threat has been neutralised."

"What does that mean?"

"After our previous chat, I asked some friends at the Security Service to send me everything they had on your recent activities, cross-referenced with any organisations that might have an interest. So I saw that you had been very interested in a particular folio in the Windsor collection, which has subsequently been withdrawn and accidentally destroyed."

"So was it you or MI5 that destroyed it?" asked Al.

"Neither. The UK government doesn't condone cultural vandalism."

"But Cecil said it was a government expert who had it removed."

"Faked ID I'm afraid. As far as I can tell it was HoHO."

"It's not funny. Cecil was very upset."

"I wasn't suggesting it was funny, I said it was HoHO. It's the House of Hanover Organisation, H. o. H. O. A sort of underground political lobbying group."

"Never heard of them." I said.

"That's the way they like it. They don't want publicity, they work behind the scenes to protect the interests of the House of Hanover." Lynn replied.

"I thought the House of Hanover died with Queen

Victoria, and now we have the House of Windsor."

"Here, yes." Al answered. "Victoria couldn't pass the surname on to her heirs, so it was her uncle who became head of the family and the ruler of the kingdom of Hanover. It all changed after the war, of course, but the House of Hanover still exists. The current head of the family is married to Princess Caroline of Monaco."

"HoHO is not an official organisation and is neither supported nor endorsed by the family." Lynn added. "Which is why HoHO feel able to use unconventional tactics."

"Unconventional? You mean illegal?"

"Sometimes. It seems they found out about your translation of the decoded folio."

"How do you know about that?" Al was looking confused.

"Don't ask. If I told you I'd have to shoot you."

"Like Cecil?" Al now looked shocked.

"What?" Lynn was obviously confused.

"Al, I think Lynn was just joking."

"Yes, it was a joke," said Lynn, "I just can't tell you."

"Not very funny in the circumstances." Al was still upset.

"We heard yesterday that Cecil had been killed. But we don't know the circumstances." I explained to Lynn.

"Ah. The curator at Windsor? I didn't know you were close."

"You don't know everything then. We'd been friends for a long time."

"Then you'll be pleased to know that they've got the driver."

"Driver?" Al asked.

"Your friend was knocked down on a zebra crossing by a drunk driver. The driver drove off but crashed not far away. He was arrested within minutes. Way over the limit."

"See," I said to Al, "an accident. Just very bad timing. Not that there's ever a good time for an accident!"

"Okay. You were right." She looked at me and gave a weak smile.

"Lynn. You were telling us about HoHO."

"That's right. They were worried that by demonstrating the invalidity of Elizabeth and Frederick's marriage, the whole line of Hanover that had ruled Great Britain would be declared illegitimate, which could have serious and widespread consequences. They were determined to stop that. So they removed the folio from the Windsor collection and destroyed it. They teamed up with another organisation with related interests to destroy copies of the folio on any servers on the internet. If you check you'll see that even Google's caches have been hacked."

"What other organisation?"

"The Rhineland Palatinate Group, R P G. They are another lobbying group who protect the interests of the Rhineland-Palatinate, including the reputation of the Electors."

"Like Frederick?" I suggested.

"Exactly. Your revelations about Frederick would have seriously upset them too. They're a bit more technically aware than HoHO, so they were better equipped to do the hacking."

"All these strange little groups, HoHO, RPG, the Mothers," said Al, "and all along I thought MI5 was trying to stop us. Even after you told us about the CIA."

"Ah! That's another interesting little wrinkle." Lynn added.

"What?" Al asked.

"Even without the intervention of the Mothers, the Americans had a vested interest in keeping the facts of your *Confessio* quiet, while ensuring that the evidence itself remained intact. They didn't know that the text was hidden in the folio at Windsor or they would have probably stolen it themselves years ago to keep it safe."

"You mean they already knew?"

"Yes. So does the UK government, or at least some people in the government."

"How?"

"Washington had been using the fact of Anne's infidelity, Elizabeth's illegitimacy and her blood relationship to her husband, to blackmail the British government for years. It's the original basis of the 'special relationship'. Why do you think it's such a one-way relationship?"

"How long have the Americans known?"

"It seems that Ben Franklin was told by the papal nuncio in Paris in 1783; soon afterwards the British signed the Treaty that ended the War of Independence. The two events are not entirely unrelated! The Americans have been trying ever since to get a copy of Anne's original confession from the Vatican, but they have always been refused. The nuncio was censured for disclosing its existence."

"So it wouldn't have been a revelation at all?" Al sounded disappointed.

"It would have been seen as a mixed blessing. Officially it would have been dismissed and the credibility of your evidence undermined. Its importance would have been seriously downplayed and a gag-order would have been put on the media, with the result that the public probably wouldn't have paid it much attention. But Washington would have been livid, as they'd have lost their leverage. In fact, now that the only accessible evidence has been destroyed, the Americans may have lost their hold anyway, without anything ever becoming public. That's a pretty good result as far as the mandarins in Whitehall are concerned."

"So it's all over."

"I think so, unless someone breaks into the Vatican's Secret Archives."

"I don't think that will happen," I said, "they have pretty good security".

Al looked at me with a puzzled expression, but knew she shouldn't ask.

Epilogue

After a few days, Al felt happy to go back to her own home. I helped her check for bugging devices – we removed one from the telephone but there were no others. We also checked the shop and repaired the damage to the door and the lock. I replaced the alarm, installing a much more modern one with battery back-up and a SIM card to contact the call centre, making it far more difficult to disable from the outside. Al took Sarah and Chris out for a much-deserved meal to thank Sarah for looking after the shop and to apologise for the fright she had received as a result. Soon Al had settled back into her normal life almost as if nothing had happened.

Lucia sent me the final annotated translation of the Mechanicant notes, a very professional job. She said that she hoped I would decide to publish them. She also sheepishly admitted that she had carelessly mentioned the project to a visiting American entrepreneur called Larry Doors who was interested in both Leonardo and robotics. He had been in Italy for a robotics conference in Catania and had been invited to visit the electronics department at the university in Florence during his trip; as Lucia's husband was head of the department she had naturally been invited to meet Larry at a small reception organised in his honour. When Larry had mentioned to her that his original interest in cybernetics was based on his fascinated discovery as a youngster that the earliest known humanoid robot was created by Leonardo da Vinci, she had told him that her British cousin and a colleague had uncovered details of an even more ambitious robotics project hidden in some of Leonardo's folios that they had obtained from the museum in Vinci. Lucia apologised to me for having told him, but was sure that Larry would be very interested and may even be willing to support the publication.

I subsequently contacted Mr Doors who confirmed it was a member of his staff who had made the inquiries at the museum in Vinci (that had concerned Simonetta) as well as trying to persuade Al to talk to Doors. It was Doors whom Sarah had managed to evade in the City; he thought that he had been following Al and couldn't understand why she was running away when she had already agreed to meet him. He apologised if he had frightened anyone, he was just keen to find out more about Leonardo's robots. When I sent him a copy of Lucia's final translations he was delighted.

Meanwhile, Lynn had been back in touch with Al – directly this time, not through cryptic emails – and they had begun to make up for the thirty lost years. Al even persuaded Lynn to call her Al rather than Alison! In passing, Lynn mentioned that HoHO in the UK was based in Oxford and that Manley Trubshawe was one of the group of intellectuals who helped to run it. She gave us sight of an intercepted email from Trubshawe arranging for the removal of the folio from Windsor. With that, the final piece of the jigsaw slotted into place. It seems that Al's meeting with him in Oxford had been the trigger for all the subsequent hassles she had endured. Needless to say, she decided she would not be consulting him ever again. Luckily, she does not seem to blame me for any of her troubles, and we continue to enjoy each other's company.

In my spare time I started to outline an account of our 'quest', with the idea of trying to interest a publisher. When I mentioned this to Al she thought it was a good idea and agreed to help, although she felt that it would not be taken seriously as a historical exposé now that we had lost the primary piece of evidence. Nevertheless I decided I would put pen to paper and, as promised, dedicate it to Iris. Larry Doors connected me with his agent Hilary who assiduously found me a suitable publisher.

However, when I was about halfway through writing, I came across a display in Cannon Street station for a new book that had just been published. From the title it appeared to concern a code devised by Leonardo. Crestfallen by the thought that someone had pre-empted our story I decided to abandon the writing, at least until the hype for this other book had died down – a few months at most I thought; how wrong I was! When I eventually read that book I was relieved to find that it had very little to do with Leonardo and nothing to do with his code. It was to be almost five years before I felt able to take up my pen (keyboard actually) again and complete this record of our own investigation into Leonardo's code.

Peter White

Postscript
I wrote to Iris, Simonetta, and Carter Philus to tell them that this book would finally be published. My letter to Carter Philus was returned from Cheyne Walk marked 'addressee unknown'.

Acknowledgement

Once a book is written, it's tempting to breathe a sigh of relief that the hard work is all over. In one sense it is, of course. The anguish and heartache about the plot, the characters' motivation and the dialogue is passed. You can sit back and watch your 'baby' as it goes out into the big wide world.

Tempting, but unjustified. All you've achieved so far is the gestation. The labour pains are still to come. For a start you have the trauma of watching someone else reading your words for the first time. You don't have to actually watch them, in fact it's better for them if you don't – it's amazing how irritated people get when you keep asking them "Where have you got up to?"! Even without that constant oversight, the torment is still there, but quietly building up to a crescendo when they deliver their verdict. On the one hand you don't want copious notes detailing errors and inconsistencies (that's what your editor is for); but equally it would be disappointing if you only got a single sentence in response, as you've been hoping to thrill, enthral and enthuse your reader rather than bore them or render them senseless. So, I would like to thank those who agreed to read some or all of the earlier drafts and the (confidently labelled) final draft, especially Alex, Hugh and Al; as you'd expect I take full responsibility for any remaining errors.

Then there is still more to be done once your publishers are sorting out the final layout, cover and all the other things that they do to make the birth go smoothly. Getting permission to use quotes and other material was largely my own efforts – I did try to ask John Dryden if it was okay to quote from his work, but the medium couldn't get through to the spirit world that day[†]. I do also want to thank the nice people at the P22 type foundry for their Da Vinci font and for agreeing to let me use it both in the text and on the cover (it was originally bought for me as a birthday present and the 'backwards' font was partly the inspiration for this book)[‡]. For everything else relating to the production of the volume you are holding in your hands as you read this, however, thanks are due to everyone at Alnpete Press who has had a hand in sending this particular creation out into the wild blue yonder; but most of all to my editor.

An especial acknowledgement is due to my remarkably talented wife Alison for the illustrations that leap out of the pages of the Mechanicant notes and bring them alive. I was almost convinced they're really by *Il Maestro* himself, even though I saw her draw them! Our shared enthusiasm and admiration for Leonardo has made the research for this book an immeasurably enjoyable experience, especially our journeys to Vinci, Anchiano, Florence and elsewhere.

Finally, I must say thank you to my family for providing support, both emotional and physical, keeping me sane (yes, really); to friends, who have encouraged me; and to those readers of *Library of the Soul* who took the time to provide feedback and encouragement, especially Iris, Stephen, Maria, Sue, Sarah-Jane, Martin, Deirdre, Corinne, Hugh and anyone else I've forgotten to mention by name – I hope you're not disappointed by Crypto da Vinci.

[†] He's been dead so long his original publication is out of copyright, of course! You can read it for yourself if you search Google Books.

[‡] If you like the font visit: http://www.p22.com/products/davinci.html

Alnpete is an exciting, innovative independent publisher.
Check out the first Peter White mystery from Simon Buck:

Library of the Soul

a P e t e r   W h i t e   m y s t e r y
S i m o n   B u c k

For years the CIA have been using a poison designed to cause a heart attack and
then disperse without a trace. Now a batch has gone missing.

On a visit to Rome, Peter White is recruited by his old friend Costanza into
the oldest secret society in the world, in order to help her solve an urgent
problem. Cardinals and other clerics around the world are dying of unexpected
heart attacks. Police authorities are not interested as there is no evidence of foul
play. But Costanza believes someone is using electronic cash and a betting
website to fund and coordinate a campaign of murders that will ultimately lead
to the assassination of the Pope. She and Peter must track down the killer
before any more people die. Using the world's largest supercomputer, deep in
the Secret Archives beneath the Vatican Library, they lay an electronic trap and
wait. But when the Library itself becomes the target of an audacious plot to
steal a 2000 year old manuscript, the problem suddenly becomes much more
personal.

ISBN 978-0-9552206-0-9 £9.99
Read an excerpt at www.libraryofthesoul.co.uk

Visit the Alnpete Press website www.alnpetepress.co.uk
for the latest information on our titles, authors and events,
to read the blog, or to place a order

Alnpete is an exciting, innovative independent publisher.
The next Peter White mystery from Simon Buck will be:

Iscariot

a P e t e r   W h i t e   m y s t e r y
S i m o n   B u c k

In 33AD Judas Iscariot betrayed Jesus for thirty pieces of silver. Nearly two thousand years later, those same silver coins still exert their malign influence over the weak and treacherous, even in today's technologically secular society.

Raffaella, one of the Vatican's secret Guardian Angels, enlists Peter White to help her investigate a cult group who are apparently looking for the coins. Do they really believe these ancient coins have supernatural power? Why are they searching the enigmatic 12th century octagonal Castel del Monte? Is the sudden arrival of an American TV evangelist just a coincidence? How exactly are the local mafia involved? What is the significance of the raunchy mermaid? Raffaella and Peter must race against the clock and answer these questions in order to stop impending disaster on the rapidly approaching saint's day of St. Michael.

Peter once again teams up with Costanza and Raffaella in the third Peter White mystery Iscariot, the exciting sequel to Library of the Soul.

Coming in 2011
ISBN 978-0-9552206-4-7 pb £9.99
Find out more at www.iscariot.co.uk

Visit the Alnpete Press website www.alnpetepress.co.uk
for the latest information on our titles, authors and events,
to read the blog, or to place a order

Alnpete is an exciting, innovative independent publisher.
Read, if you dare, Alison Buck's horror thriller.

*"I really enjoyed the filmic style, and found a distinct creepiness in turning
the pages late at night."*   The Bookbag

"This book has all the ingredients of a really good horror story"
*"Buck's imagery is extremely vivid, tapping into the most primeval
of humanity's fears"*
"a superb read"   DeathRay

Abiding Evil

A l i s o n   B u c k

A sleeping menace is roused deep in the darkness of the forest. For decades it grows, biding its time, reaching out to tug at the ordinary lives of those living beyond the shadow of the trees.

Their children begin to disappear.

Unaware and unsuspecting of the danger, a group of families, friends for many years, journey to a newly opened hotel. It stands alone in a clearing a mile or more within the forest boundary.

For some this will be their last reunion.

ISBN 978-0-9552206-3-0 £9.99
Read an excerpt at www.abidingevil.co.uk

Visit the Alnpete Press website www.alnpetepress.co.uk
for the latest information on our titles, authors and events,
to read the blog, or to place a order

Alnpete is an exciting, innovative independent publisher.
You won't be expecting the twist-in-the-tail in

Devoted Sisters

A l i s o n   B u c k

Elderly sisters Lizzie and May live quiet, ordered lives in the house in which they were born; their self-imposed seclusion and the unchanging predictability of their lives shielding them from the changing world beyond.

But the day comes when this protective isolation is broken; the world outside forces its way in. A stranger appears, unsettling them, bringing with him the threat of danger, upheaval and violence.

Fearful and alone, with all semblance of comforting routine wrenched from them, Lizzie and May are driven to desperation. Dark memories emerge from their buried past as the sisters gradually slip from reason into their own confused realities, within which even their former carefully regulated world seems only a distant memory.

ISBN 978-0-9552206-1-6 £9.99
Read an excerpt at www.devotedsisters.co.uk

Visit the Alnpete Press website www.alnpetepress.co.uk
for the latest information on our titles, authors and events,
to read the blog, or to place a order

Alnpete is an exciting, innovative independent publisher.
A thrilling new story from Alison Buck coming soon:

Female Line

Alison Buck

Anna sits in the darkened kitchen, the knife in her hands. Looking down at the blade, she feels nothing. She absently reads the name on the cold metal and then closes her eyes again, lost in thought.

He'll be back soon.

But, for the moment, the silence of the flat is unbroken.

She carefully touches the side of her face. Her teeth are jarred and sore, but she looks down again at the blade and still she feels nothing.

He won't be long now.

As Anna waits, she dreams. She is, in this moment, detached from all of this; from her life with him, from the pain, from the failure of all her dreams, from life itself. This is not revenge. It's too cold for revenge. It's an ending, that's all.

A key rattles in the lock.

He is home...

ISBN 978-0-9552206-5-4 £9.99
Coming soon
Find out more at www.femaleline.co.uk

Visit the Alnpete Press website www.alnpetepress.co.uk
for the latest information on our titles, authors and events,
to read the blog, or to place a order

Alnpete is an exciting, innovative independent publisher.
Look out for the first volume in a thrilling new fantasy trilogy:

Queens of Antares:
Bloodline
P . R .   P o p e

A new fantasy trilogy for readers of all ages from 8 to 80. Already compared to
CS Lewis and CJ Cherryh, PR Pope weaves an enchanting tale around three
young people who are accidentally transported from their mundane lives to a
new world, where they must find the strength to lead a revolution in order to
find their way home. On the way they discover who they really are, where they
belong and the enduring power of a bloodline.

Volume I **Bloodline Returned**
coming next year
For more information visit www.queensofantares.co.uk

Visit the Alnpete Press website www.alnpetepress.co.uk
for the latest information on our titles, authors and events,
to read the blog, or to place a order

Simon Buck has been a consultant for many years to blue chip companies including banks, retailers and telecom service providers. He has been widely published in the fields of internet security, electronic commerce, data communications and identity management. His first published novel, *Library of the Soul*, introduced the Peter White mysteries. He was born and brought up in Kent by an Italian mother and English father. He still lives in a village in the Garden of England and has a wife, two adult children and an Apple Macintosh habit to support.